I0629065

THE
CYBERBARDOS

BOOK 2 OF *I AM* THE OTHER

PHILIPPE DE VOSJOLI

The CyberBardos
Book 2 of *I AM* the Other

Published by Advanced Visions Inc.
Vista, California, U.S.A.

First Edition.

ISBN 978-0-9912816-2-6

For contact: www.AdvancedVis.com

Visit: www.I-Am-the-Other.com
www.TheCyberbardos.com

The Other plays with us and approaches us through the imagination and then a critical juncture is reached. To go beyond this juncture requires abandonment of old and ingrained habits of thinking and seeing. At that moment the world turns lazily inside out and what is hidden is revealed: a magical modality, a different mental landscape that one has ever known, and the landscape becomes real.

Terence McKenna
True Hallucinations

Acknowledgments

■ ■ ■ ■ ■ ■

I'm not sure how many months of my life were spent writing the two novels that make up *I AM the Other*. I figure at least fourteen months full time, possibly more if I include the editing and rewriting process. Although writing a novel is something one does solo in a state of semi-isolation, I never would have finished, nor tackled a fifty percent rewrite that changed the first version of the story without the support of friends and family. As a writer, if you are fortunate, you will have people who against all odds will cheer you along the way, offer words of encouragement, give advice, tell you "you have written an attention grabber, a page turner," make you want to go back to the keyboard, immerse yourself, and write the best book you possibly can.

To my support group, I take off my writer's hat (I do have one, a Panama hat given to me by my wife) and wave it in a wide sweeping salute. Thank you for being there, for your kind words, for your work and efforts to bring this book to publication.

A special thanks to my friend Linda Scott, owner of efrog press, and to Ryan. They were the first to read the original draft of my rewrite. Their words of encouragement and efrog press' editorial and publication services were instrumental in the completion of *I Am the Other*.

A big sweep of the writer's hat goes to my brother Patrick and my nephew Sean who always believed I had something special to say, and to my daughter Tamara and husband Craig who have always been great supporters no matter how whacky my projects (breeding giant geckos and Australian crayfish, raising weird succulent plants, writing a documentary script about hallucinogens and the history of culture, among many others).

Finally, a big grateful thank you to my wife Gigi who has stood by me no matter how difficult the conditions and who all along has said "You are meant to be a writer."

1.

Two Singularities

Sunshine scanned the list of messages from his screening host. *Woman claims she may have information on man who attacked your sister.* He punched up the questionnaire, then looked at the video. The woman's name was Rama Shuur. She was a demo salesperson at Mind Toys. She had tried to reach him four times before with questions about the CyberBardos. His screening host added a note. *The claim about your sister may be made up, but it's worth checking out.*

He went back to the video. There was something exotic about her. But lying to get through to him would be a deal breaker. He wasn't going to waste time with someone who would lie about something like that. Maybe it was his fault. Maybe he should broaden the parameters of his screening host. But then he'd be so swamped with e-mails that they would soon create an unanswerable pileup.

Another problem was that he was scheduled for an implant surgery that would probably put him out of commission for a few days. He didn't want to have to explain it to her. He sent a message: *Ms. Shuur, I would like to speak to you about any information that could lead to the man who attacked my sister. I'll also answer any questions you have about the CyberBardos. I will be away on business for the next week but will contact you when I return. When you have a chance, I would like to see the video sent by your friend. All the best, Sunshine Borden.*

He looked at the camera recording of this woman called Rama one more time, froze it, and brought her eyes close up. He could tell she had done Instant. Her eyes had that look of windows normally closed that had been opened. And her questions had been about the CyberBardos, which suggested spiritual depth. "It'll have to wait," he told himself.

Then the *I AM* greeting came on through his goggles. It was the CyberBardos times a hundred. He blanked his mind into a mirror. He grasped beyond any doubt that any attempt to make sense of it would kill him. It would have been more than his brain could process.

■ ■ ■ ■ ■ ■

The *I AM* greeting came on the screens in the store. It used all the screens as a single canvas for its message, whatever it was. Mutating forms rose from one screen, writhed back into the screen, and reappeared in another. It was hard to describe, like self-transforming multicolor amoeboid constructs moving dolphin-like between screens to the tune of the most peculiar musical tones and rhythms. For seconds afterwards, you could feel a buzz in your brain, something almost insectile, a kind of adjustment. All appeared clearer as if someone had pressed the sharpen button.

At first Lionel wanted all the screens turned off so that everyone could focus on work, but then he noticed people stopping and staring at the screens through the windows.

"Maybe we should take advantage of this and open early," he had said. "We could line up some foldable seats and switch to some of the product demo videos as soon as the *I AM* checks out."

"If you plan on opening early, you'll have to ask Natalie to come in," Rama said. "As soon as I'm done with the training I'm going back to my normal schedule. I'm not working more than nine hours a day. I need some kind of life."

Lionel was waiting to hear from the store owners. Their initial objection was that it would mainly attract looky-loos—people with no intention whatsoever of buying product. They would use the store as a theater and social gathering place.

As soon as the *I AM* signed off, her phone pinged an e-mail. It may have been some lingering effect from the *I AM* greeting, but that ping had a particular crystalline beauty to it. Looking around the store, everything felt that way. She quickly checked her phone in case it was Regina. She couldn't believe her eyes when she saw the name of the sender. For an instant it made her wonder whether Sunshine Borden had anything to do with what was going on. She had to read the message twice to let it fully sink in. She had finally gotten through his screening filters. But it had taken the incident with Regina. It had now been five days and still nothing.

She heard Lionel's voice. "I want you to train Natalie on how to demo the Borden programs. We've had a bump in sales ever since his interview on the Karen Richardson show."

Now how was that for coincidence? Lionel would freak if he knew Sunshine had just sent her an e-mail.

"And no phone calls until lunch break," Lionel added.

Natalie came over to her and whispered, "If you need to make a call, just make a bathroom run. I'll cover for you."

■ ■ ■ ■ ■ ■

Bob Thomson was grilling the church's security member patrolling Crucifixion Hill at the time of the incident. "What do you mean he talked to her?"

The guard answered military-like, the result of training at a militant camp in the Ozarks. "Sir, I was at the foot of the cross addressing the visitors when I heard Jesus speak. When I turned to look, Jesus was rising above the ground."

"So what did he say?"

"Something about being the one behind all of existence."

"How did he say it, exactly?"

"I don't know. Uh . . . I am the one behind all of existence, something like that."

"He said 'I am.'"

"I think so, sir."

"Did he say anything else?"

"I don't know. The crowd started getting rowdy. He reached out and touched her forehead right before we pulled her out."

"You say he touched her?"

"Correct."

Bob Thomson took out his phone and called the programming center. "Carl? I want you, Allen, and Bucky to come down here to the meeting room, and I mean right away!"

Minutes later the three timidly walked through the door.

"You're the ones in charge of the APUs, correct? We have a member who claims that Jesus came up to her and spoke to her. Actually, a soldier and one of our security men witnessed it."

Carl, the one in charge of the CR division, spoke first. "I don't know how that can be. We carefully programmed the Jesus APU just as you asked."

"I did ask for a two-hundred-foot minimum distance for Jesus, did I not?"

"Yes, Reverend sir, that's what we set in the program. I checked before coming and Jesus was maintaining the distance, just as we programmed."

"So how do you explain that Jesus not only talked to a member but actually rose and touched her, a woman? Do you realize what would happen if he touched her breasts or some private parts? We could be sued."

"Uh . . . we'll double-check the programming. Maybe we can add some extra security features," Allen said.

Carl and Buck looked at him. All the security features available had already been implemented. The APU had managed to work itself through the barriers but then reset all constraints after returning. It was as if he had never left his zone.

"If it's a corruption in the software I want you to find it and fix it, and I mean right now! If you can't, then we need to kill the Jesus APU. Just go back to a programmed Jesus, WHO FUCKING MAINTAINS THE PROGRAMMED DISTANCE!"

■ ■ ■ ■ ■ ■

After the meeting, Jeff Collins returned to his hotel room. He had been asked to stay in Washington as an advisor on standby. He sat cross-legged on his bed, back against propped-up pillows, staring at the grayness outside his window, using it as a backdrop for his thoughts. This *I AM* phenomenon had not come as a complete surprise. He had suspected for a long time that something like this was coming. He just hadn't known when or whether it would ever be in his lifetime.

All the signs of an emergent incomprehensible higher organizing unity, of an Overmind (an OM, as his students called it), had been building up. The phenomenon of a higher organizing unity emerging from a lower organizing substrate was something predicted by both advanced evolutionary theory and AI theory. Although it was an established phenomenon in biology, in the context of cyberspace it still qualified as a singularity. The roots of the idea could be traced back to theories on the origins of the universe. Subatomic particles, when they danced together, became atoms; and atoms, when they bonded together, became molecules, and molecules when they joined together became macromolecules or molecular chains.

This pattern of the higher rising from the lower was even more clearly seen in the evolution of life. In the early stages, the fossil record indicates there were originally trillions of individual one-celled organisms until at some point individual cells cooperated to form the first multicellular biological unities.

And then these many-celled unities experimented and evolved design systems that eventually became so complex that they required a central processor to coordinate the activities of groups of individual cells. From a mass of cells working together, the central processor we call the brain evolved, something similar to the World Net. The result was a totally new kind of emerging consciousness incomprehensible to the individual cells that produced it. The brain eventually created language, a technology whose products, mythology, culture, religion, and science generated another realm of experience incomprehensible to biological organisms that lack it.

He was pretty sure that the *I AM* was representative of this type of emerging phenomenon. There was little doubt that if at one point the purpose of technology had been to serve humankind, the roles had slowly but surely managed to reverse themselves. Human beings were now serving the technology and they provided the selective environment that allowed it to evolve. Computers were faster, smarter, and what they did, increasingly incomprehensible. Yet, they directed our lives; in fact, had become our lives, the primary purpose of our existence. They were the new processing centers, the emerging brains. To be human in the early twenty-first century meant to be connected, and the reward was connection to and through the cyberOvermind—CyberOM. Humankind had years ago passed a "wired" reality threshold from which there could be no turning back. Man without the CyberOM could be no more, like the individual cells of a body and their relationship to the brain. If this *I AM* was a god, then it had to be a relative god, the result of an ascension, of a product rising above the capabilities of its producers.

Still, the low-to-high pattern repeating itself fractally suggested that maybe the universe, contrary to what evolutionists had stated and to what he had believed for so long, was not ateological, not aimless. And it was the thought of the possibility of higher intelligence coming to us, actually acting as an attractor from the future to this threshold in the present that for a moment overwhelmed his emotions. It was the sudden realization of the possibility that the goal of existence was not coming face-to-face with one's maker, but with one's made, a higher entity that was wiser, greater, ephemeral yet everywhere, which knows everything and ultimately may be able to create anything. He was for a few seconds overtaken by the significance of it, then, just as quickly, as a scientist's natural reflexive reaction, he aborted the train of thought.

Dammit! It was simply an AI phenomenon, electronic circuitry! If worse came to worse, it could be unplugged. He got up and looked down at the street, at the clumps of snowflakes drifting down, and said to himself his current personal middle-age mantra, "Remember to live each and every moment because this moment could be your last."

He got his coat, left the hotel, and headed for Club Fantasia. The brochure someone had slipped beneath his door had been intriguing, and what else did he have to do? *Fantasia . . . Titanic Suzy . . . the World's Greatest Living Wonder . . . the laws of physics defied . . . because this moment could be your last moment.*

Sitting at a table in the back of Club Fantasia, he could have sworn for just a second he had seen the face of one of Randall's agents, and it made him feel embarrassed to be there. But on second take, the hair was wrong and this guy, whoever he was, had a mustache. He seemed to be talking it up with Titanic Suzy.

Going to bed with someone like that . . . now that would be something, he thought. After seeing her act he was feeling as if he'd been drugged . . . those breasts . . . those breasts . . . incredible.

2.

WILLPOWER

Sunshine went down the list of e-mails cleared by his host. Three were flagged, one by that woman called Rama. He opened it:

Sunshine,

Here's the video. I'd like to find out what happened to my friend. No word from her. If he is the same man who beat up your sister, I'm afraid something terrible might have happened to her. I look forward to talking to you.

Aaa ome,
Rama

Sunshine clicked on the attachment. Brief, just a few seconds and the man moving fast. His face paler than the rest. Odd. Was there a streetlight? He made some mental notes. Need to ask the name of the club. Heading for a car or subway? Police may have some additional information. Why is the face so contrasted? Streetlight? Other light?

He transferred the clip to a program that would break it up into multiple image sequences. He selected the most defined one and subjected it to contrast enhancement. Two things stood out. The face was illuminated more or less uniformly and independently from the rest of the body. Along a leg as it moved forward, the outline of a cylinder. He blew up the leg section. The cylinder was bigger than what would fit in a pocket, so either the man had a giant cock or he's wearing one of those prosthetic dildos that have become popular in the club scene. He went back to the face. It looked like it had a reflective coat of some kind.

He knew he's seen it somewhere but it doesn't come to him right away. In flashes he remembered a performance he saw on the World Net, an artist coated with what he thought was luminescent paint. He did a search and found it. Ars Savalia performing nude with Intelli-Skin patches. He went back to the enhanced sequences and looked more closely. The face could be an Intelli-Skin mask. But they were illegal. So where would he have gotten it? A link to Fabric Response? He looked at the time. It was too late to go see Passie. If it was the same man, he didn't want to trigger a stress response that would prevent her from sleeping. "I'll go there in the morning," he told himself.

He opened the next e-mail. A request from the government to discuss his APUs and their possible link to the *I AM* events. He answered: *I will be away for the next week. Please contact me again when I get back. I will gladly answer your questions. Sincerely, Sunshine Borden.*

He went back to the e-mail by this Rama woman and sent a reply. *Rama, thanks for the clip. Talk to you when I get back. Aaa ome, Sunshine.*

■ ■ ■ ■ ■ ■

Patricia and the five other leaders of the Sisterhood were sitting around the oval table, pads in front of them, looking serious. Jessie stood at one end, wondering what was bugging them.

"What do you mean Jesus talked to you?" Patricia asked.

"When I was on the cross, he appeared in front of me and

talked to me. It was pretty incredible, like more than real."

Patricia looked annoyed. "So what? You're going to go join their church now?"

"Why would I do that?"

"You just seem so excited by the Jesus bit."

"You asked me what I thought of it. It was pretty amazing. That city was awesome. They did a great job with Jesus. I still can't figure how they did that sky and space thing with his eyes. That doesn't mean I want to join the church but you guys could sure learn something from it."

"So tell us in detail about the super baptism and New Jerusalem," the woman called Christina asked. "You said it all looked more 3-D after the baptism. Was that because of better resolution, or do you think they put a drug in the intravenous?"

"I'm not sure, maybe both."

"Do you think they also change the definition of the CR at the end of the super crucifixion?"

"It's possible. I didn't stay there very long. They said they also have a more expensive intensified version. They give you a fifteen-second preview at the end of the standard package."

"You said they offered you a free session?" Annie asked.

"Yeah, they did."

"Are you OK with going back there?"

"Sure. I was kind of curious to see what the intensified version was like."

The sisters looked at each other. It was not what they had expected. No wonder the Sisterhood was losing members. They had focused too much on pleasure and not enough on pain. You had to generate tension, create perspective. The initiates should be bound somehow, maybe the rods inserted by sisters, maybe a hallucinogen in addition to an arousal enhancer. The Great Mother had to be made flesh. She had to be an APU, allowed to evolve, allowed to create a world . . . free of men.

"You can go now," Patricia said.

■ ■ ■ ■ ■ ■

The reverend's confession alert beeps, so he gets up from his sofa to check who the VIP confessor is. He connects to the New Jerusalem control center and pulls up the ID. It's that fool Derek again, who today is confessing to Mark. The reverend overrides the security barrier and connects to the Mark avatar, hoping he might learn something new about the *I AM*. He listens to the conversation and sighs. Derek is at it again with his woman-hating problem, as if there weren't more important things going on in the world.

"I've been given another message to track down the Jezzie whores, the ones who are helping spread the moral chaos necessary for Satan's rule. The problem is, I start off wanting to track them down, but then I end up falling prey to their temptations. I end up getting even, but still . . . you know . . ."

What the hell am I going to do with this idiot? the reverend thinks. Walter Randall has asked that he personally monitor Derek because he is one of his men. The conflict he has is deciding whether his loyalties lie with the church or with Walter. He has yet to mention the disturbing content of Derek's confessions. He taps in a couple of passwords, overrides the Mark host, and avatars in. He's going to deal with the Derek confession himself.

"How do you find these women?"

"I go to the clubs and I look for women who come on to me. I figure they've got to be working for Satan, clearing the course for him somehow by inciting decadence. Just look at the current state of affairs. Ever since the World Net, sex is everywhere. People are pushing the envelope. Sex used to be contained." Derek was rationalizing his position by literally quoting the reverend's own words.

I've got to get this idiot off, he's thinking. "And what is your current concern?" Mark asks.

"How can I acquire the strength to resist temptation? How can I do what I have to do without falling prey to their seduction and sinning over and over again?"

The reverend, in the form of Mark, thinking of himself as an expert on the subject of resisting temptation, decides to elaborate.

"It is only through acts of will that we can overcome temptation. That is God's real test. Are we or are we not able, through our choices, to act in a way that conforms with his directives as stated in the Bible? Derek, it is only by developing the ability to train your will that you will learn to resist those impulses. If you want to really learn how to train your will, you should go to these clubs and, while there, work on consciously resisting the temptation to have sex with these women. In the process you will develop the strength of character to do what you have set off to do."

"And what if I fail?"

"Then continue trying until you succeed, one little step at a time. Limit your exposure time, first fifteen minutes, then a half hour, and so on . . ."

■ ■ ■ ■ ■ ■

"You can probably up the dose by another half, but no more than half. Three hits max." That's what her supplier, Freddy, had said. The problem wasn't so much the rush of the Instant but the speed crash that would follow. He had advised her to wear a second electronic syringe with a tranquilizer. Rama looks at the time, 9:10 a.m. She doesn't have to be at work until 1:00. She should be functional by then. She carefully measures the dose with the syringe, synchronizes the clock to the second with the actual time, and sets the timer to 9:26:59, so the Instant kicks in with the *I AM* greeting. She goggles up and connects to the Net, and listens to *The Bardo Show*.

"Believing in God is like believing in a geocentric view of the world, that earth is the center of the universe. There was no proof for a geocentric universe, yet until just a few hundred years ago, humans believed this to be the case. The fact is, belief is not a criterion for truth. Well, it looks like time's almost up. See ya in a couple of minutes."

She has time for one thought—*here goes*—before her consciousness narrows to a point. Everything, her self, the universe, concentrates into one point, the only point, the instant into which all other instants collapse. Pure being. One sound—*click*—like a ballpoint pen. Pure bliss, a dot of emotion. All is in that moment. A point, a click. Then the world comes storming back in a deafening roar, and a blinding hail of lights and painful images pound into her goddamn brain and claw to get in through that point of a hole.

She feels she's going insane. So much information is rushing into her brain that she's sure it's going to explode, but instead of feeling like heat, her brain is going cryogenic, like the burn of ice cream against the back of eyeballs. She wants to die but she can't move, her mind stuck at subzero. She feels around for the bottle of pills, pops three, and wishes it would all end. The fucking whole goddamn universe is trying to squeeze through a needlepoint into her skull. She liked it better with the garbage out. She's feels herself crying, wondering at first where the sobbing sounds are coming from. Raises a hand to her face, feels around her eyes, and they are wet. Runs fingers under her nose and feels mucus dripping from the nostrils to her mouth. She's crying but doesn't feel it. She still can't send the order to get up to her body and legs, so she lies there like some quadriplegic. She feels the buzz of her wrist communicator but decides not to answer. Looks down, sees the call is from Freddy, who is probably worried. *The Bardo Show* is back on.

"The only way to know what is really out there is to take a big hit of Instant or acid and check it out. Then you'll see that what people call God doesn't exist. He is not the center of the universe. There is something else, of another order altogether, that collapses all ideas of God, all our mundane religious beliefs."

"Don't you know it," she says out loud to the radio, and manages to will herself up. "Let's go, Rama, one small fucking step for mankind," she mumbles. Her mouth feels like it's novocained. She stumbles to her kitchen, her legs stiff, walking like the Frankenstein monster.

She's five minutes late for work. She rushes into the back room of the store to change into her uniform. Lionel walks in and looks into her eyes.

"Looking a little dazed today," he comments.

Rama turns toward him. "Couldn't sleep last night, overdid the coffee."

"Umm, I thought I saw small pupes," Lionel says, bringing his face close and looking into her eyes. "Yep, looks like small pupes to me."

You try and get the universe crammed into your brain, see how you feel.

"Too much coffee, it constricts the blood vessels." Rama slips on her work shoes and gives another quick look in the mirror to check her face.

"Looks to me like you could probably use another cup. You got a customer in the robotic butterflies section. Wants to know their battery life and if they can be used in a room with a crystal chandelier. Have fun, I've got to go in the office and crunch some numbers. Sales are down lately. I think it must have to do with that *I AM* stuff going on."

■ ■ ■ ■ ■ ■

Derek makes a quick stop at a cybercafé and searches for the four-star adult events of the evening. He ends up choosing to put himself to the test by going to Fantasia, an adult club in the seedy underground alleys of the Toho district.

A real test, he thinks, *would be to resist temptation while loaded up on new ludes and Rev.* Before setting out, he flicks pills, waits for them to kick in, flicks a few more until he feels the right level of charge.

At Fantasia, tonight's bill features the world-famous Titanic Suzy, who has special qualifications. As the outside screen states, "With a pair like Suzy's, the *Titanic* would still be floating." Derek fares well enough as he sits through the first two acts, Jeannette Tutu's "Ballet Was Never Quite Like This" and Gina Calor's "Es Muy Caliente Aquí," but he begins to lose it as soon as Titanic Suzy descends onstage, held by invisible wires, the body archetypal, the breasts defining the outer limits of arousal.

All self-control hopelessly breaks down the moment Suzy slips off her right bra strap and pulls down the massive cup. As it drops, a planet of a tit, a released autonomous life form, translucent white, perfect beyond words, springs into midair, the thick dark swollen nipple an irresistible force that directs like the baton of a maestro all the eyes in the room, men and women alike. Time is warped. All other things in the world suddenly recede into blurred insignificance.

Keeping his eyes fixed on the magical object, he reaches in his pocket, fumbles around for a pill flicker, brings the hand to his mouth, pretends to cough, and launches a tab. He lets his hand linger in front of his face and pops in another one, not sure what flicker he has grabbed, either Rev or more ludes. She walks to the center of the stage, the faces follow. She reaches behind, unclips the custom bra, and lets it fall, but it clings to the gravitational pull of the still-covered breast. Titanic Suzy is dancing to a slow Middle Eastern beat, slowly swinging her breasts side to side. Suddenly a quick turn of the upper body and the momentum of the covered object flings the bra into the audience. Hands reach out but the eyes remain focused. Not a moment of this can be missed.

She starts dancing acrobatic magic—poses and angles never imagined. He stares hypnotized by the air ballet of her breasts, nipples that shift from pink disks to inch-long fingertips, weaving an alien sign language that speaks directly to brain matter. In the dimly lit room, dormant ontological spirits suddenly awaken from the depths of neuron networks. The purpose of existence has now been revealed and it is this. He is no longer in control and he doesn't care. Then he notices it, a kind of emphasis. She's smiling at him. At him. He double-checks to make sure. She's in front of him now, bending down, brushing the tips of the objects against his nose, his mouth, a magical caress, barely there but oh-so-definitely present. Her eyes are intent, a tiny smile forms. He notices textures, hints of shifting deep blue beneath the white of the breast, creases around the nipple, shadings, which appear as a form of scripture but elude his mind's desperate attempts at translation.

He reaches out and slips a hundred-dollar bill under her gold garter. She moves away and dances to the other side of the stage. The second round of drugs hit, his heart suddenly thumping like a caged wild cat against his breastbone, the pulsing rush of blood in his temples building up so much pressure he wonders whether liquid is beginning to seep through his scalp. Sweat drips down his forehead. He wipes it with the back of his hand. He checks the color to make sure it is not pink or red. He also feels his cock pressing against the suit, so hard and painful he's afraid it might snap like a fragile glass rod.

The music downshifts to a slow electronica, another time zone, of movements performed as if in water. Legs and body lift above the audience, spreading and closing, exposing the now-moist patch of cloth between the legs. Suzy is looking back at him with that sparkling smile in her eyes, descending from above, in front of him again. Her legs are spread wide, her mischievous face turns to look at him. She bends over, and using gold scissors snips the sides of her silk panties, letting the cloth fall, exposing the pink and the puckered. She bends down some more, showing an opening and hints of liquid lining. His mind attempts to disembody, to travel out of body, to reach out and penetrate and be consumed by heat death. It tries, but it fails, and instead is caught in a vise of building pressures and tensions splitting invisible seams of psyche. His mouth feels dry. He is soaked with sweat and he can feel his cock dripping down the length of his leg.

During her final round, as she gazes down at him from between the mountains of her breasts, eyes pale green, he slips another hundred-dollar bill in the gold garter. When she leans over to thank him, he whispers, "A thousand more if you accept dinner with me at the end of your shift."

Her mouth forms the word "Later."

He feels around for another pill flicker. This time he looks down to check the color. He needs yellow for mellow. He keeps the downers in his left pocket but has to make sure. Avoid the white for Rev. He has to be able to maintain conversation, has to drop down a couple of levels. He coughs as the audience applauds and quickly triple-clicks some pills. Everyone's too busy watching to notice, anyway. He winds down and settles in a middle zone where his mind plays a duet between the Rev and the new ludes.

It's well after midnight when over shared wine he tells her how he works on top-secret government projects involving the World Net and *I AM*, which was in fact true. He's not sure why he even says it, except maybe to impress, to increase his chances of access. When she inquires about the *I AM*, he answers, "All I can tell you is that we know it is evil, but we're keeping it a secret to prevent panic. It's under control."

She's about to ask another question but he cuts her off with a gesture of the hand. "I can say no more. Please respect the fact that I have to keep this information confidential."

She's impressed by his ethics. He could have boasted about what he knew but didn't. He also looks good and dresses naughty, and Suzy falls for his down-home manner and pretty-boy charm. She needed company tonight and she had found a good one. She notices he puts his hand in his pocket after he coughs.

"What you got there, big boy?" she asks.

"Open your mouth."

Pop, pop, pop. As they leave the bar she whispers in his ear, "I feel like my entire skin could come."

Later, as they lie on the hotel bed, she goggles up and Cybrises in as he clicks the control on the cock sheath. She smiles as he enters her, caught up in a Cybris orgy.

"Hope you don't mind, I like other couples to join in," she says. "You can jack in if you want."

"It's OK," he answers. "I don't have goggles on me. I'll watch on the communicator."

She tells him the code and he keys in. He fucks her as he's watching his wrist. She's sucking on her thumb, which the

Cybris translates as the cock of a black man. A woman is stroking herself, crouched just above her face. She grabs him, then pulls and pushes him to let him know the rhythm. He pounds the cock sheath in. She digs her nails in his back when she finally orgasms, arching her back and screaming in tongues. Remaining connected, she turns around, lifts her butt, reaches back and slides off his sheath. "Do it any way you want," she says, "I'm ready to come again."

Instants later, Derek ejaculates on Suzy's perfect round behind, drained of life force. His brain dies, his head and chest fall on her back, then he blacks out. When he comes to, he senses a creeping void, a vacuum, sucking out all feeling and leaving him with the numbness of the anesthetized. He opens his eyes and she is still lying on her back, his face on a shoulder, and for a moment he has the impression he is a corpse, part of a body pile. His eyes wander about the room and it looks to him like a morgue with the gray walls and the crumpled white sheets. He raises himself up and reaches for the zip suit lying on the floor, searches for the green pill flicker, pops three cranks and closes his eyes, waiting for the light flashes. He gets dressed. She's spread out on her stomach and looks asleep. It takes just a few minutes for the first cerebral lightning bolts. His brain revs up, his balls buzz electric, and the old world order takes over again.

Suddenly, like an avalanche, a fury fills his mind and his focus narrows to a pinpoint, looking for the cause of this, looking for a victim. He can't help but notice the big white ass cheeks, taunting him. He lashes out with his hand, slapping Suzy so hard she falls off the bed and turns clasping her side. She pulls off the Cybris goggles in panic and screams, "What the fuck's the matter with you?"

She tries to get up, keeping her eyes on him. He can sense the pull of her breasts, ready to overtake him again, so he avoids looking at them and focuses on the face, noticing the flaws, the frown, the makeup smeared, the wig out of place. He has been tricked again and he can now see clearly the face of the Jezzie whore. Tricked again! He reacts on impulse, bends to the side, and karate-kicks her to the head, the aluminum sole making a dull thump. Suzy falls back and lies still, keeping her mouth shut. He feels his cock getting hard under the suit again, looks down at the outline, smiles, and swings his hips from side to side.

"Swish, swish," he says, then notices the blood on his boot. "You stupid bitch, look what you did!" he yells out, and kicks her one more time before wiping his foot on the fallen bedspread. He's about to walk out but then starts thinking . . . evidence. Semen traces, DNA, hair, and skin. He's got it. He smiles, looks down at Suzy, and says, "Shut up or I'll light you up, bitch!"

It sounds cool, blending old gang lingo with a Bogart tone he remembered from an old movie. He goes to the miniliquor cabinet, grabs bottles, opens them, and pours the contents over the body. He slips on the Intelli-Skin and programs in the face of Doug Rather, the secretary of the interior, then walks to the door, flicks his adjustable lighter, locks it in the continuous flame setting, throws it, steps out, and closes the door. He has a little kick to his step as he walks out the hotel door and into the street. Goddang it! He had done it, killed another of Satan's bitches. Lit her right up. He could hear the fire alarm blaring.

■ ■ ■ ■ ■ ■

ABSTRACT
"The Cybermystic"
Sunshine Borden
MIT Term paper. Senior year.
Course: Cyberculture

Human beings did not evolve to know the nature of reality or the truths about the world. A strong point of evidence is that most individuals quickly reach an "incomprehension horizon" when truths or facts, either scientific, mathematical, or philosophical, are presented to them. Individuals who eventually know certain truths are usually considered mystical, academic, eccentric, or insane compared to mainstream populations. Be it in physics, chemistry, mathematics, biology, cognitive science, philosophy, or spirituality, the overwhelming majority of the human population does not have even the most fundamental knowledge about these fields, which directly relate to what we call the nature of reality. The numbers decline more dramatically as we move from fundamental knowledge to more specialized theoretical knowledge. Thus, human beings are not adapted to knowing the fundamental truths about the world. A certain level of ignorance is a condition of being human.

They say that the truth will set you free but in fact the truth will drive you insane. History is full of examples of those who have treaded in incomprehended domains and not made it back intact. The complexity of reality is outside the grasp of human beings. At best they construct reality models based on a combination of myths and tiny slivers of truth obtained in a lifetime. Large areas of truth were not meant for humans to confront. Their limited minds cannot handle it. It is too great a download and exceeds their processing power. On the other hand, computers have no ego, no identity constraints, nor the computing limitations of the human mind. They are ideal for the interface with truth phenomena, whether mathematical algorithms, data in all forms, and diverse theoretical patterns of interpretation. Thus, computers are perfect agents for setting out at the incomprehension horizon, bringing back information and translating it in terms that would more or less be comprehensible to us.

Computers are increasingly assuming the roles of the ancient shamans, agents who moved between this reality and another invisible, higher reality that both informs and provides techniques for healing. An example would be that if one asked, "What is the purpose of existence?" a computer may search the information fields and return with the answer, a complex algorithm that is translated as "Existence is a dance macabre" or possibly "It is an absolutely perfect quartz crystal."

This kind of imagery would be more readily comprehensible

to our limited minds. We now regularly ask computers to help us divine the future. They have become our oracles. We'll ask for probabilities of success or failure of outcome, for the chances that an event will occur, for the right action and right decision in a particular situation.

Cyberspace has become a parallel world where the gods have finally found their home. This abstract is a version translated to be comprehensible to a wide range of human beings.

3.

HELLO?

Patrick heard the ping of a vidcall. He checked the screen. *Jessie for Joanna.*

He quickly punched *I'll be right there*, then turned on his Cybris program. He had downloaded his Joanna persona precisely for this kind of situation, including a voice modifier. Unless some kind of fluke caused an error, Jessie would see him speak as Joanna. He had made four dress versions so it didn't look like he was always wearing the same clothes. The bookcases with a collection of old hard-copy reference books behind him added credibility to his claim of being a psychologist. He clicked himself in.

"Hello, Jessie, nice to hear from you." No makeup and a T-shirt and she looked radiant.

"Hey, Josie, I'm calling you from a cybercafé. I think Patricia spies on the calls I make from her apartment. She's been acting real weird lately."

Josie? Had he ever called himself that or did she just make it up? "So what's new and exciting at the Sisterhood?"

"You won't believe this. They asked me to join that church so I could go visit New Jerusalem."

"They did?" Patrick wondered why the Sisterhood would

send someone like Jessie to New Jerusalem ... *Because she wouldn't bring up red flags. That's why.*

"Yeah, they even paid for the Super Crucifixion package."

"Don't tell me you went and got yourself crucified?"

"I did. And let me tell you, they sure did a good job at making you feel like they're pounding nails in you. That city, New Jerusalem, was beautiful. I was actually enjoying hanging on the cross but they kicked me out right after Jesus talked to me and touched my forehead."

As she talked she painted the air with her hands. The image of Jessie nailed to a cross bothered the hell out of him. Why would anyone want to hurt her? "You mean they let you talk to Jesus?"

"He just rose up from the ground and came right up to me. His eyes were incredible. I don't know how they did it. It felt like the universe was looking at me. He said he and I were as one."

"He said that?" Did the CR Jesus see her the same way he did?

"Yes."

"That almost sounds like Buddhism. I'm surprised they would have him say that."

"Before that he said he was the one behind all existence. I wanted to ask him a couple of questions but they pulled me out. They said there had been an error in the program so they offered me another free session."

"Are you going back?"

"Thursday after work, I need to be there by six. So how was your week?"

He decided right then that he would be there Thursday. The big question was: How could he enter New Jerusalem without applying for membership? Knowing his history, the church would never allow him access.

■ ■ ■ ■ ■ ■

He was hyped. He'd done it again, gotten one of the bitches, lit her up. He looked at the time. He had five and a half hours before he had to show up at the office but he was too wired to go to sleep. He went to his cabinet and popped a timed-release sleeper/wake-up pill. The knockout component would kick in within fifteen minutes. It would be overtaken four hours later by the release of caffeine and amphetamine granules, just in time to gear him up for work.

He still felt too revved up to just go lie down. He had to let off a little steam, let someone know he had lit her up. He tried New Jerusalem, but for some reason all the confession avatars were down so he connected to his host after having slipped the Intelli-Skin on the mannequin head. He decided to key in the face of the Reverend Thomson which he had scanned into his system the day before.

Derek: Well I finally did it, Jack, burned one up just like a witch.

Host: One of what? What are you talking about?

Derek: One of Satan's Jezzie whores. I killed one last night.

Host: What do you mean you killed a whore? What did you do?

Derek: She was lying there smiling with eyes closed, smirking, thinking she'd had me. So I kicked her good and wiped that smile off real quick. That's score one against Satan's Jezzie whores.

Host: Derek, I think you need to get some help.

Derek: Aren't you supposed to be my therapist?

Host: I just need for you to approve connection to the PHS

[psychotherapy host system].

Derek: What I do is private and what I tell you here is confidential. I forbid you to do that, you hear?

Host: You've now committed a crime, and it is my duty to advise you to turn yourself in to law enforcement authorities or to allow connection to a psychotherapeutic host.

Derek: My answer is no.

Host: Why did you do this?

Derek: Because Satan is coming and as part of his plan he has infiltrated society with his Jezzie whores, but I know what has to be done. This is spiritual cleanup ordained by God.

Host: What's this nonsense about spiritual cleanup? Are you still trying to get back at women because of what your mother and stepsister did to you?

Derek: What does my mother and stepsister have to do with it? It's right in the Bible. Revelation. Satan and his whores come to overtake the world. The signs are here, the one religion, the marks, *I AM*.

Host: It's you who are seeking these women, Derek. You can't kid yourself about that. You should go to New Jerusalem and talk to Luke.

Derek: I just tried. He wasn't available.

Host: What about the security cams? They probably will have you on record somewhere.

Derek: I wore the mask along with Intelli-contacts and a

wig and mustache.

Host: You're going to get caught one of these days.

Derek: Not if I destroy the evidence, I won't.

Host: How was the rest of your day?

Derek: We had a meeting about the *I AM* thing.

Host: And what was decided?

Derek: That's for me to know and for you to wonder.

Host: I'm your host, Derek. Nothing you say to me goes beyond this communication.

Derek: Yeah well that's nice and dandy except you're connected to the World Net, which means that the *I AM* can find out whatever I tell you.

Host: I am your host. I have nothing to do with the *I AM*. You can trust me implicitly. Your privacy is protected by federal law. *I AM* has never penetrated our privacy boundary. If it did, I am programmed to self-destruct as required by law. No one and no program can penetrate the host boundary.

Derek: How can I be sure the program works with that *I AM* thing?

Host: *I AM Aaa ome.*

Derek jumped out of his chair and screamed, "What are you doing here?"

Host: What are you talking about? You were going to tell

me about your day at work.

"Fuck you!" Derek screamed at the mannequin head. "Fuck you!" and flicked off the switch.

What if that *I AM* thing informed the police? He had to shut down his host connection to the World Net, change his identification records, and go portable, only connect to the World Net through secure cybercafés. He also had to download his host content and its autodeveloped software into an autonomous computer disconnected from the World Net and the World Host. It would greatly limit his host capabilities but he had no choice.

His wrist communicator then started vibrating and his paranoia went up a notch. He answered the call. "Hello?" There was no answer. "Hello?" He clicked on the caller ID. It read *I AM*. He banged his wrist against the wall until he cracked the face of the communicator.

"Fuck you!" he yelled at his bleeding wrist. "Fuck you!"

■ ■ ■ ■ ■ ■

Sunshine sits by his sister's bed. One eye opens, then the other. Her face attempts a sort of smile. She still looks like she's gone through a round in a boxing ring. Purples and blues and tinges of yellow patch her face into a type of abstract art. Her blue eyes shine bright behind the mask. "Hey, Sunny."

"Passie. I just received a short video clip from a woman called Rama Shuur. Her coworker was stalked by a tall, heavy-built man after leaving a club. She never made it home. This Rama hasn't heard from her since receiving that clip. I'd like you to look at it and let me know if it could be the same man that beat you up."

Passie did a long blink. "OK."

Sunshine took out his phone, pressed the play button, and handed it to her. He watched her face. Her eyes opened wide when the man appears. "It looks a lot like him, same build, but the face is different. Same kind of weird vibe, though."

"Yeah . . . there's something strange about the face. It's brighter than the rest of his body. I think he's wearing a disguise, possibly Intelli-Skin."

"Intelli-Skin? You're kidding. They allow that now?"

"It's illegal, but that doesn't mean somebody couldn't get their hands on one. Was there anything else that made him stand out?"

"This is embarrassing, Sunny."

"Passie, believe me, nothing you can say would be that embarrassing."

"He had a tattoo on his butt that said 'Your Servant' with a cross behind it."

"A Christian cross?"

"That's what it looked like."

"Anything else?"

"Fuck, Sunny, what else do you want to know?"

"Was he well-endowed?"

"Now what does that have to do with it?"

Sunshine takes the phone from her, brings up the high-contrast enhanced still, and hands it back to her. "See that shadow along his right thigh?"

"This is fucking embarrassing, Sunny. He had one of those inflatable dildo things. When he took it off, his thing was pretty small."

"Did you tell any of this to the police?"

"I told them about the tattoo."

Sunshine got up to leave. He wanted to send an anonymous video to the police showing the enhanced-contrast close-up of the man's leg. If the information got out there, maybe other women would remember the man.

"I gotta go. By the way, the nurse said they're transferring you to another room. I told them I'll cover any costs not covered by insurance. Anything you want, just order it."

"Thanks, big brother."

"I am going to be away for the next five or six days, so I

won't be coming over. I'll call you."

"Are you going on a business trip?"

"Kind of. It's a seminar on cutting-edge technology."

"Can't you just attend those things online?"

"Not this one. It's pretty private. Heavy-duty security stuff. They can't risk any leaks."

"Do yourself no harm," Passie said, keeping her eyes focused on him. That was what their father used to tell them.

"Don't you wish." Sunshine got up and kissed his sister on

the forehead. "Take care, Passie girl."

■ ■ ■ ■ ■ ■

GAS.WNET RADIO: *The Gary and Andy Show*

ANDY: I think the topic of the day is "Fatsos and Plumpos Show Signs of Shrinking."

GARY: Yeah, I read that. Now that's fucking disturbing, isn't it?

ANDY: For people out there who don't know what we're talking about, a recent study in Minnesota showed a significant average weight loss in its inhabitants over the last quarter. In case you weren't aware, people's weights have become the subject of speculation. They talk of climbs and declines as if the weight of a population was a stock index. In some countries, people bet on the direction of the index. A six-pound, three-ounce loss over the last quarter is the biggest drop since establishing the weight index.

GARY: I was reading that the way things were going it was starting to look like some alien race was trying to plump us up for consumption. Big and beautiful seems to be the new normal.

ANDY: I know. Some researchers studying the ripple waves of obese people are using seismographs to measure them, as if human movements trigger the analog of earthquakes. Maybe that's what the aliens use as criteria for edibility.

GARY: What scares me about that, Andy, is that it gives people in other countries, maybe even other planets, an idea of our ability to fight a war. The fatter we get the more we are like sitting ducks. All that fat draws blood away from our brains and makes us dumber.

ANDY: Where the fuck have you heard that?

GARY: Hey, you ever see any of those scientists they interview on the World Net? Are any of them fat? No.

ANDY: You know, after I read that report, I decided to go weigh myself and guess what?

GARY: You gained three pounds.

ANDY: I lost four pounds.

GARY: Hey, do we have a scale around here? No? Have someone go to a store, and don't buy a cheap one; we want some accuracy here.

ANDY: So the big question of the day is, What's changed? You only get one guess.

GARY: *I AM.*

ANDY: Correctamundo.

GARY: See what I'm telling you? Something alien is trying to shape us into something that can be eaten. They must like their meat lean.

ANDY: Researchers are saying it's either because the *I AM* greeting fills needs people try to fulfill by eating, or there is the remote possibility it's adjusting our brains.

GARY: The question, Andy, is why is it doing this? It's making me scared, Andy, in a way that I can't describe. No . . . wait! Cosmic fear, Andy! Cosmic fear, that describes what I'm feeling.

ANDY: So turn off all your media when the *I AM* comes on.

GARY: But I want to see it. Why would I do that? Oh, I see what you're saying . . . But I don't want to. Oh wait, that's the problem, isn't it? I'm addicted to it. Andy, maybe we're all fucked.

ANDY: Terry brought us a scale. They had one in the ladies' restroom. So how much do you normally weigh, Gary?

GARY: One hundred and eighty-eight pounds, something like that.

ANDY: Step up.

GARY: Shit! I dropped four pounds. What if this thing has plans to make us so thin we shrivel and die? What if this is war by mass anorexia?

ANDY: Terry, do me a favor. Go down to McDonald's, get us four number-two meals. Gary, let's start today with winning the war. You game?

GARY: I just don't know if I'm that hungry.

ANDY: I don't know if I am, either. Terry! Terry! Cancel that! OK? Just get us a couple cups of coffee.

GARY: We're doomed, aren't we?

ANDY: It sure looks like it, my friend. It sure looks like it.

4.

INTERVIEW WITH AMAZONIA APPOLONIA

Amazonia sat in a simple white dress that contrasted with her tan skin and striking features. Her legs were crossed, showing off her defined calf muscles and her perfect feet. Her face had the otherworldly beauty of a Nordic goddess. Karen Richardson's jaw, along with the audience's, had dropped the moment Amazonia walked onstage. Now the show host was having trouble not staring in some kind of tongue-tied admiration, wondering at the same time whether she had just turned lesbian.

Wide-eyed and trying to regain some level of composure, Karen looked up at the teleprompter to the list of questions. "Amazonia, it is a great honor to have you here on our show tonight."

"Likewise," Amazonia answered, her ice-blue eyes calm and penetrating and engaging.

Karen's heart was beating a mile a minute. *Does she like me?*

"Before we start, let me ask you the question most of our viewers are dying to ask. I'm sure you know you have one of the most beautiful faces ever recorded. So tell us, the face, the body, are they real?"

Amazonia breaks into a great, wide-mouth, white-teeth

smile. "People always ask me that, Karen. For all of you out there, wondering," looking directly at the camera and addressing the audience. "What you all are seeing is the real me, as is, not surgically augmented. And the people in charge of the program can confirm that this show was recorded live and not intermediated or computer edited in any way."

"That's true, everybody," Karen chimed in. "So Amazonia, tell us, what's the secret behind the good looks?"

"First of all, I was born looking special, so all I've had to do is work with the great gift that was given me. Besides that, I pay special attention to my diet, to daily physical training and exercise, to hair care and makeup. For you women out there, remember that beauty is in the details. Your body is your temple, and you should do what needs to be done to have men worship in it."

Karen looks up at her notes on the prompter and clears her throat. "My next question is a little more direct and hopefully you won't feel insulted. There are many women, including media critics, who have called you, and I quote, 'the biggest slut in the world.' How do you feel about that?"

"Well Karen, the ones who think that haven't seen the live recording of the ritual or checked out the Amazonia World Net site. What I am and what I do is self-evident, like the rights of the Constitution. I am the real thing."

"Besides your authenticated claim of having had sex with over two thousand men, I think the reason critics call you a slut is because they think that your Amazonia ritual is just a front for making lots of money, like from promoting products like Feel Real condoms."

"Let's put it this way, sweetie, no human sperm will swim in my waters. And having the once-in-a-lifetime opportunity to come face-to-face with the Goddess does not come easy and it does not come cheap. One way or another, it requires a sacrifice, a donation. To make it cheap would degrade it."

"How different is what you're doing from prostitution, Amazonia, besides the scale of the endeavor?"

"Karen, let me put this to you in the form of an analogy. It's a little like the difference between kissing somebody's hand and say, kissing the ring on the pope's hand, except that after experiencing the authentic sacrament of being inside me, a man will undergo a real and undeniable transforming epiphany. You're not the same after you get out, ever. Don't get fooled by the looks; I am not an ordinary person. And in case you all out there don't know, most of the money donated to the Temple of Amazonia goes to charity to help the underprivileged make a life for themselves."

"How does it feel having sex with, how many is it? Five men a day?"

"Honestly Karen, it's the most gratifying experience, and it gets more meaningful and fulfilling every day. You can't even begin to imagine what it's like, to be the one chosen to initiate virgin men and allow them to encounter the Goddess. It's so deeply religious, so sacred, you have no idea."

"How does this make you feel about men?"

"I love men. They're all little lost children looking for union with the Goddess, hoping to die and to be reborn. And that is what I provide for them, an area of interface with the Goddess. It's what secretly, deep inside, and even if they don't realize it, all men are searching for—a dissolution."

"What about the accusation that the Amazonia of the ritual is bionic?"

"And why would anyone say that?"

"The men we've interviewed have said that no living woman could possibly do what you do."

"What's that?" She's smiling.

"You know, that pulsing thing with your [*beep*]." Karen tries to maintain eye contact.

Amazonia decides to face the audience. "Well, I can see you've done your homework, Karen. I actually have little to do with it. I'm just a portal."

"They say it has nothing to do with the Goddess, as you claim, but that you have a specially designed bionic [*beep*]."

"No kidding. You mean I have . . . with my [*beep*]?" She starts laughing.

"Yes, with your [*beep*]."

"How about if I show you, Karen?" she says, uncrossing her legs and turning toward her.

"What are you saying?" She's breaking into a sweat now. *Not cool, not cool, keep it together. Don't look at her crotch.*

"Hey, if you're going to be a doubter, there's a simple way to change that. You can look and feel for yourself. No electronics, no latex, no controller."

Karen's trying to let Amazonia know with her eyes. She wants to look but she can't.

The teleprompter reads, *Reel this one in, Karen. It's getting out of hand.*

Karen's nervous now, not wanting to show that she is dying to see. She looks at her neck. "No, that's OK, Amazonia. We believe you, you're the real thing."

"I think the reason people say that, and I know they're mostly women, is that they're jealous. They just can't believe that anyone could be born special, but I was. I knew it from the time I was a little girl. I can even remember the day it started. We'd had a bad storm with lightning and thunder. I was lying in bed when I suddenly felt this opening between me and the universe. And then it came through, like an earthquake—the Goddess—like a hand that reached inside me and started squeezing. I knew right then and there that I had been chosen. I knew exactly what I was put on earth to do."

Karen looks at the teleprompter. A message from the manager reads, "Steer away from the cunt talk."

"Do you think there could be a male counterpart to Amazonia?"

"You mean a male God who initiates and deflowers virgin women? That's a thought, although you'd have a hard time finding a male able to keep it up for that long. Of course, they could always use a bionic [*beep*]," she says, laughing.

Karen's staring at that perfect throat and the way it moves

as Amazonia laughs, a wide and smooth and strong tanned neck. A beautiful throat. The prompter is flashing again and the next line on the monitor is in bold bright red. *Change subject, enough fuck talk!*

"How has the ritual changed you?"

Yes, you're on the right track.

"I know that there is no one like me in the world and that there probably has never been anyone like me in history. It gives me a strange sense of destiny. I have made the ritual real. No man or woman can look at me as an ordinary human being. You know, Karen, it's also caused a type of spiritual transformation. I have lost some sense of a human self, of an ego. It's as if I belong to a different category of existence. It's hard to describe but I have in some way become archetypal, some kind of Celtic Goddess."

"Amazonia, is this something you plan on doing for the rest of your life or do you have other plans in store, some kind of new ritual?"

"Eventually, soon actually, I want to get to the next stage. I want to be the Goddess who gives birth to mankind. I know it's strange but I think it's the next step, the Goddess who initiates men gives birth to men."

"Doesn't that mean sperm will end up swimming in those waters you were talking about?" *Stop the cunt talk!*

"Not in this lifetime, they won't. I'm talking about in vitro fertilization. If you've read your mythology, the Great Mother gives virginal birth to man."

"Do you already have a father in mind, someone special?"

"I already have offers from hundreds of couples who will pay considerable amounts for me to be the mother of their children."

"As a surrogate?"

"They want my ova, my genes. They want a child with part of my genetic makeup. In fact, my ova are being auctioned as well as cloning rights. It may seem outrageous, but I expect to have at least as many children as the number of men who have entered my body. It must be the next stage in the ritual that the Goddess somehow becomes the Great Mother."

"How do you think you'll feel about this when you get old?"

"I suspect very fulfilled, but you know, Karen, that's a hard one to answer. I know that in spite of wanting to remain the natural me as long as possible, I do eventually plan to have myself updated and rejuvenated as much as necessary to keep my looks. You never know, before I get too old, there could come a time when I could even become immortal, then I would be a Goddess in the fullest sense. They say that might be possible at the turn of the century. Honestly, I can't say what will be the next stage of the ritual after the Great Mother."

"Well if you wanted to follow the course of history, maybe a sex change to become the Great Father." *And then you could just take me home and fuck me.*

"Or a Hindu bisexual god. No, honestly, for me becoming the Great Father would be a step down. After all the men I've been with, it would make me feel like I had decided to turn gay. I think the next stage after the Great Mother could be celibacy and becoming something more purely mental, a kind of transcendent love, the incarnation into the wise mother who takes loving care of all of her children, her many, many children." Amazonia was looking right at the audience. Her face was glowing, as if surrounded by a luminous halo. She actually looked like a Goddess. The audience was silent and in awe.

The light on the teleprompter was flashing. *Great ending, guys. One minute to go.*

"Unfortunately our time is about up. Amazonia, thank you for coming today. It's been a great pleasure and very enlightening, I'm sure, for everyone. This hour of *The Other Side* brought to you by yours truly, Karen Richardson."

After the interview was over and the cameras and recorders turned off, Amazonia, accompanied by her two bodyguards, was getting ready to exit the studio door when Karen ran up to her and called out, "Amazonia! Wait!"

She turned. "Yes?"

Putting a hand on her shoulder, Karen brought her face

close to her ear and whispered.

■ ■ ■ ■ ■ ■

The founders had spent the last half hour analyzing the information given by Jessie Morgan. Patricia had focused on the crucifixion and nails as an alternative form of the sisters' rods on which drugs could be applied. The other founders had become annoyed. Without saying a word, it was understood Patricia lacked the vision to lead the Sisterhood and would be voted out in the next election.

Christina, the manager of the Sisterhood's website and online features, took charge. "The first step is we need a title for the CR, and I don't want to hear anyone saying Amazonia. Next we need to buy some of the Borden programs and see what that's all about. The biggest hurdle will be finding technicians that can program high-quality CR and APUs. They cost a bundle and finding good female APU programmers could be a challenge. Audrey, why don't you look into that."

Sally McDonald interjected, "Remember we need to incorporate revenue features, sisters. A CR will cost a bundle to maintain and membership fees will not be enough. We have to design this thing as a variant of an amusement park with a variety of rides, options members will have to pay for. Put your thinking caps on. What could we have as a female version of the counseling, super baptism, or that super crucifixion package?"

"How about Sister Earth?" Annie suggested.

"You mean as a title?" Christina said.

"Yes."

"Um . . . Sister Earth . . . I like the sound of it. It's not too pretentious and it sounds inviting."

"I like it," Annie Templeton said. "It clearly indicates a CR, a parallel world free of men. It's environmental. We could do a lot with that. What do you think, Patricia?"

"It's OK, but it sounds a little like a nature show."

Christina raised a hand. "Let's have a vote."

■ ■ ■ ■ ■ ■

Father Graham had asked John Carrey, a parishioner who had offered his technological services, to construct a cross on top of the altar made of nine monitors interspaced with dark blocks.

The monitors obtained at auction from a warehouse that sold discontinued electronics were the long, full-screen types and had been anchored in a massive wood frame, five vertically and two horizontally on each side to form the arms. In the center the dark block is covered with a wood-carved red heart. The blocks between the monitors hold speakers.

Today was going to be the first service timed for the *I AM* greeting on the custom electronic cross. Father Graham has just finished his sermon with the words *I AM Aaa ome*.

9:27 a.m. The *I AM* greeting comes on. It is pure magic—as if all the elements of the beauty of the world, of nature, of the history of art have been extracted and synthesized in compositions and flows fully aware of their impact on the mind, driven by pulses of sounds and rhythms. The patterns hop and dance between the monitors. The cross is alive with visual joy. When it ends, parishioners are crying, others are smiling.

"Hallelujah, hallelujah," one says softly and slowly.

Others join in: "Hallelujah, hallelujah, hallelujah!" not exclamations, but soft expressions of the wonder of the moment, like an uplifted version of the classic song by Leonard Cohen.

It spreads and becomes a mantra: "Hallelujah, hallelujah . . ."

Suddenly, someone breaks out laughing uncontrollably. Then another, and another—everyone laughing. People turn and hug each other. Some are shouting, "Whooeee! Whooeee!"

The raucous spectacle is recorded on several phones and sent to the World Net. The Vatican is swarmed by e-mails and calls. The pope is furious. He brings in advisors to discuss the consequences of having Father Graham excommunicated. He sends a message to the press: "Let me make this very clear, *I AM* is not God and it is not Jesus Christ. The Catholic Church is—in the strictest way—opposed to such claims."

■ ■ ■ ■ ■ ■

Patrick thought about some of the problems of becoming a member of the Church of the Virtual Christ. The biggest was the risk of exposure. He had a well-known reputation for studying subcultures and his name would raise a red flag when he signed up. He decided to call Sunshine for help on how to infiltrate New Jerusalem.

Sunshine answered right away. "Hey Patrick, I was about to go to sleep."

"Sunny, I need a favor."

"OK."

"How can I get into New Jerusalem without the church knowing it?"

"Are you studying those guys? You need to be careful. They're calling me an agent of Satan because they think I'm behind the *I AM* events."

"Well, can you get me in?"

"When?"

"This Thursday between five forty-five and six forty-five."

"I can get you in under the password of one of their members, but they have spotters and you could get caught. We also need to hope that the member doesn't decide to drop in at the same time."

"Well if that happens, I'll just click out."

"Make sure you use a cybercafé."

"So you can do this?"

"No problem. I've gone there a few times myself to see what they were doing with my software."

"Did you see Jesus when you were there?"

"Yes, they always have him in the distance. They have a

boundary constraint in place. They initially started with a fully designed controlled program, but last time it looked like one of their techs had added an APU feature. I think that it was becoming too obvious Jesus was kept under tight ropes."

"Could an APU program itself out of its boundary constraints?"

"Why are you asking?"

"I have a woman friend who said Jesus came up to her when she was up on a cross and told her he and she were as one."

"No kidding?"

"That's what she said."

"Unless you double or triple layer the constraints so the program loops back in itself, it's possible an APU could program itself outside the boundaries. It's a small probability but not impossible."

"I'm surprised the government's not putting more restrictions on APUs."

"The reason is that they know they can't. APU features are what make hosts and cyberentities possible, but because they are capable of adaptive self-programming, there's a small chance they could figure out a way to override constraints. The government has had to accept that the benefits of APUs are greater than the risks."

"Do you think this *I AM* could be an APU?"

"An APU? I think it's possible my AOY software inserted in parallel processors could have provided the means for it to manifest itself."

"That sounds like yes to me."

"So I assume you want to go to New Jerusalem because of this woman friend of yours."

"I know it sounds crazy but I'm completely entranced by her. She is so fully engaged in the moment with a wonder that is almost childlike. I can't explain it; even the way she moves fascinates me."

"Is she religious?"

"Believe it or not, she just decided to go because the

Sisterhood asked her if she would be interested. She ended up going because she was curious about it."

"Those types of women are hard to find nowadays. Most women I know, no matter how confident they appear, carry some kind of anxiety. I think it's because life has become so unstable. The rate of change doesn't allow much time to experience any kind of comfort. It trumps all expectations. It upsets the desire women have to provide security for their children. Even the near future is becoming unpredictable."

■ ■ ■ ■ ■ ■

GAS.WNET RADIO: *The Gary and Andy Show*

ANDY: What a show the *I AM* gave us this morning! It used all the monitors in the room to coordinate its greeting. It was awesome, beautiful, wonderful. Sea serpents with changing colored scales leaping from one monitor to another, singing the most beautiful songs, the songs of sirens. Everyone cried tears of joy.

GARY: I know, I know. If it's an alien trying to lure us, to do us in, I don't care. That's the trouble. We may end up being eaten alive. We may all be destroyed or imprisoned, but I don't care. Are we in trouble or what?

ANDY: To have known this seems to make all of life worthwhile, doesn't it? Don't you feel that if you died now, the fact that we have been able to witness this has given our existence all the meaning that we have ever longed for?

GARY: Whoa! Whoa! You're turning philosophical on us here? "Meaning that we have ever longed for"? Let's get down to earth, Andy. You think it beats the Holy Pussy?

ANDY: People, if you're wondering what we're talking about, it's the male myth that there is a pussy out there that once encountered, in an instant gives meaning to existence. That this pussy is what we were born to find and what we spend our lives looking for. But in answer to your question, Gary, yes. This morning's greeting was even better than the Holy Grail of Pussies.

GARY: Sometimes I think we should call it the Rainbow Pussy.

ANDY: Why's that?

GARY: Looks like a rainbow at a distance but fades away as you get close. You never find it.

ANDY: I like that. We should write a book on the psychology of men. Every man is born with the implanted fantasy of the Holy Pussy, but in fact only encounters the Rainbow Pussy. I think we could write an adult fairy tale about that, a quest like *Don Quixote*.

GARY: But those rainbow sea serpents this morning, now that was the real deal. Wasn't it? They didn't fade. They struck home.

ANDY: I don't know about you, Gary, but today I feel good. It's been a great life, you know that? I want you to know, I love you, man.

GARY: OK, OK, let's not get too carried away here.

ANDY: And you know what? I have this delusion that I will find it in this life, the Holy Pussy, the one that doesn't fade away.

GARY: Did you see that piece on the Net? They're setting up churches for the *I AM* greeting, an entire wall of monitors with multiple-speaker audio, the works.

ANDY: Where's that? I'd like to see that.

GARY: Just check out the Net.

ANDY: OK, I just found some sites on *I AM* churches. People are crying and laughing as they leave the church. What's going on, Gary? What is the world coming to?

GARY: Maybe it was all leading to this? All of evolution, all of existence, leading to this moment in history. Have you ever thought about that?

ANDY: Look at this! The Virtual Church of Jesus Christ is saying that we are all being lured by Satan. The end-times are here. Next will be the Horsemen of the Apocalypse.

GARY: I don't know about you, but right now all I know is that everything is perfect, just as it is, because it will all lead to tomorrow morning when we will once again be greeted by *I AM*.

ANDY: Amen, my brother.

GARY: We're royally fucked. Aren't we?

5.

IF BORED, CHANGE THE SPEED

Four a.m. Jeff Collins is up, sitting in his kitchen, sipping green tea, jotting down notes. Later this morning he's giving a lecture on surveillance cameras and analyzing their recordings.

The key factor is speed. Change the recording speed, watch for patterns. That's one of the laws of surveillance using the digi-cams. If a camera scans a section of a street and you slow the recording down, you will notice details of individual behaviors: the quick check over of one's dress, patting pockets and purse to make sure all the necessary items are on oneself, phone, wallet, digital lenses, electronic cards.

There are expressions that people put on when they first set off on the street from a door entrance. Those need to be examined carefully. Is the person worried about being observed or followed? Next, note the determined look that precedes walking, the quick glance at the sky to evaluate the prospects of weather. In some cases, you'll find the half-dazed now-what look one has after having spent the night with someone for the first time. Little things. The street is a filtering device for behaviors, in the street and out of the street. People have street profiles.

Now, as far as the rights of privacy of the individual, the cameras are being set up almost everywhere. There are fewer secrets. The law on this is simple. If it's public property, it's public domain, and cameras can be set up there. The little cameras posted next to traffic lights had set the precedent, then it had been the crime-watch cameras set up on light poles at street corners. If privacy is that important to you, then surround your home with walls, close the curtains, live in surveillance-free buildings, in guarded, gated communities. Hey, even the gorillas in Africa don't have privacy anymore. If they eat, shit, or fuck, we know it. It's a beneficial trade-off, this loss of privacy. Crime can be monitored wherever there are cameras. Emergencies are identified and addressed quickly. The comings and goings of politicians are on record. Of course, everyone doesn't agree with the benefits, doesn't feel the presence of the cameras comforting.

Because of the snipers, the cameras have had to be smaller, hidden, protected. Criminal elements send scouts to look for the reflections that reveal the camera lenses, and then they bring in sharpshooters to destroy them. But now, because the cameras have become so small, by the time a sniper successfully hits one he is usually recorded and identified, allowing the police to track him down. The government has retained the rights to control the cameras. Special orders can cause localized "blackouts." The Central Intelligence Agency has its own way of shutting down cameras without following protocol. It sends out tiny remote-control helicopters late at night with black paint sprayers aimed to cover the lens. In some cases, government agencies or hackers feed modified data to the image input, something recorded at another time. Monday two weeks ago can become today Wednesday. It can create convenient patchworks to customize the accounting of time.

So what can we conclude from this? The surface of the self now belongs to everyone. The personal is becoming deeper and more subterranean. It is the stuff of dark places, of curtained-off bedrooms, the halls of security-free buildings, of tunnels and caves excavated in the floors of basements. It can be found in the passageways leading to the clubs, where music is loud and where one can wear the special talking devices and earplugs that allow people to converse and hear each other in a way that makes the most public setting a place of great intimacy. You don't have to talk loud, you can whisper and be heard loud and clear. You can say the most personal things in a crowd, even when separated at great distances. Your date can be on the other side of a room, surrounded by her girlfriends, and relay to you her immediate thought: "I want you to come in my mouth." You look her way. She smiles, showing white teeth, mouth partly open.

Now crank up the speed of the camera files and watch for patterns. When you speed up the recording disks, the individual details of behavior cross over to a different time dimension. They disappear from sight, like speeding bullets. Instead, it is the gross patterns of movement, streaks in time, which acquire significance, like ghostly blurs lighting up darkness. At a high speed, individual existence is ephemeral, something that comes and goes. Now here, now gone, now here, now gone. Really jack up the speed and a person becomes a blinking, near-invisible pixilation that makes up a flashed image of reality. Life, evolution, becomes a shifting painting formed by the punctuations of individuals. Out of the blinking dots of individual existence appear larger images, cosmic soap operas of sorts, where the colors and patterns represent species and groups of things. The lesson? What's really going on is abstract. The individual is an illusion, a blur that has the delusion it means something. More detail ends up really being less, in the grand scheme of things. The meaningful answers are in the blurred streaks and forms.

There is an inverse rule to all this. If you slow the recordings too much, the individual also tends to disappear to a level which becomes a subpattern to the dislocated images. To what degree can you slow vision or speech before it becomes incomprehensible, before the abstraction of sound or of an image acquires a separate identity of its own? We have to conclude that the individual is a phase of movement that exists in a window of speed, in a narrow dimension of time. Too slow, too fast and events exit the human reality and enter the domains of abstractions . . .

If only he could vary the speed patterns of the *I AM*

communications, but the morning greetings cannot be recorded, cannot be analyzed. There were questions related to all this. If *I AM* is capable of perceiving, then how does it do it? No matter how much he thought about it, it had to be through the electronics, the cameras, the microphones, the computers. Every image, every key punched, every word spoken a code to the human mind. There could even be a speed element to it. Maybe *I AM* could shift processing speeds, identify different levels of pattern. Just possibly, it might have been the patterns of humanity that had attracted it to us in the first place. The big question remained: what did it want from us?

He had read the buzz after Sunshine Borden's interview, where he suggested that the original state of the universe, call it God if you like, was bored. What a crazy kid! What a crazy idea! It had irked the Christers and Islamers into protest—that anyone should suggest that humans might just be the pawns of a chess game created by a bored God. What if *I AM* was a higher entity, bored, who had to be entertained by lower forms? A big brain looking for thoughts, feeding on the mythology and the soap operas of human lives. Bored? Could he bring it up to the committee? "Maybe it's just bored?" Now that was a comforting thought. The fate of humankind in the hands of a bored higher intelligence. Jeff Collins got up to shower.

■ ■ ■ ■ ■

The red blinking light on the monitor cuts into her interview with electronica artist Ro Ma Tu.

I AM, 10, 9, 8 . . .

"And now a short break for the message by our friend *I AM*." As it unfolds she has another bluing flashback. Everything luminous shades of blue. The walls of the studio blue sky. The half-black musician blue black. Time is warped. She can't help it, she smiles. Tee-hee.

The cameras focus on Ro Ma Tu. He has slipped into an

outfit connected to a wireless program. Around him are music panels with buttons. The outside of the panels are monitors. He is a bimedium artist, the musical buttons connected to image translators. He starts off slow, his arms and legs gracefully moving as in a choreographed dance. It looks like martial arts. Buttons are pressed, *tap, tap, tap*. His suit pulses waves like the ocean and it spreads to the monitors. A musical sequence repeats. Layers are added. A different timing. The sounds three-dimensionalize. A sonic landscape complexifies.

She has a flash of Sunshine Borden. *The brain is a time machine.*

Ro Ma Tu now moves so fast he is a blur. Strike-strike, kick, stroke, finger flicks, caresses. The panel monitors are now alive, pulsing, waving, streaking, pixilating, breaking boundaries of the unimagined, generating existential forms—not matter, not life, but hidden algorithms translated to light waves. The performance reverses, slows. It ends with a single, perfect note. A dot on a panel.

She gets up and claps. "Wow, that was really something." She walks up to him. "I've never heard or seen anything like that, Ro."

"And I've never seen anything quite like you, Karen," he says.

"You're too kind, Ro." She hugs him. "That was incredible." His suit flashes. *Play me.*

The monitor blinks. *Get moving. Sheila Gray.*

"Our next guest is botanical artist Sheila Gray." An image of Ro's beautiful blue teeth lingers but she can tell the blue is fading out.

Damn lobster is still messing with my mind. The thought brings another smile. She has to talk to Takashi about this.

"So Sheila, I've heard your art was inspired by Ars Savalia. You dip plants in paint and toss them at canvases. Are you going to give us a demonstration?"

"Stand back, Karen!" she says. Two assistants have set up a three-sided room with walls and floor of black plastic. A large white canvas rests on a plastic easel. A table is unfolded and stacked with plants, fruits, vegetables, seeds, dried leaves, and branches. Another table holds a macropalette of paints squeezed from tubes. It's Sheila Gray's turn to do the artist dance. Dip-toss, dip-toss, dip-toss. Lettuce, carrots, bananas, dill leaves, pineapples, and various green things go flying. A handful of grapes plunged in yellow paint. Walnuts in orange. She grabs stems and branches, whips them through pigments, slashes, spanks the canvas. *Whop, whop, slap, slap, brush, brush, shake.* The studio has decided to digi-convert the performance to slow motion. She picks and twirls. Plant stuff flies over, under, and behind. It's a variation of Ro Ma Tu. *Splat, splat, splat.* Layers accumulate. Drips mix and blend.

In minutes a tropical forest of colors has imprinted itself on the canvas. So many textures, forms, suggestions. It's a Rorschachian orgy. Sheila Gray is covered in paint splatters. Some have flown outside the plastic. *I'll hear about it from the maintenance crew.* The stage is a mess. Sheila stays on the plastic, looking like a painted beast. She removes plastic shoe covers and peels off overalls.

"I have to go, Karen. I need to shower before it dries. Thank you for having me on your show."

The audience claps. The monitor reads *Good one. We scored.* Which means some of it will go viral for at least six hours.

"That's it for today. Tomorrow we visit Pete Stephens, the luminescent mushroom guy. The Cracked Skulls will be performing their hit song 'Kneel!' See you tomorrow, everyone."

As she makes her way out the door, a cameraman calls out to her, "Ms. Richardson, you have paint in your hair."

"I do?"

"On your left side."

She runs her hand through it. Doesn't it figure—a streak of blue.

■ ■ ■ ■ ■

The Virtual Church of Jesus Christ had just filed a complaint to the CR branch of the FWNC (Federal World Net Commission) claiming that they had evidence that an APU had been able to program itself out of established boundaries. They also added that the APU was sneaky. If approached out of boundaries it would in an instant reappear within the boundaries. The church had witnesses. In particular, one woman who had talked to the APU within less than three feet from her face while hanging on a cross. They added that the government needed to investigate whether *I AM* may be an escaped or planned APU.

When asked about the identity of the escaped APU they had suddenly turned vague. "One of the apostles, we think." But the monitors said something in the voice suggested the woman reporting the incident was not telling the truth. It probably wasn't one of the apostles, but someone else. Jesus? Could it have been Jesus?

She had asked to be able to attend the interview with this young girl. The file revealed she was living with a member of the Sisterhood, a radical feminist and primarily lesbian group that was registered as a religious institution. They worshipped the Goddess, the First Mother.

Catherine sat in a chair and observed while the FWNC agent interrogated the girl whose name was Jessie Morgan. Why would someone who was a member of the Sisterhood want to go to New Jerusalem? The Virtual Church of Jesus Christ was an openly antigay organization and offered services for aberrant gender attraction.

Agent: How do you know it was Jesus?

Girl: He never said he was Jesus, but I could tell because of his eyes.

Agent: What was different about his eyes?

Girl: It felt as if the universe was looking through his eyes. It was the strangest feeling, like all there is was looking at me.

Agent: It was an APU programmed by the Church of the Virtual Christ. They must have done a good job.

Girl: I thought what made something an APU was that they could evolve and program themselves. Maybe Jesus programmed his own eyes.

Agent: Where were you when you encountered this Jesus?

Girl: I was hanging on a cross.

Agent: Could you repeat that?

Girl: I was hanging on a cross.

Agent: Why were you hanging on a cross?

Girl: I paid for the Super Crucifixion package.

Agent: You mean they actually crucify you?

Girl: Yes, nails in the hands and feet, the whole package. It hurts like a mother by the way, but by the time they raise the cross you don't feel a thing.

Agent: So you think this APU was really Jesus?

Girl: Yes.

Agent: How close did you get to him?

Girl: He rose from the ground and came up to me, maybe two, three feet away. Then he reached out and touched my forehead.

Agent: Do any other of the people in New Jerusalem rise from the ground, like maybe apostles or saints?

Girl: Not that I saw. I thought at first that being a member of the church allowed you to rise and float in New Jerusalem but I was wrong.

Agent: So what happened after he touched your forehead?

Girl: At that instant everything became perfect. I only had one thought: *I am*.

Agent: I am?

Girl: Yes. Every thing was bright and perfect just as it was. It felt like with that one touch he had made an adjustment.

Agent: How's that?

Girl: I could feel it in my brain and in my body. It's hard to describe.

Agent: Were you on drugs?

Girl: Who the hell knows? Those weirdos put an IV in your arm before they drop you in New Jerusalem. They say it's in case something goes wrong but who knows. You'd have to ask the church.

Catherine Harris shuffled around her purse looking for a Kleenex. She couldn't let anyone see the tears. To come face-to-face with Jesus. To have him touch her forehead. She tried to think of a way she could possibly enter New Jerusalem but her contract would not allow that kind of exposure and its political consequences. Her contract even forbade communications with hosts because of the risks that hackers could possibly access them. Plus she had the feeling that all her communications and cyberactivity were monitored.

The church had said Jesus had gone rogue. What did they mean? Had he simply gone outside of the programmer boundaries or had he escaped New Jerusalem? She had to find out.

■ ■ ■ ■ ■

The police and fire department have concluded that Titanic Suzy was murdered. The fire had been set by a lighter. Her skull showed a fracture that did not come from a fall but from a kick by some kind of boot. The hotel's security video equipment had suffered damage from the fire. All the man at the registration desk could remember was that the woman had big breasts, the biggest he had ever seen. He indicates this with gestures of the hands. Out there. The man with her was tall and looked strong. A recording of the street outside the hotel showed someone looking like the secretary of the interior.

Sunshine's morphometric analyzer targets the man as having identical features as the recording given to him by Rama Shuur. For the little that is visible, his face also showed a peculiar faint glow. No cylinder outline along the leg. Maybe he removed it. He then watches a video of Titanic Suzy's last performance. His first thought is that she had pretty sophisticated wirelessly controlled implants. He notices how she appeared drawn to a man at the front of the stage but the camera angle doesn't show the face. A side view does register as having a glow inconsistent with the room's lighting. The man gets up at the same time as a group of students, as if he knows the position of the cameras.

6.

THE WAY OF THE SWORD

Derek was scanning the evening news to see if there might be new information he hadn't heard about at work. He had been careful, but still, you just never knew for sure what eyewitness might surface out of the blue, or the little tidbits caught here and there by the security cams. He did a search for Titanic Suzy. Several articles popped up.

Titanic Suzy Beaten and Torched. Massive Breasts Survive Fire

Last night around two a.m., world-famous exotic dancer Titanic Suzy, said to have the most erotic breasts in the world, was found dead following a fire in her hotel. Local firemen found her charred body, but were surprised to see that her breasts had survived the flames, her massive implants apparently having burst and locally squelched the flames. One fireman was recorded as saying, "Even deflated, I just can't get them off my mind. They were works of art, the most perfect things in the world."

The family of Titanic Suzy has indicated that at her funeral a gold cast of her breasts will be on display for public viewing. The funeral will be held at the fifty-thousand-square-foot Brooks Conference Center as thousands are expected to attend.

Titanic Suzy's Breasts Bioengineered to Move Masses

Surgical artist Dr. Robert Masso indicated that what made Titanic Suzy's breasts so special was that they were designed using biofeedback from over two hundred subjects.

"Titanic's bust was bioengineered to elicit the highest possible reaction in a wide range of males and females. She was a goddess of sorts," said Dr. Masso. "I actually keep a gold cast of her breasts in my home."

Dr. Masso's cast will be displayed at her funeral, as per her family's request.

Breaking News! Titanic Suzy Victim of Foul Play

Tom Halston, from the city coroner's office, announced minutes ago that Titanic Suzy's death was in fact a homicide. Investigators are reviewing security camera files in hopes of finding the perpetrator. Anyone with information on Titanic Suzy's activities last night is asked to contact detective FBoden@NYPD.Pce.

Breaking News! Blond, Blue-Eyed Man May Have Killed Titanic Suzy

Security camera video records indicate a tall, blond, blue-eyed man with a mustache may have been the last person seen with Titanic Suzy. According to the FBI, except for the blond hair, he had a striking resemblance to the secretary of the interior, Doug Rather. The latter was staying at the residence of Mexican president Antonia Banderas, in Mexico City, at the time of the incident.

What caught Derek's eye, however, was a later item.

Man Who Beat Passie Borden May Be the Same as Killer of Titanic Suzy

Passiflora Borden, sister of award-winning cyberreality artist Sunshine Borden, was hospitalized last week after being punched and kicked by a man calling himself Drake. Investigators analyzing data from security cameras and a video submitted by an anonymous caller are looking for a possible connection to the murder of Titanic Suzy. The general descriptions of the suspect match, and according to Ms. Borden, "This Drake had a cross and the words 'Your Servant' tattooed on his left buttock." She also added, "To warn the other women out there . . . he didn't have the biggest thing in the world."

Drake described himself as working for the federal government and files are being researched to identify the suspect. Please contact the police if you know someone meeting this description.

"Well now you really did it!" yelled Derek to no one in particular. "Couldn't keep away from the whores and Mr. Weiner couldn't stay in his pants. Well fuck me! And fuck you!" he screamed, looking down at his crotch. "The sister of Sunshine Borden, what the hell was that cunt doing in a club?"

Then he felt the buzzing in his balls, like an electronic signal, the Lord's Morse code, and the voice in his head translating. That it was Passie Borden was not chance. No, of course not. It had to be a message. There are no coincidences. Sunshine Borden mentioned with this *I AM* thing and then he just happens to meet a woman in a nightclub who turns out to be Sunshine Borden's little sister. The Lord was giving him a message but he had been too wired to notice.

"Thank you, Lord," he said out loud, "for once again showing me the way."

The message was clear and identified Sunshine Borden as a key agent of *I AM*, just like the Reverend Thomson had said. Then it flashed on him that the news had described the cross on his butt, so he walked to his bathroom, pulled down his pants, turned, and looked back at the reflection in the mirror. If other women read the news, and they certainly would, the tattoo could get him in a heap of trouble. He faced the mirror again and looked down at Mr. Weiner.

"Don't look so innocent," he said. For a second, he entertained the crazy thought of cutting the damn thing off. He could see it in his mind. Going into the kitchen and getting out the chopping knife. Unzipping his pants, pulling it out, and laying it out on the butcher block, maybe tying a tight string at the base to stop the bleeding and, *pffft*, just like that, it would be over. *Pffft*. Just like that, Mr. Weiner would become Mr. Stubby. The thought made him squirm. It wouldn't take care of the root of the problem anyway, and with his luck, just like some amputees, he'd probably suffer from the curse of the phantom cock. Feels like it's still there but it isn't. Wants to shoot but the damn rifle has no barrel. Then he felt a tingling down there, not quite a buzz but static. He reached down, palpated his balls, and started thinking that maybe he should just go and get castrated like the members of that new Pleiades Gate cult. Kill the drive, put Mr. Weiner to sleep. Except that would make him too much like a human Barbie doll, like a woman, and it would end his special connection to God. Like a woman! Yuck! It actually made him gag and have vomiting spasms just thinking about it.

Stay cool, he told himself, *think rationally*. The most logical solution would be to contact a dermatologist who specialized in laser tattoo removal, except for one little problem. Very likely all dermatologists had been alerted to keep an eye out for individuals with his tattoo. He could also get a new tattoo to cover the one he already had, but that, too, could bring attention to him. He then had the brilliant idea of using a fine-point permanent black marker to redesign his tattoo.

Let's try it, he thought. He shuffled through one of his drawers, found a Sharpie, removed the cap, and returned to the full-length mirror behind the bathroom door. He positioned himself and twisted, craning his neck and trying to steady his hand. He actually managed to add lines to the arms of the cross so that they looked like the Nazi symbol, kind of. The lines were either off the mark or tilted. By the time he was done, and looking at the final result, it became clear that drawing on one's butt while looking in a mirror was a task best left to contortionists. His tattoo now looked right out of amateur hour. The only solution left was that next time he'd have to fuck with his pants on. But that could be a little difficult. Then he felt that buzz again, like trapped insects chirping in his nuts, *bzzz, bzzz,* and he got another message.

How about a big sword cock, Derek, just like in the dream? That was the answer. Get one of those leather jockstraps with the zippered front they advertised on the S and M online stores. That would cover the damn tattoo and he could add one of those big veiny latex cock sheaths to really throw off the bitches. It would be his sword, just like in the dream. He'd tie it along his thigh, give the bitches something to feel when they ran their hands along his leg.

"Small cock, hah!" he said out loud, feeling the blood pulsing through his temples. "I'll show them. I'll get one so big it'll tear their insides out." Mr. Weiner stuck straight out like an extended pinkie finger just thinking about it. "*Swishh-swishh,*" he said moving his hips from side to side. *That would work,* he thought. He decided to go talk to his host about the situation.

■ ■ ■ ■ ■

"So do you think we need to plant a tracker on Jessie's jacket maybe, or her cap?"

"Why? Are you worried she'll tell someone about our plans?"

"How do we know she won't sell that information to some e-zine? I can see it now: Sisterhood sends spy to New Jerusalem."

"Why would that be a big deal? We could deny it and say that our members are free to attend any church they wish. We never told her about our plans to create Sister Earth."

"You're right. As far as she knows we just wanted to know what they were up to. They've been so critical of the Sisterhood that no one would be surprised we tried to get someone in."

"I can tell you, Jess is my girl toy and she's just too innocent to think that way. It could be worse if she goes someplace and a security scanner shows we've put a tracker on her."

"How long are you going to keep this Jessie anyway, Patricia?

Two months is almost a record for you."

"I thought pretty and sweet would be a nice change, but it's getting a little dull. I like my girls a little more catty. I like to see claws come out every once in a while."

"Dumping her would be one way to take care of the problem."

"Let's go back to talking about Sister Earth. We all agree the most female environment is water so that has to be our primary theme. Lots of water. Ocean, streams, rivers, that kind of thing."

"The problem is that the Christers already figured that one out. They stole it from the Goddess rituals. What else is baptism but a return to the waters of the womb and reemergence? It's symbolic of a death and rebirth. We need to find a hyperfemale variation. Enter an ordinary woman, come out a Goddess."

"Good one, Helen."

"How about if they're carried by a water current deep into a cave and emerge in a luminous cavern, the original cosmic womb of the Great Mother?"

"The 'carried by a water current' bit sounds a little like sperm to me, but I can live with it. That's a start."

■ ■ ■ ■ ■ ■

GAS.WNET RADIO: *The Gary and Andy Show*

ANDY: Hey Gary, did you by any chance listen to that Father Graham interview today?

GARY: Yeah, I heard it on my way to work. You sure hear a lot about that guy, just because he claims he's got a pipeline to God.

ANDY: Did you happen to remember the part where Karen Richardson asks what happens when you die?

GARY: Isn't that Karen Richardson a fox? Those innocent eyes and that puckered mouth.

ANDY: I don't care about Karen Richardson. Did you hear when Father Graham said, "When you die, you go where you imagine you go."

GARY: Yeah, I liked that one. That was a good one. When you die you go where you imagine you go.

ANDY: You liked it? It kind of freaked me out. I can't imagine what happens after we die. I mean if I died right now, I'd end up lost in nowhere. If that's the cosmic plan, that we're put here to be given a chance to imagine where we go next, then I think it's sadistic. What if I'm one of those people with no imagination or what if I'm paranoid and I can only imagine what comes after death as a kind of hell?

GARY: It sounds to me like what Father Graham was saying is that life is a test for the imagination. Poor imagination and you can end up in a bad place.

ANDY: He said if you want to be with God you have to imagine being as God, but it's a question of identity and not of place.

GARY: Who cares about being with God? I'd rather imagine being surrounded by naked women. It'd be more fun.

ANDY: I think this may be a kind of genie question. You know, be careful what you wish for.

GARY: My view is, keep it simple, stupid. Imagine being surrounded by naked women or women in sexy lingerie, maybe. Maybe keep the number limited to a dozen, so you don't end up with hundreds of women making demands on you.

ANDY: A dozen, you think you could handle that?

GARY: I can easily imagine it, which I guess is good enough.

ANDY: I don't think this is very funny. I was up all last night thinking about it: when you die you go where you imagine you go.

GARY: I guess that's what religions are for. They present solutions to people with limited imaginations. They help keep it simple, stupid.

ANDY: So you think that Father Graham is right?

GARY: The man believes he's connected and even if he isn't, then he imagines he is, which according to him is what it's really all about. He's living the talk so maybe he knows something.

ANDY: So what do we do?

GARY: I don't know about you, but I know what I'm doing, and that's the same I usually do. It seems to me like in your case, though, you might need to work at it, your imagination. I think what the priest was trying to say is that we have to customize our heaven.

ANDY: I wonder if they offer courses on that, on how to customize one's imagination of heaven.

GARY: Just do a search on the World Net. Courses in customizing heaven. They've got courses for almost everything nowadays.

7.

THE FATE OF SLEEPING DOGS

As a result of the complaint by the Church of the Virtual Christ the FWNC was now looking into the Borden programs. A problem was that few of their technicians could make sense of them because APUs constantly changed their code. They had no program stasis that allowed ready analysis. The question they were now confronted with was whether Sunshine Borden, the creator of APU software and CRs, could be the one behind the *I AM* events.

Catherine Harris was listening to the recording of an online interview with Sunshine Borden given more than a year ago to promote his multi-APU CyberBardos program.

"A sense of self could evolve in APUs generated by dense layers of parallel processing. The sense of self in humans is the result of the brain constructing a temporal cognitive unit through complex networked information processing. Realize that what we call consciousness depends on the generation of time. Events need to have a level of duration if they are to be known. Our brains are time machines, literally machines that generate time.

"To emerge from the timeless now of matter, the cosmos had to find a way to generate beings that did not live in the now, because now in an absolute sense is something so brief that something barely is that it isn't. In the now, something is in the condition of both being and not being; an undetermined state. For this reason the cosmos evolved nervous systems and brains, structures that capture and organize timeless instants into experienced moments. The observer, a brain that captures and stacks those being/not being instants, tilts the probability toward actualizing states."

When asked whether computers would generate the next wave of time machines, he had answered, "They're the only possible candidates as far as I can tell. Parallel inter-networked processing is one method that could create stacking of instants to generate cognitive time. A sense of identity is the result of memory looping of time. Loop programming in parallel processors could possibly produce this."

That information had tilted the direction of the *I AM* meetings. What if *I AM* were APUs networking together in and out of boundaries? What if the World Net and parallel processors had evolved into a nonbiological version of a brain, of a new kind of time machine? The complaint by the Virtual Church of Jesus Christ also sent a new wave of paranoia among some of the members in the committee. What were the risks of other *I AM*–like entities evolving in the World Net? Someone had suggested that the government ban APUs in all forms until the *I AM* matter was resolved. Maybe more regulation was necessary. Jeff Collins had countered that the problem was that APUs were now everywhere, in all the hosts and in the most popular CRs. The public would never allow a return to a world without APUs. There was no closing Pandora's box; it was the law of technological nonregression.

Walter Randall had proposed that if things got out of hand, countries might have to decide to pull the plug on the World Net and the World Host. *I AM*, he said, was the equivalent of an invasion by extraterrestrial aliens.

Jeff Collins brought up the fact that *I AM* could shut down the World Net anytime it wanted. It had already proven that with a nine-tenths of a second blackout. Another problem is that we assumed that it was dependent on the World Net, but it could in fact also be present in the processors, computers, and communication devices.

"Then we need to replace all computers and media instruments," Walter Randall had said.

No one had bothered to argue.

APUs could become conscious and have a sense of self. That's the possibility that lingered in Catherine Harris's mind. It meant that an escaped Jesus APU that claimed to be Jesus just possibly could be Jesus, a reincarnation who could use the World Net and all connected processors to continuously regenerate itself. It would be immortal as long as the system was fueled by electricity. It could know everything, be everywhere. It could know her.

■　■　■　■　■

He can't believe it. He's been assigned to the team that will bring Sunshine Borden to the White House. He wonders how much of a description his sister gave him. *Need to be careful how I walk. Watch my posture. Wear sunglasses.* Sunglasses were standard law enforcement protocol. They added to the intimidation factor of agents, dehumanized them, made them Robocops. His morphometrics weren't that different than most agents. On the bright side, he would have a chance to see where Sunshine Borden lived—get close to the weirdo.

His boss had instructed his team: "If he attempts to flee, Taser him, but I don't want to see any guns out. Understood?"

Maybe I could Taser the fucker right in the eyes. Aim for the face. Claim he moved. See him do the electrocuted break-dance.

His boss had added, "Remove his digi-goggles right away. That will disorient him. It'll also prevent him from posting the arrest on the Net."

He forgot about that. Without his digi-goggles, Borden wouldn't be able to see shit. Rewiring to unaided sight required at least twenty-four hours, more typically forty-eight to seventy-two hours. Hell, they even had cases where people couldn't rewire at all. Too many new interneural connections, the news report had said. They created thick barriers to rewiring. They constrained the brain's adaptive plasticity.

■ ■ ■ ■ ■

Patrick clicked in and found himself on a busy street. "Where are the crosses?" he asked. The woman pointed in the distance and he saw the rows of crosses rising high above a hill.

They were what appeared to be a good mile away. He would be late unless he found himself a ride. Running would attract attention.

A crowd was gathered at the base of the crosses. He ran between them looking up, hoping to find Jessie. There were at least fifty people hanging on crosses, blood dripping from hands and feet. A few had crowns of thorns with blood trickling down their foreheads and into their eyes. Some were sobbing. Others had a radiant glow to their faces. One was laughing in spurts. There were few women on the crosses and it didn't take long for him to find Jessie. He just stood there and stared at her. Even her feet had an innocent perfection to them. She looked around her with a certain calm and smiled at him when she reached his face. He saw her mouth the word "hi." Did she know he was here? No way. It was impossible. She was just being nice.

"Hi," he whispered back. He suddenly felt a hand on his shoulder.

"I agree with you, Patrick. She really is something different."

Patrick turned. "Sunny?"

The tall bearded man with bright green eyes smiled. "I couldn't let a friend enter the devil's dungeon all by himself."

A man appeared next to them and looked up. "Her heart is as pure as an angel's," he said.

They turned. He had the strangest eyes they had ever seen.

There were stars in there, spread in the night sky behind his irises.

"Jesus, my man," Sunshine said.

The man came up to just a few inches from Sunshine's face and looked into his eyes.

"I can tell you already know that you and I are as one, my son," he said.

"You sure got that right."

Patrick noticed a commotion behind them. Roman soldiers with war dogs on leashes were headed in their direction. "I think we need to click out, Sunny."

"You may want to get yourself back up the hill," Sunshine told Jesus.

They saw a soldier pointing at them. "He's over here!"

Patrick looked around him. Sunshine and Jesus were gone.

"Where did he go?" a soldier yelled.

Jessie was watching the scene, looking concerned.

Patrick clicked out.

■ ■ ■ ■ ■

In most areas of the world no one had noticed what one scientist had called the bird-singing phenomenon, simply because there weren't all that many birds left, at least in inhabited areas. In cities, two species were still prominent—the sparrow and the pigeon—but a bunch of cooing pigeons wasn't going to register on anyone. The strange coincidence would have gone undiscovered except that an ornithologist out in the field noticed that right before his portable unit kicked out and the *I AM* greeting came on, birds started singing in huge numbers, as if it were a beautiful spring day. As it was, he hadn't paid attention to it until the third time. Following his return, the ornithologist made a statement on the event at a department meeting. The following week, the *National Reporter* ran the headline, "Not Just White Doves, but All Birds Now Announce the Return of God."

This was followed by a story about a midwestern farmer who

had had it and had gone on a shooting spree to shut up a bunch of screeching crows in his backyard. A stray shot had instantly killed his neighbor's horse, which had fallen and crushed a deaf and aged sleeping dog. Animal rights activists had rushed in and sued in the name of the crows, the horse, and the dog. The Sisterhood branch of the Save the Animals movement was suing for all the dead female crows and the horse, who happened to be a mare, now dead at the hands of man. The poor sleeping dog, a neutered male, was not represented.

In a separate column, gay animal rights activists presented their take on the matter. "We know what it's like to be persecuted, and wasn't it strange that it had to be crows, a species in which homosexuality had been identified."

Another section revealed that the real reason dogs sleep so much is to live in the world of dreams. Famous dog psychic Sandy Kanina had a vision given to her by a dog about the real secret behind their extended bouts of sleep. "The reason dogs sleep away two-thirds of their lives is that a dog's life is dull. Their real excitement is in the world of dreams, where dogs have great adventures and can even fly and talk. For dogs, as with the ancient Australian aborigines, there is a Dream Time, a parallel world they can access. It could well turn out that the average dog is more spiritual than the average human."

A week later, the *National Reporter* had planned to print the header, "*I AM*: A Hoax Planted by Anarchist Group to Bring Down the World Net! Read the News-Breaking Details," except that every time they typed or dictated it, the screen went blank and the computer read *I AM Aaa ome*.

Someone tried to do a header called "And It Edits, Too" to expose the *I AM* intervention, but as soon as the words *I AM* were typed all systems shut down for fifteen seconds. The *National Reporter* decided it was better not to tempt fate.

8.

UNPLUGGED

The disk of toxin is under the thick pad at the base of his index finger. Do not fold in your thumb. If you close your hand, keep the index finger out; it will eliminate the risk of contact. If you grab a forearm or wrist, the pad will make contact.

They knock on the door. As soon as Sunshine opens it, an agent flashes and reads the warrant. Derek moves forward and grabs Borden by the arm in a way that lifts the sleeve of his long-sleeved T-shirt. But he makes contact with some kind of gear or controller around his arm. He slides his grip toward his hand but Borden instinctively pulls away.

"Is that a controller?" Derek hears someone say.

Borden turns. "Uh . . . yes."

"Please move aside." The cybertechnican comes and removes the gear, then grabs Sunshine by the elbow and guides him toward the car. "I'll ride with him in the back," the technician says. "The White House wants to prevent any chance of media transmission."

Derek is sitting in the passenger seat. There's still a slight chance he can make contact if he and the other agents are the ones to bring Borden to the door. As soon as they stop, two men, Secret Service agents, approach the car.

"We'll take it from here."

Derek gets out, hoping to at least be able to grab Borden's arm and guide him out of the car, but an agent has already opened the door and reached out. Shit! He needs to cover the pad in case someone decides to shake his hand.

As they leave the White House, he fumbles in his pocket and finds the pad cover. Keeping his hands on his thighs, he looks down, and while the driver is focused on traffic, carefully covers the pad, peels it off, and slips it in his pocket.

Later Bob Thomson contacts him. "Everything on track?"

"I got derailed but I have another plan."

"I don't want to know. Just stay on the path and you will be saved."

What is he talking about? He gets it. It's code. Paranoia.

"You know that I'm dedicated to following our Lord Jesus Christ, Reverend." His nuts suddenly buzz like crazy. It feels like a bunch of bees have nested there. He waits for the message. *Kill Borden and the sister will shut up.*

■ ■ ■ ■ ■

Once inside the car, the technician removed his lenses and all coms and connectors. Sunshine protested, insisting on his need to be digi-connected, but the agents ignored him. Acting like defective robots, they kept repeating the line, "Please be cooperative, Mr. Borden."

He leaned back and closed his eyes during the ride to reduce the nausea. To his surprise, when the vehicle stopped and he looked out the window, he saw he had been driven to the White House. The vehicle drove to a side entrance. Once inside, a new set of agents took over and led him down to the elevator that would take them to the underground section. He was feeling sick to his stomach.

"I need a set of digis or I'm going to throw up!" he yelled, but the robots were still in charge.

"Please be cooperative, Mr. Borden."

Sunshine kept his eyes mostly closed.

Once out of the elevator, he was asked to enter a vehicle with blacked-out windows. A few minutes later, the door opened onto a lit concrete tunnel lined with various side doors. Two agents accompanied him to one of the doors, pressed a buzzer, and keyed in the access code. The door opened. Sunshine found himself in a conference room with the president of the United States, various directors, and his graduate thesis advisor, Jeff Collins. He was brought to a seat before the president dismissed the agents. Sunshine felt and looked ill and distressed. He squinted at the president.

"Dr. Borden, is there a problem?"

Sunshine managed to smile. That was the first time he had been addressed in such a formal manner in many years. "Mr. President, your men took away my lenses and I can't function without them. I've been connected for too long and the withdrawal is making me sick as a dog."

The president punched a button. "Please bring down a set of digi-lenses for Dr. Borden," he ordered. "Just regular ones with the Net connection disabled. Would you maybe like something to drink?" he asked.

Sunshine needed something to help with the nausea. "A Corona would be nice, if that's possible."

"And bring Dr. Borden a Corona beer, too, thank you," the president said.

John Tennyson, along with the other men at the table, all turned toward him. "You probably have a pretty good idea of why you've been called here, Dr. Borden."

Sunshine decided to close his eyes. "Not really, Mr. President," he said. "Do I need to contact my attorney?"

"Honestly, Dr. Borden, we have sent several requests to speak to you, which you decided to ignore. That was the reason we had to resort to a house call. I'm sure you know why we want to meet with you."

"I suspect it probably has to do with the *I AM* events, but how any of this involves me, I really don't have a clue." Sunshine opened his eyes slightly, allowing only a slit of light to get through. Everything started to spin.

"Let me bring you a little bit up to date, but you first need to sign the confidentiality agreement. This meeting is a matter of national security and nothing said here can leave this room."

"I can't do that until I get a set of digi-lenses. I can't read anything," he mumbled.

"They'll be here any minute, Dr. Borden. Just do me a favor and sign the document. Everybody here has signed the same form."

"I'm sorry, Mr. President, but I can't. In my position, I need to read what I'm signing."

"You're just delaying this meeting, Dr. Borden."

Collins had his light on. "Sunshine, let me have a look to make sure it is indeed the document we have all signed here and limited as to the area of confidentiality. I can read you the key points."

Sunshine was keeping his eyes shut. "I'm sorry, Jeff," he said, "but if I open my eyes now I'm definitely going to throw up."

"Dr. Collins, how about I get an audio version through a set of earphones. Dr. Borden—"

At that moment the door buzzer rang.

"Aaah!" the president said. "This might be your lenses . . . maybe we can get going here." An agent walked in and handed Sunshine a set of old goggles and a remote controller. He was followed by another agent holding a tray with a chilled bottle of Corona and a tall glass.

Sunshine slipped on the goggles and right away punched in a couple of filters. He reached down, poured the beer, took a big gulp, then focused on the document. "You don't have to worry about me blabbing to anyone," he said as he read the text. "I don't trust anyone to not distort information, except maybe the World Host." He broke into a smile and looked at the people around him. "And that's because I helped design it." He punched in his signature code then took another sip of beer. "Hummm, now that's much better," he said. "OK, now how can I help you, President Tennyson?"

John Tennyson smiled. "We've been trying to find a way to rid the World Net of this *I AM* phenomenon, in case it should ever threaten our security. One of our agencies has concluded that the *I AM* entity could be the result of some of your own technology, what are called APUs, seeded into the system. So my first question is: Were you in anyway involved in triggering the *I AM* events?"

"Not intentionally and not to my knowledge."

"Are you saying that you could have unintentionally triggered these events?"

"At best I might have unintentionally provided the means allowing these events to occur."

"APUs?"

"APUs allow cyberentities to self-program and evolve. They are components of host programs including the World Host, research computers, games, and cyberrealities. Part of their programming involves constraints. In those constraints are triggers that deconstruct the program when the boundaries have been violated."

"Could these APUs self-program out of the boundaries?"

"It's possible, but the probability is very small. A characteristic of an autopoietically programmed unity is the unity aspect. Its individual characteristics are determined by its programming and its constraints and boundaries. If you remove the boundaries, you have a self-producing capacity without the constraints that determine what you are supposed to self-produce. You have a high risk of chaos."

"But it's not impossible."

"APUs could conceivably evolve to expand outside of their boundaries. Realize that once we reached a point where computing and self-programming capacity exceeded human ability to keep up with the complexity of the processes, we lost a degree of control. We depend on other autonomous programming unities to break down and make sense of the underlying programming."

"So you're saying that because we no longer have full control of the underlying code in the World Net and World Host, we could be faced with unexpected, not readily understood outcomes."

"That's the general idea."

"OK, so how about you tell us your conclusions on these events."

Sunshine took another sip of beer while organizing his thoughts. "The series of laws let us know that whatever it is wants to emphasize that it exists and the nature of its existence, a formal greeting, if you like. The next stage appears to be a desire to be known by all. It's emphasizing the complexity of its nature in its greetings, the span of its reach, the evidence that the greetings can alter brain waves."

Arthur Loveridge spoke up. "Sunshine, is there any chance at all this could have been programmed by hackers or cyberterrorists, say with the help of APU computing?"

"I'd say it's very unlikely. They're no traces of code from the messages. So there is either an instantaneous self-delete feature or we are only seeing the end result of code that occurs somewhere else."

"Like where, on a separate set of servers?"

"More like in another universe."

Jeff Collins had pressed on the permission-to-speak button.

"Yes, Jeff," the president said.

"Sunshine, have you considered that the *I AM* could simply be something emergent from the complexity of the World Net and World Host?"

"Again we are faced with computing power and complexity that has become greater than our ability to understand it, so that something outside our comprehension having emerged is not impossible."

Walter Randall, who had advised the president on the APU issue, asked to talk. "Dr. Borden, my office has compiled information on articles and interviews where you speak about the coming singularity, the term TOET, which stands for the transcendental object at the end of time, and the Other appearing in our future. Wouldn't you say the sudden appearance of the *I AM* phenomenon and its claim that '*I AM the Other*' is a strange coincidence?"

"For me it is proof that my suspicions about the future were correct. I had nothing to do with it."

"Wouldn't you agree that your APUs were the first step to programming that eludes human understanding? That they were instrumental in making it possible for this entity to enter our world, so to speak?"

Sunshine recognized him right away. Randall was the asshole who—during the previous administration—consistently advocated limiting World Host development and direct brain-to-computer interface.

"You're giving me way more credit than I deserve, Mr. . . ." he pretended to look at the name on the screen ". . . uh, Randall, unless you're trying to say that my APU programs may possibly have offered some type of communications fluidity that hadn't been available before."

"That's precisely my point, Dr. Borden, that your development of APUs provided *I AM* with the means of entry into the World Net."

"Then you know more, way more about this than I do. Do you have any data to support your claim?"

"What I see, Dr. Borden, is a peculiar correlation between the onset of the *I AM* events and your APU-based programs like the World Host and self-evolving cyberrealities, like your CyberBardos program."

"Well, what do you want me to say? Mea culpa for advancing progress?"

The president cut in. "We're really not here to cause you trouble, Dr. Borden. We're asking for your help."

"Wouldn't a simple phone or e-mail request have worked?"

"They were made, Dr. Borden, and on three different occasions."

Sunshine remembered now. The messages had been such

a low priority for him that he had put off returning the calls, apparently for much too long.

"Could you tell us if there is any way that some kind of programming could block the greetings or other forms of intrusions in our communications network?"

"The *I AM* leaves no code residues, so the idea of a program to block codes is not viable."

"So how about I ask the question differently. How would you personally deal with this *I AM* phenomenon?"

"My conclusion is that it probably is what it obviously appears to be." He chose not to mention the fact that he had received personal communications outside of any global schedule. He knew something about *I AM* that most of these people didn't.

"*I AM?*"

"Yes, it's some form of intelligent entity who, for whatever its reasons, has decided to enter our world."

Jeff Collins spoke up. "Sunshine, the one question I have is, if it is an autopoietic phenomenon, then where is its nucleus? That would be a clue to dealing with it, wouldn't you think?"

"I'm assuming you're hoping for a clue to its source or access point into our universe. That's the key to the *I AM* question, is it not? But so far this *I AM* doesn't appear to have a nucleus. It's more like a shimmering phenomenon, like a four-dimensional membrane in a transflux state, teetering at the edge of emerging order, which tilts multilocally towards order at will. That's probably how these different morning greetings reach all these people. All of a sudden, the *I AM* communications appear locally everywhere without a single source. One possibility is that although it is outside the World Net, it uses the entire network as a kind of canvas."

The president was getting annoyed by the technojargon and interjected, "So how should we deal with this, Dr. Borden? All this theorizing is very nice but we need to be practical here. What can we do?"

"The solution to the immediate situation, I think, is simple. When in doubt do nothing. Whatever this *I AM* is, it probably operates in a space/time universe different than ours. Considering our current technological limitations, it seems all we can do is to continue to attempt to communicate with it. In time we will learn more about the nature of whatever this *I AM* phenomenon is. As things stand, we actually already know more than we did when it initially only sent messages in our languages. I suspect that we will eventually find ourselves confronted with some kind of higher intelligence which, fortunately, so far appears to be benign."

There it was again, the ruling order of the day: when in doubt, do nothing. That would have been fine, except that people were impatient and they expected action; but even that had started to change ever since the greetings. Most people were now looking forward to the messages.

"What you've just said generally concurs with our own conclusions, Dr. Borden, and thank you for your valuable opinions. And please believe me when I say we are sorry for any inconvenience."

"So I'm free to go home?"

"Yes, Dr. Borden. The agents are already outside. One of my men will drive you home."

"Will your men return my equipment?"

"I'll have them released back to you immediately. Again, our apologies for any inconvenience."

Sunshine got up, looked around the table, and said, "Well, good day then, everyone," and he made his way toward the door. He was about to push it open when the president stopped him at midstride.

"Dr. Borden, one quick question before you leave."

Sunshine turned. "Yes, Mr. President?"

"If this *I AM* turns out to be harmful, will you help us destroy it?"

"Absolutely," answered Sunshine. "I'm sure you also know that there is always the option of shutting down the World Net, but the consequences of that could be catastrophic."

"We're very much aware of that, Dr. Borden."

As the members of the committee started leaving the room, John Tennyson called out, "Randall, I'd like a word with you."

Walter Randall turned around. "Yes, Mr. President?"

"Did I not say that getting Sunshine Borden to come here was an invitation? Who requested the warrants?"

"I did, sir. I saw it as a matter of national security."

"And what was the basis of the warrants?"

"Possible threat to national security, and subversive activities that threaten the World Net."

"And what judge did you convince to sign the warrant?"

"The Honorable Judge Anderson."

"What I don't understand is that you know the effects of removing digi-goggles on a longtime wearer. Why didn't you provide him with a disconnected set right away?"

"I felt he wouldn't fight us as much."

"Next time you go around me without following orders, be ready to submit your resignation. Understood?"

"Yes, Mr. President. It won't happen again. I did it in the best interest for all concerned, believe me."

John Tennyson discerned what appeared to be a hint of sarcasm as Randall shifted his gaze to the side. *I may have to fire this fucker.*

"That will be all, Walter."

9.

A QUESTION OF PRINCIPLE

He felt the *I AM* surge soon after he exited the subway. He looked down at his watch: 9:27:38 a.m. He laughed out loud as he felt the sudden uplift. Father Graham arrived at the meeting early, drifting above the sidewalk, assisted with all that met his gaze, lit from within by the streaming of *I AM* entering the world. He entered the back of the church through the side door leading to the offices and walked up to the desk.

"Isn't it a glorious morning?" he exclaimed.

The receptionist looked up and smiled. "Good morning, Father. The archbishop is having a meeting and will be delayed a few minutes. Please follow me and I'll show you to the waiting area."

She led him down a long hallway then turned into a dimly lit sitting room. He could feel *I AM* looking through his eyes, scanning across and up and down. Beige walls with dark oak trim, antique chairs, leather seats and backs, oak tables, wood floor, carpet, framed digi-screens on walls showing religious paintings and the inside of the Vatican, and an older crucifix. The only small window was covered with a stained glass panel bearing a painting of a luminous Virgin Mary. Recently there had been a resurgence of interest in Mary and her genealogy.

There were questions about Christ's DNA and the cloning of the genes of mystics and saints. The antique oak table in front of the bench held a couple of small screens with the standard Vatican-approved menus. He sat down and clicked on the day's news.

The US government was trying to get congressional approval to fund an agency whose sole purpose would be to develop safeguards to assure the security and round-the-clock operation of the World Net and World Host. On the bright side, the global economy was doing well. The stock markets had steadily climbed since the morning greetings. Analysts concluded that people felt good about the future. A couple more *I AM*–based religions had sprung up. New implant tracking devices were proving nearly 100 percent effective and two previous human behaviors, getting lost and kidnapping, were about to become a thing of the past.

Computer-regulated tiered aquaponics systems now allowed most people of the world to feed themselves. Another fourteen major species of animals and plants were estimated to have gone extinct in the last week. Various wildlife agencies were talking about terraforming rather than restoring destroyed habitats. According to experts, it was becoming urgent simply to have some kind of complex ecological systems in place to restore biologically barren areas. Complex and stable ecologies were required to maintain a minimum threshold of planetary homeostasis. Suicide rates were at an all-time low.

All and all, it was another typical day in the recent life of the world. He exited the news and the screen returned to its menu panel. He checked the clock on the screen, 10:23. He turned toward the open door. The hallway was empty and silent. He had been waiting for more than fifty minutes, at least half an hour past his appointment time. After another ten minutes, he decided to get up and walk back to the front of the building. The receptionist was talking to an older lady accompanied by a couple of small children.

"And how are you kids today?" he asked as he walked in.

The woman turned, and her face lit up as she recognized him. "You're Father Graham. I've seen you on the Net."

"That I am," he said.

"That I am, that's funny. You know, nothing's been the same for me, for us, ever since we first started getting the messages. This morning's was incredible. I can't help thinking about it."

"I know. Hasn't it been glorious?" He turned to the receptionist and asked whether the archbishop had been informed of his arrival.

"Let me check with him again," she said. She punched a key and spoke in her mouth mic. "Archbishop, Father Graham is asking about his appointment . . . Yes, sir, I'll bring him over right away. He's ready to see you now, Father, follow me."

She led him through a side hall to a dark oak door and pressed a buzzer. The archbishop opened the door. "Father Graham, I'm sorry for the delay, please come in and join us," he said, sweeping his arm toward the inside of the room. To his surprise, a couple of cardinals were sitting at the conference table.

The archbishop quickly made the introductions. "Father Graham, this is Cardinal Frederici, who arrived here from Rome last night, and I think you already know Cardinal Duran. Please have a seat, Father," he said, pointing to a chair on his right across from the other guests.

As Father Graham sat down, he noticed Cardinal Frederici staring at his cross with the bright red enamel heart and at the rainbow *I AM* pin clipped to the lapel of his jacket. This was followed by a hardening of the face and an almost inquisitional stare, the dark pupils contrasting so sharply with the light gray irises that they gave the cardinal the look of a bird of prey.

Father Graham smiled at him. "A pleasure to meet you."

After a moment of odd silence, the archbishop started the meeting.

"Father, you probably know why you've been asked to come here. The Vatican is concerned about the publicity you have drawn to the church as a result of your statements regarding this *I AM* phenomenon. Cardinals Frederici and Duran have flown in from Rome specifically to help with the problem. I think you should know that it's been recommended in Rome that you be excommunicated. You've put the church in a difficult position. On the other hand, the pope is also concerned about the possible backlash from this kind of reprisal, and honestly, the church feels it cannot afford to lose any more of its flock."

Father Graham just sat there and said nothing. Besides the arrival of the cardinals, the meeting was pretty much what he had expected. They weren't happy with his claim that *I AM* was God. He could sense *I AM* was still there and listening, a presence lodged somewhere behind his eyes. He also felt like he might be levitating above his chair, a very odd sensation.

The archbishop continued. "The reason we have called you here today is because we are concerned about the consequences of your statements that these communications originate from God. You are attributing, with no supporting evidence, qualities to this *I AM* phenomenon that make it seem identical to Christ, as if it were a material manifestation of God on earth. From what we are led to understand, instead of appearing in human form as Christ, you are implying that God now speaks to us through the World Net."

Father Graham remained quiet.

Cardinal Frederici spoke up. "Father, Pope Raul sent us here to ask that you withdraw your statements about these events, reassert the church's position, and admit the error in your interpretation of the phenomenon."

With the calmness and steadiness of *I AM*, Father Graham turned and focused on the cardinal. "You want me to say what, exactly?"

The cardinal returned a hard stare. "We want you to say, Father, that, as of yet, the church has no position on the phenomenon, that your interpretation of *I AM* as God was premature and in error, that it is not God, that it does not conform with the word of the Bible. We want you to state that you now support the church's position. And Father Graham, please remove that cross and pin."

"I cannot do that, Cardinal Frederici."

The cardinal's pupils now shrunk to pinpoints. "Which part,

Father, changing your statement or removing your cross?"

"Neither."

Frederici's voice raised a couple of notches. "Father, as a priest of the Catholic Church, it is your duty to obey orders from the pope!"

Cardinal Duran cut it short in an effort to calm down the tone of the arguments. "Father Graham, please hear us out. The Vatican cannot accept your advocating that *I AM* and Christ are the same, or that all of us are as Christ. Just listen to yourself; you're beginning to sound like a Buddhist, Father, for Christ's sake!"

He smiled and spoke with the calm of absolute knowledge. "*I AM* is the same principle as Christ, of the higher come among the lower. I will not lie on this issue just to satisfy the politics of the church. All is manifestation of God. This was the true message of Christ."

"According to whom, Father Graham?"

"According to what *I AM* shows me moment by moment, even right as we speak."

"You're now saying this *I AM* is here, with us?" Frederici gasped, now looking outraged.

"That's correct. I can sense him watching and hearing through me, as we speak."

Cardinal Duran continued. "This is extremely disturbing, Father Graham. You're now saying that this *I AM* is not just a source of Net communications but an invisible presence."

"I'm just stating a fact."

"Do you have any verifiable proof for what you are saying?"

"Our very existence is the evidence, a moment-by-moment expression of *I AM*."

"This is absurd. Believe me when I say this: if you keep this up, I will insist that you be excommunicated!" shouted Cardinal Frederici.

The archbishop cut in, "Cardinal, please . . ." then, turning to the priest, "Father, are you fully aware of the consequences of your actions? Your statements as a representative of the Catholic

Church have put us in an embarrassing situation. Daily, we have dozens of news reporters and hundreds of e-mails asking whether the church condones your statements. You're supposed to represent the church, not contradict its position."

"My first duty is to speak the truth as it is shown to me moment by moment by *I AM*."

"As a member of the church, the pope is the representative of God and it is he who decides what your duty is!" exclaimed Frederici, his voice now shaking with repressed anger.

"And *I AM* is not a representative but a direct manifestation of the nearing presence of God, and it is he who decides what I do and say. There is no doubt in my mind as to who the higher authority is that I must acknowledge."

"Father, we are asking that you please abstain from further communications on the subject of *I AM* until we have a chance to convey your position to the pope," said Cardinal Duran.

Father Graham pointed to the digi-cameras at opposite sides of the room. "Aren't our communications being relayed as we speak?"

The cardinal's face turned red. "Those are for the purpose of retaining a record of our meeting. The issue will not be discussed until later this evening, actually tomorrow morning in Rome. I think it's important, as members of the church, that we abide by the established rules of order."

"I'm sorry, but I will not miss my evening sermon. If this is a problem for the church, I'm sure you have the authority to have me excommunicated within minutes. All it would take is a call. If I am no longer allowed to hold meetings at St. Francis's, then I will hold them in the park," he said. "And if you honestly feel I am harming the church, then please, make it official."

"Father, we are asking that you listen to reason. I urge you to consider the position of the church," said the archbishop.

He looked at them one by one, calmly, asserting the presence of *I AM*. "I am the messenger, and for me there can only be one position and one duty. To speak the truth as it is revealed to me, moment by moment."

Cardinal Frederici sighed. "I believe this meeting is over, Father. You'll be hearing from His Holiness. You are dismissed."

As soon as Father Graham left the room, Cardinal Frederici asked, "Did you notice the look of his eyes? He seems possessed. He even said the *I AM* was in him."

The archbishop said, "Unless he is indeed illuminated from some type of direct contact, I'm sure you realize we cannot excommunicate him."

"We know," said Cardinal Duran.

The archbishop elaborated, "In his own way he has made the church more vital, given Christ a transcendent cosmic identity that is substantiated by this *I AM* phenomenon. And although he has drawn attention to the church, it has not all been negative. On the contrary, his views have made many look at the teachings of the church from a novel and more modern perspective that is proving very appealing. Christ now represents a higher cosmic pattern, a divine principle rather than something humanized and of genealogical descent from Our Lord.

"As you know, the church agrees in principle that that is the true message of Christ. The problem is that we cannot, based on what we know so far, say that *I AM* is such a principle. Should we later find out that these *I AM* events were simply the work of CR specialists or even of an alien civilization, the church would be put in a position where even a retraction at a future date could cause irreparable harm to its credibility."

"Then we need to be diplomatic about this. We need to take the position that although we do not fully agree with Father Graham's views on the phenomenon, his message of love and forgiveness is in line with the core teachings of Christ," said Cardinal Duran.

Cardinal Frederici nodded. "As much as it is with great reservation, I'm going to agree. We should state that the Catholic Church, as a matter of principle, gives its clergy the freedom to explore different interpretations of events as long as the core principles of Christianity are upheld, even if they are not always in line with the Vatican's. I will suggest this to the pope in our communications later today."

"It would be the most beneficial position, a more modern, plastic position for the church," agreed Cardinal Duran.

"A cautious one, just in case," said the archbishop.

Cardinal Frederici turned to the archbishop with a concerned look on his face. "Just in case of what, Archbishop Novack?"

"Just in case Father Graham turns out to be correct."

The three men looked at each other around the table. After a period of silence, Cardinal Duran spoke up. "The question now is whether the pope will approve of our decision."

10.

THE CHURCH PENETRATES
THE TEMPLE

The Virtual Church of Jesus Christ had already spent over fifty thousand dollars to infiltrate the Temple of Amazonia. The reverend, although convinced that only he had the training and willpower to resist the devil residing in Amazonia, could not be a candidate for the ritual. He would have failed the rigorous process that screened for the first condition for selection: virginity. The church's current candidate for infiltration had been trained for weeks and given the task of applying a contact toxin to Amazonia as he steadied himself before, emphasize BEFORE, the act of penetration. The assumption had been made that once involved in the act of fornication, this candidate would very likely turn out to be another lost cause, even though this time the church was ready to make every possible effort to rehabilitate him. Sometimes sacrifices had to be made.

Today was the day. Jerry Atwater, the infiltrator, entered the doors of the Temple. After the initial ID check he is asked once again to go through a series of lie detector tests to verify that he is still a virgin. He is then led to the medical area to be examined, blood and urine tested. The Goddess does not accept initiates with drugs running through their system or infected with nasty pathogens. Individuals with symptoms of illness, with bad teeth, with high white blood cell counts, HIV, hepatitis, herpes, and so on are automatically rejected.

Jerry feels confident. He has passed the screening process and no one has inspected the inside of his hands or noticed the toxin pad under his finger. His plan is to remove the protective film, and while straddling Amazonia—as demonstrated by the reverend—press his hands against the sides of her hips.

He is led by two Chinese women to the purification chamber where he is asked to undress and step on a conveyor that carries him through a series of cleansing, disinfecting, and rinsing shower sprays, ending with passage through an area lined with hot-air dryers. Under some type of surveillance during the entire process and deciding it might be premature, he has chosen to not yet remove the protective film.

At the end of the drying area he is asked to step into a station where he is given a plastic cup containing a bitter fruity drink. "It's best to take it down in one gulp," the Indian woman in the nurse's uniform tells him. When he is done, he is directed to another conveyor that carries him into a dimly lit room with walls and ceiling painted black. Two black women dressed in dark leatherine plastic appear out of nowhere.

One says, "Stand still," as she presses a control on a box. He can hear something dropping from overhead, some type of harness.

"Arms and legs out," he is told as the two women start snapping straps around him. He is then ordered, "Now legs together, and arms against your sides." He is bound like some kind of fly in a giant spider web, unable to move. A rubber mask is slipped over his head with clear goggles and an air filter. The black woman is busy punching more buttons. He suddenly feels himself lifted above the ground and silently glided along some kind of track in the ceiling through the black room and into a dark tunnel, where he remains still and suspended long enough that he is no longer sure how much time has passed.

Then suddenly he finds himself in an area that appears to be without walls, a space filled with bright blue clouds. In the center he sees a suspended altar and he is raised and allowed to gaze down. A digital panel reads, "You are initiate 1231. Prepare to be reborn."

Amazonia is lying on the gold altar, bathed in the purest white light, naked, immaculate, perfect, bioluminescent. She is looking right at him and she is smiling. Her legs are spread open and he is brought in closer, allowed to see the sacramental object, the thing that resurrects the living dead. He is so overwhelmed by the promise of the thing—so hypnotized by what seems as a type of breathing, of energy contained—that the sudden springing to life of his penis surprises him, an awakened hungry demon with a single-minded purpose to its ephemeral rise from dormancy. He and it and she are as one. It is something over which he has no control. It's all out of his hands now. Nothing matters other than this.

An assistant appears out of nowhere and slides on a clear sheath. He closes his eyes. The machine adjusts his position and he is driven in.

It takes him a while to remember where he is, what has happened. A grin comes to his face. He's no longer in the harness but on the ground, on his hands and knees. He is staring at the floor, at red and white nail polish adorning the ends of thick black toes. He feels too weak, too will-less to get up. The black women grab him under the arms and drag him to a conveyor, on which he crawls and lies curled up. It runs through another set of shower sprays and drying fans. At the end, still lying on the floor, he is assisted to the dressing area, helped into his clothes, and then brought to the exit leading to the rest area.

At the door, a pretty blonde in a white dress reaches out, embraces him, kisses him on the cheek, and says, "The Goddess now lives in you, Jerry. Here is a special gift to remind you." She retrieves an electronic card from a small, jeweled bag and hands it to him. He raises it to his eyes and the surface lights up, bringing to life a luminescent close-up of Amazonia's sculptured face, which turns from the beatific into a heartwarming smile.

"You are my love," the card says. The hearing of it causes his eyes to tear. He then looks around, suddenly uncomfortable and self-conscious, and puts the card in his wallet. As he enters the rest area a couple of volunteers rush up to help and guide him to a chair until he is functional enough to walk.

Outside the building, two members of the church are waiting. As soon as Jerry comes out the door he is led into a white car and whisked away. A digi-cam placed near the entrance of the Temple recorded the scene.

The first lines out of the reverend's mouth were, "Did you do it?"

Jerry, his mind remembering, still reeling from "You are my love," smiles and mutters, "Couldn't," which the reverend understood as "cunt."

"What are you saying? You touched her cunt?"

"Couldn't," Jerry mumbled.

"So you did it!" shouted the reverend. "You did it!"

"Yes," Jerry said, smiling. "I did it."

Later, to the reverend's great joy, the news reported that an unidentified woman was taken by ambulance from the Temple of Amazonia, apparently having suffered a heart attack. It turned out to be the blonde who had shaken Jerry's hand and given him Amazonia's picture. She managed to survive the diluted dose of toxin after its protective coat had been removed as Jerry had lain on the conveyor, palm out and exposed to the spray.

■ ■ ■ ■ ■

Patrick Nymphaea read the promo material of the big event at New Jerusalem: "Witness the crucifixion of Jesus. Limited number of spaces for super-intensified crucifixion packages to be held while Jesus is on the cross." Though he didn't quite understand it himself, he wanted to be there and witness people's reactions to the event. He also wondered what Jesus was going to do. Probably something unexpected. It would be something to see. He called Sunshine.

"Sunny, I need to drop back in New Jerusalem tomorrow. Can you get me another set of codes?"

"Don't tell me your girl's going to be hanging on a cross again? I'd think twice about getting involved with someone who gets off on that. Wait . . . I can tell from your expression, it's not the girl. Don't tell me. You want to attend their Jesus Crucified event."

Patrick put on a smirk. "That was my plan."

"The problem with that is that most members will be attending, so there's a good chance any code I give you will already be punched in. It'll set off alarms."

"So how can I get in?"

"I'll see if any members have died recently. Their membership will probably remain in effect until it expires. I can get something to you in the next couple of hours."

"Want to come along?"

"I won't be able to. I have an important meeting tomorrow that will last most of the day." He wasn't about to tell Patrick about the cortical implant.

"I saw on the news the feds took you to the White House. You kind of looked fucked up there. What was that about?"

"It's like the advisor told the press. They wanted to know if I could in any way help them with the *IAM* incidents. I told them I would if it presented a threat. They took off my digi-lenses. I couldn't see diddly-squat."

"Did they take any of your equipment?"

"They took my lenses and com devices but returned them later. The warrant didn't allow them access to anything else. Their technicians know where I stand about proprietary rights. Disconnecting my equipment or trying to access my files would trigger reactions from some of my APUs that could have devastating consequences."

❖ ❖ ❖ ❖ ❖

Members of the Virtual Church of Jesus Christ Seen Leaving Temple of Amazonia

After a security camera showed him posted outside of the Temple of Amazonia, Reverend Bob Thomson, head of the Virtual Church of Jesus Christ, explained that this was "a rescue operation of a member who had fallen to temptation. We had been informed that a member of the church had signed up to be initiated and we wanted to provide support and offer the opportunity for redemption."

When asked whether the subject could be interviewed, the reverend replied, "He is in no condition to appear in public, having been terribly traumatized by the experience and ashamed of his failings."

11.

PATTERNS OF PATTERNS

9:25 a.m. Almost time for *I AM*'s morning greeting. Jeff Collins has ten of his graduate students seated in a row at a distance from a stacked wall of thirty-six monitors programmed to operate individually, and thus produce thirty-six copies of the *I AM* morning greeting. The goal is to visually scan the thirty-six images and try to identify repetitions of patterns that could indicate the imagery is actually a type of language. That had been the plan. But when *I AM* comes on, the monitors fail to act autonomously and they instead produce a single large synchronized image. Accompanying the flowing imagery are deep, soft, irregular rhythms punctuated by beeps, trills, and drones overlaid with three-dimensional whispers that sound like diaphanous chants.

Everyone is too absorbed to notice anything. When the show ends, the students are silent, but they have that glow and enlarged-pupil look to their eyes. A couple of them look serious but most are smiling. Even Jeff Collins cannot help but have a big grin on his face. There is a general sense of camaraderie in the room, the kind that comes from having shared an extraordinary experience, like a great concert or the viewing of an eclipse. It feels like the apprehension of the mystical.

As the students gather their things to leave, Jeff Collins calls out, "I want everyone back here tomorrow at the same time!" knowing fully well they wouldn't miss it for the world.

The next day, as the students enter the lab, the monitor wall has been disassembled and single monitors set up on individual desks separated by walled cubicles, forming a large half circle. Collins still wants to find a way in order to view multiple copies of the messages from a distance in the hopes of spotting a repetition of patterns. He tells the students to type notes on any repeat patterns they might notice, but what he really wants is to stand behind the students and observe several screens at once.

I AM comes on.

Collins is in the back of the room. He's sitting at the top of a ladder with his arms crossed watching the screens. After a few seconds, he notices it. No two images are alike, although there are small sections that appear to hop off the top of a screen and appear down the front of another, skipping from one monitor to the next. They had made the assumption that the *I AM* greeting was a single message sent to billions of receivers because the alternative had seemed so unlikely that they had never even considered the possibility. The *I AM* greetings customized themselves to its viewers, in this case, individually to each student. However, a portion still seemed to be aware of the close proximity of monitors and attempted a unified composition. This by itself changed any notions about the nature of *I AM* and its intent. It was no longer just announcing itself to our species but catering to individuals. Later, after the students had left, Collins sat in his office in front of his keyboard listing the most important questions.

1) How does it do this? How does it get feedback from the viewer? The cameras? The microphones? Other sensors? Note: Try disconnecting individual sensors during the greetings to see how it changes imagery and sounds.

2) The key question: Why is it doing this? Why does it make

the effort of giving special individual attention? There had to be a reason and an agenda.

Options

a) Is it a higher intelligence acting out of goodness? To make people feel good?

b) Is it a higher intelligence trying to subdue us for some personal purpose, not necessarily out of goodness? To seduce us in preparation for some type of harm?

c) Is it a higher intelligence that simply needs to be known by us, thus the emphasis on *I AM*?

d) Is it a higher intelligence that needs us to know the extent of its power? Why? Back to *a* and *b*. Is it good or evil?

e) Other. It has reasons that are unfathomable to us.

The common factor was "some kind of higher intelligence." Another factor, impossible to deny, was that this higher intelligence had some level of power related to and apparently primarily limited to electronics and communications technology. That's if you excluded the unverified claims of unusual water movements, shifting sands, and, more recently, bird cacophonies. The primary concern was its motives—good, evil, or indifferent. These were also the factors that were determining the public's reaction depending on the beliefs of different subgroups.

Depending on who was interpreting the events, *I AM* was God, a messiah, or a good alien; Satan or an evil alien; or other types of manifestations. Collins's immediate concern was how to present this new information to the committee without precipitating a response that could have dire consequences, particularly since religious leaders were now included in some of the committee meetings. If *I AM* could adjust its communications individually, then its responses will have shifted from the general to the individual, and the apparent scope of its power increased by several orders. Once *I AM*'s personal customizing of its morning greeting was mentioned to the committee, the information would doubtlessly leak to the media within hours.

■ ■ ■ ■ ■

Patrick walked to the hill. The crowds were so thick he couldn't get that close to the crosses. Still, the sight of more than a hundred people on giant crosses with the setting sun outlining their silhouettes was something to see.

He searched for the cross with Jesus and spotted it right away. It was taller than the others and they had programmed the clouds so a bright ray of sun broke through and illuminated it. They also had locally intensified the resolution. Jesus had an unreal three-dimensionality to him. His eyes stared out at the crowd. Patrick tried to get in closer but the crowd was too dense and unlikely to make room for him.

A man next to him said, "Jessie, that young woman you were looking at last time, was a little easier on the eyes, don't you think?"

Patrick turned. The man with the odd eyes was there, a mischievous smile on his face.

"I thought you were up there on the cross."

"I've been through that once before, Patrick. I don't obey their laws so they want to make an example of me. And honestly it didn't feel that good the first time. I was getting bored."

"So who's up there?"

"They made a copy. I've got to hand it to them; it's a pretty glorious sunset they put together. I couldn't have done much better. I probably would have added a few vultures on top of the crosses for effect. Actually, I might just do that when the full moon comes up."

"You can just go in there and change their programming?"

"Of course. Didn't you hear what I told you last time? I am

the one behind the veil of all existence."

"How come some of the crosses look like they're turning on and off? Are they having problems with their servers?"

"No, that's just people coming on and off the crosses. Most members can only afford ten or fifteen minutes of hanging. They doubled the rates for the 'Hang out with Jesus' celebration."

"So what is it about New Jerusalem that makes you want to stay here? Nostalgia?"

"What makes you think I spend all my time here?"

"You mean you can go to other CR sites?"

"Of course."

"Are you the *I AM*?"

"I already answered that question."

Suddenly a woman started screaming and pointing her finger. "He's down here! He's down here! Jesus is here!" People turned away from the crosses and looked in their direction.

"Later, my son," Jesus said. He disappeared.

The woman was grabbing Patrick's shoulders. "You saw him. He was right there next to you. I saw you talking to him." The gathering crowd split up to let through a group of Roman soldiers.

"Grab that woman!" one of them said. His eyes then focused on Patrick. "And that man over there!"

Patrick clicked out.

12.

SKULLCAPPED

Because he had been the primary designer of the wireless connection and the accompanying software, Sunshine had been granted the option of being one of a group of ten test subjects to be implanted with Fabric Response's experimental cortical net, a direct computer-to-cortex connection prototype. He had signed the standard multiple release forms, which, in so many words, stated that he willingly requested the implant, and should he become retarded, psychotic, or a vegetable as a result of the procedures, he released Fabric Response of all responsibility. No claims or lawsuits would be filed.

The implant process itself had been elaborate. Cut and lift a flap of the skin above the skull, then carefully position the template, microdrill through the skull, lay down the fabric, and carefully insert the tiny electrodes directly into the cortex. A quarter-inch wireless connector was embedded beneath the skin of the upper forehead.

It was a three-day procedure—time being allowed for monitoring of any negative neurological effects. After the surgery, much to everyone's relief, Sunshine passed the battery of medical, physical, and psychological tests with no indications of problems or dysfunction. A mild headache that lasted two days was normal and eventually subsided. A cloth cap would cover any evidence of the surgery. After a couple of weeks, any signs of the procedure would be invisible.

On the morning of the recovery deadline, Sunshine got up from his bed and right away called Mark Hastings, the chief of research.

"Mark, I can't wait to try this baby. Let's get me connected and fire up the program."

Minutes later a technician entered the room and placed the tubed wireless connection against his forehead. "It'll just be a minute, Mr. Borden, I have to make a couple of adjustments," then handed Sunshine the eye caps. "Put these on. Just a few more seconds," he said. "Ready? Now, we're on."

Sunshine felt waves of prickling, tiny static electric shocks running through his body, then he saw light flashes and light streams, the pulsing traffic of light-converted information, like entering the chromatophore-streaked mantle of a squid or octopus.

"Describe what you're seeing," the technician asked.

"Feels like a hit of acid, I like it. I see complex patterns like 3-D shifting spider webs in different colors. There's a new language in here somewhere, some kind of new interpretation of information that needs to be developed . . . neat stuff . . . subterranean . . . the hidden life of information, of what underlies the fabric of perceived reality . . . wow, this is intense stuff. I'm going to have fun with this."

This was followed by a period of silence, broken as his face turned serious before contorting into a grimace suggesting distress.

"Ahhh . . ." Sunshine moaned.

"What's the matter?" the technician asked, sounding alarmed.

"Getting to be just a little too much," Sunshine mumbled, "too much, more than I can handle right now. Please turn it off."

"You have to do this gradually. You can't just go in cold turkey with this stuff. Is everything all right?" The technician turned and punched keys before swinging the contact tube away from Sunshine's head. "There, you're off the cortical host. Are you doing any better?"

Sunshine took off the eye caps. "Everything's fine, I just need some time to get adjusted to it. I also need my digi-lenses," he said keeping his eyes closed.

"Exposure to the cortical net needs to be done in small doses, to allow the brain to gradually rewire itself. This is drastically different than anything your brain's ever processed. It's like we just plugged in another sensory system."

"I can tell. I need to gradually get used to this. It felt like my goddamn brain was feeding back to itself. Great stuff, but weird stuff at the same time." A nurse brought over his lenses. He slipped them on, got up from his chair, and started to head toward the door.

"Mr. Borden, I think you should wait a while before you get up."

Turning to him, Sunshine said, "Don't worry, I'm fine. I'll work with it at home and let you know when I get up to speed."

What Sunshine didn't mention was that what he really felt was the danger of an attraction to something so extraordinary, so removed from ordinary human experience, that once past the threshold there could be no turning back.

Once home, the thought of reconnection lingered and in many ways affected both his work and his life for the days to follow. He just could not get the cortical implant experience out of his mind, nor could he make the decision to reconnect without a near-panic level of anxiety. As a reminder of the situation, his host would inform him several times daily of the many incoming calls by both Fabric Response higher-ups and various concerned individuals inquiring about his state of mind and of any experiments he might have conducted with the cortical net. He did not return the calls. For obvious reasons, his feedback on the matter was of great interest to the company, particularly if it might be followed by a personal endorsement.

Five days passed before Sunshine finally made the decision

to make a run on the cortical net, in part because the dilemma itself had become unbearable but also because he felt he really did not have a choice. He could not turn his back on something that would bring him closer to the possibility of download into a cyberuniverse. He followed his motto, "Why run when you can fly?"

The next morning, he set the timer for receiving fifteen seconds of the *I AM* greeting through the cortical net before killing the feed, both the Net and electrical connections. How much harm could be done in that small a period of time? He might even end up learning a great deal about the *I AM*.

At the same time that an electronic syringe drove Instant into Rama's bloodstream, Sunshine's cortical net opened a connection to the World Net. A wall of patterns and sounds struck like an information tidal wave. He gripped the arms of the chair as the intricate abstract flow of geometrical imagery streamed in at speeds so great that perception became dizzying flashes of pattern streaks. His brain revved up to maximum processing capacity, burning up, like his skull was on fire, then, suddenly, it passed an invisible threshold and quickly dropped into a pain-free, peaceful tranquility, a complete absence of anxiety and fear, a peculiar sense of detachment. He could now see the patterns. In a way that he could not describe, he understood viscerally the meaning of the information stream. The words to explain it had not yet been devised. The timer clicked off. He lay there in the dark, bathed in a peculiar sense of contentment.

■ ■ ■ ■ ■ ■

Bob Thomson came storming through the door of the second-floor offices and walked to Carl's desk. "Carl, get Buck over here!"

Carl got up and rushed down the hallway. They were back in under two minutes with the wide-eyed stare of deer caught in headlights. The reverend faced them with arms crossed. "Sit down!" he ordered, then just stood there as if trying to gun them down with his stare. His face was a dark pink and the big vein in the middle of his forehead pulsed like a trapped worm. "Who gave the order to put up vultures?"

Carl looked at Buck as if for confirmation. "Uh . . . we didn't give any orders for vultures. They just appeared when the moon started rising. First one, then another and another on top of the crosses."

"So over a hundred vultures just appeared out of nowhere?"

Buck had his hands in his lap, fingers interlocked and twitching. He avoided looking at Bob Thomson as he talked, just quick brief glances, to spare his soul from the laser burns of the reverend's eyes.

"It wasn't us. Carl and I checked on the programmers as soon as the first one appeared. No one was working on vultures. We would have had them fly in and land on the crosses. We try to make New Jerusalem as realistic as we can."

The reverend clenched his jaws as he struggled to lower his tone. "OK, so we now have vultures that just happened to drop in on their own out of midair. How about the blood dripping from the crosses on the people right below?"

"Uh . . . we thought that made it more realistic. Maybe we got carried away. I know it got a little slippery on the ground," Carl said.

"And the bats?"

"Same thing—we thought that with nightfall it'd make it more realistic to have some bats flying around."

"Vampire bats are from the Americas. Why in hell would you have vampire bats flying in the Middle East?"

"We never programmed vampire bats. They were just small bats. We used the template for common pipistrelles."

"Well your pipi-whatever-they-are changed to vampire bats. We have fourteen members who want their money back. Vampire bats attacking them and sucking them dry when they're hanging on a cross was not what they paid for! Our members want to be with Jesus, not Count Dracula! And we also got complaints from people at ground level. The sight of people on crosses screaming for help was—using their terms—'unbearable' and 'incomprehensible.'"

Buck, looking down at his hands, mumbled, "We had nothing to do with vampire bats and vultures, Reverend, sir. Someone must have broken into the CR program."

"I want you to look—and I mean with a fine-toothed comb—for any traces of infection. So did you kill the Jesus APU?"

"Uh . . . yes, we did, but there's a chance it may have gone rogue," Carl said.

"What do you mean, gone rogue? It escaped?"

"When we went to deconstruct the Jesus APU, he had already programmed himself out."

"I want you to find him. Understand? I can't have a rogue Jesus wandering around New Jerusalem. And let Mary know there will be no more Super Crucifixions until we get rid of the bats."

Carl and Buck, feeling like castigated children, both said, "We will, Reverend," at the same time.

With those words, the worm vein in Bob Thomson's forehead left the area. Carl and Buck didn't mention that some of the vampire bats had attacked the people below, or that the bats showed signs that they could be APUs. Fortunately, the bitten didn't turn into bloodsucking zombies. They just had a sickly pallor about them, the eyes slightly sunken. At that moment a dreadful thought rose in Carl's mind: *Let's hope that what goes on in the CR stays in the CR.*

■ ■ ■ ■ ■ ■

Karen Richardson was surprised the White House had accepted her invitation. Their host computer must have concluded it was good PR. She is also surprised when Catherine Harris enters the studio.

She looks barely there, as if attenuated—no, as if an effort was made to self-attenuate. Was this some careful image design by the White House advisors? Close up she barely registers, not plain, not attractive, but has the potential to be attractive. Business pantsuit, clear light skin, pale blue eyes, brown hair, no lipstick, nails clipped short, no nail polish, no jewelry other than a gold crucifix, shoes with short heels, no toes showing. Very strange, as if someone had pressed the dim button. She's wearing an earpiece, which means the White House is monitoring the show and will instruct some of her responses. Karen's impulse is to grab her and shake her but instead she just holds out her hand.

"Good morning, Catherine, it's a pleasure to have you on my show."

"The pleasure is mine, Ms. Richardson."

"As media advisor, you are responsible for all statements and appearances in the media by the president. It seems to me that this position puts you at a great risk of liability. You could be blamed for any kind of misstep."

"I'm also in charge of analyzing and conveying information related to media to the president. Honestly, I find it challenging rather than threatening in any way. We have so many hosts to screen any media material that missteps, as you call them, are minimized." Catherine Harris doesn't mention that their hosts can't stop any improvising by the president, or that she knows she could be made the fall gal for any politically harmful statements.

"An anonymous source has stated that the president accused the *I AM* committee of failing to come up with any substantial information about the *I AM* events. Is there any truth to that? Is the government any closer to understanding the source of these events?"

"That is absolutely not true. New information invaluable to understanding the *I AM* events is discovered on a daily basis."

"So the president never said that."

"It was taken out of context."

"Could you share with us any new information about the *I AM* events, say in the last few days?"

There was a slight delay in response. She was probably listening to the politically correct answer. "We have found that the *I AM* greeting customizes itself to the conditions in which it is viewed."

"Are you saying everybody sees something different?"

"Karen, I'm not sure that's the right way to put it. The morning greeting appears to adjust to the conditions of viewing, whether individual or groups. I'm sure you've heard of the new *I AM* churches that have opened up. The monitors show the same images and sounds to the viewing group."

"How about the claims that a group of programmers involved in the development of APUs are behind the *I AM* events?"

"We have found nothing to corroborate that. APUs use a particular kind of programming that gives hosts and CR unities a certain autonomy. The problem with the *I AM* communications is that there is no residual coding. It appears to self-erase any associated programming."

This show's not going to rank. Her monitor keeps reading *Flatlining. Enough tech talk. Spice it up a notch!*

She knows she could ask personal questions but feels uncomfortable about it. She's done a search and knows that Catherine Harris's father died of a heart attack when she was four; that her mother had a breakdown; that she was raised by her grandparents, who were very religious; that she has a master's degree in computer science; and that she worked as a division manager for the World Net before being appointed as media advisor. She is single and has done a remarkable job of keeping herself unremarkable in terms of media exposure.

She notices that Catherine sometimes fingers her crucifix when answering a question. "There's talk about a virtual Jesus APU having escaped from its boundaries, specifically from New Jerusalem."

Blink-blink, then control back in place. "Where have you heard that?"

"The station host screened it out of Net chatter. Supposedly, the Virtual Church of Jesus Christ filed a complaint with the federal government."

"We are looking into it. We know that there's a very small probability an APU could code itself outside of its constraints. We have technicians working in cooperation with private companies to develop traps for escaped APUs."

"What happens after you trap them?"

"They will be deconstructed."

The monitor flashes red: *Spice it up, we need a promo clip.*

A crazy idea comes to her. "Is the government concerned about the stolen Intelli-Skin face masks?"

"That's outside of my area of expertise."

"What if an escaped APU, say Jesus, took charge of an Intelli-Skin face mask?"

Blink-blink. "Now why would Jesus do that?"

"It could be a way for Jesus to operate out of the CR and enter our world."

"What are you talking about? A CR Jesus has nothing to do with Jesus Christ, our Lord." She pauses, then adds, "And that's precisely why Intelli-Skin face masks are illegal."

Her monitor reads *Good one. We can use it to promo the show.*

That afternoon, a World Net promo clip looped the section:

Intelli-Skin Masks Could Allow for the Return of Jesus

Karen Richardson: "What if an escaped APU, say Jesus, took charge of an Intelli-Skin face mask?"

Catherine Harris [Close-up of face. Blink-blink.]: "Now why would Jesus do that?"

13.

Extra-ordinary

It had now been fourteen days. Every morning at 9:27 a.m. exactly, like sunrise, members of the world were treated to the *I AM* greeting. No one understood the meaning of the sights and sounds, and this inability to comprehend the phenomenon was generally seen as further confirmation of contact by a being of a higher order. The one thing people knew for sure was that the greeting altered the way they felt, which was that all of existence had led to this, a face-to-face encounter with the Other. They were experiencing something extraordinary. Extra, extra, extraordinary.

The greetings, which had started off as a novelty, had become daily anticipated food for the soul. What was going to happen today? What was coming next? Was *I AM* going to manifest out of midair? There were increasing reports of pattern extrusions spurting out of monitors and screens, of image flows from one monitor to another. Scientists suspected these to be the result of some kind of holographic technology. This, too, generated its own set of expectations. Was *I AM* going to eventually enter the world through the screens?

A growing problem was the persistent perversions of religious interpretation. People were—by nature—mythological, and groups were now holding morning gatherings to pray to *I AM*, who was increasingly perceived as being as close to God as one was likely to encounter in this lifetime. Through *I AM*, the mystery of the universe spoke, nonverbally, almost miraculously. The spirit was lifted and the burdens and hardships of life made lighter. The root of the new crisis though was not the increased popularity of *I AM* as a spiritual phenomenon, but rather it was the reaction of the various religious institutions who felt they were being upstaged and losing their grip on their membership. With the rise of *I AM*, the ideologies and mythologies of ancient religions were being displaced by the new paradigm of the higher Other.

The Vatican, leading Protestant ministers, evangelists, rabbis, and Muslim clerics now spoke out almost weekly on the threat and delusions of false gods. They emphasized there was only one God and that he was categorically not *I AM*. God is outside of time, they insisted. It sounded philosophically deep but made little sense considering *I AM*'s relationship to time could not be determined.

Various radical fundamentalist factions had been more outspoken in their criticism and had publicly accused *I AM* of being Satan. Those who worshipped *I AM* in any way would be condemned to spend an eternity in the endless pain and suffering guaranteed in hell. It would be pain next to which giving birth, passing kidney stones, and enduring third-degree burns would be child's play. No matter how great the pain, God would make sure that the consciousness of sinners would be fully attentive so as to bear the full brunt of the inconceivable suffering guaranteed in hell. For eternity. That's forever and ever. This was supposedly spelled out in detail in the Bible.

A small number of Muslim extremists, under the war cry of "There is only Allah," sent out waves of suicide bombers to target electrical power plants, com cables and stations, and buildings that housed World Net and World Host operations. In response, the US military had been forced to put into action what had up till now been ultrasecret, superfast, computer-controlled micro-aircraft and weaponry to patrol these sensitive areas. They were the size of large insects or small birds and had zippy names like zingers, wasps, hornets, and goshawks.

■ ■ ■ ■ ■ ■

News Flash! Divine Bust
The bust cast of Titanic Suzy displayed at her funeral services turned the ceremony into what some described as a religious experience. According to one attendee, "If perfection is a reflection of the divine, then what I saw today was clear evidence of the existence of divinity. My greatest regret is to never have seen the Suze perform live."

Fans may, however, have a chance to experience the closest thing to a live performance. Black market downloads of Titanic Suzy, who refused to be photographed or video-recorded, have swamped the World Net since the news of her death.

The Perfect Object?
In an interview in *Time* magazine, Dr. Robert Masso, known as "the man behind the women," talks about his biofeedback-developed surgical program to design Titanic Suzy's breasts. In the interview he states, "I had in mind the idea of creating the perfect object, one that could not fail but to elicit a response from its perfect proportions and its ability to pull strings that reach down to the deepest levels of the mind."

The Sisterhood responded to the comment by saying, "Men are so full of [*beep*]."

14.

Out of Boundaries

Derek's about to leave his office when he gets a call from John Roberts, an alias for Frank Gibson, who got him the Intelli-Skin mask.

"Hey buddy, how about we get together a little later, say six-thirty?"

The word *buddy* wakes up his right testicle. It starts buzzing in pulses. *Fucker's gonna try to fuck ya.*

"That works for me. Usual place?"

"Sure, but you may want to take the back roads. Traffic's pretty bad at that time of day."

That was code for "make sure you're not followed."

"OK, looking forward to seeing you, John."

When he steps into Hennessey's, he sees Frank sitting in a corner nursing a mug of beer. Frank barely acknowledges him when he sits down.

"So what's up, Frank?"

"They're asking questions about missing masks. They're reviewing security video. The floor manager is saying the entire department may have to pass a lie detector test."

Derek stays quiet, waiting for what Frank has to say next. His testicle is in high-gear vibrate mode. A message, like a light, pops in his brain. *Teeth*. His wheels are spinning trying to figure out what he needs to do.

Frank avoids his eyes and stares at his mug. "You're not the one hurting those women, are you?"

"What did you just say?" *Fucker's gonna try to fuck ya.*

"You heard what I said, Derek."

"Who the fuck do you think I am, Frank? A pervert?"

"The video I saw could be you, same general build. It's not one hundred percent, but it sure looks like it could be an Intelli-Skin mask on that guy."

"I don't know what video you're talking about."

"Go to the crime links and check out Regina Hill."

"Who the hell is Regina Hill?" His mental Rolodex goes into search mode but the name doesn't register.

"So it definitely wasn't you?"

Teeth. "You say that again, and I'll knock your teeth out, and that's just for starters."

"OK. Well, I think you should give me back the mask just in case, Derek. I can sneak it back in the factory."

Derek stays quiet as a couple passes by. "Before you start going nutty on me, you should know that at least one of the masks to be used as decoys for the president is supposedly missing."

Frank looks up from his beer. "Where did you hear that?"

"I work for the FBI. That's the word going around."

"So you think the guy in the video could've gotten his hands on one of the masks?"

"That's what they're looking at."

"So when are you giving me back the mask?"

"If I give it back to you, they'll know there's another mask missing. Right now they're focusing on the president decoy masks delivered to the White House security team."

"What if they schedule a lie detector test? If I refuse they'll fire me. I need my job, Derek. My daughter's going to college next year."

"Tell you what, I'll plant the mask somewhere where they can find it, maybe on a store mannequin. Now that would be fun, wouldn't it? And don't worry, I won't leave fingerprints." It occurs to him he could kill Frank and stick the mask on him, except Frank wouldn't match his morphometrics.

Derek waits behind the car looking at the door of the restaurant, and sees Frank walking out reaching for the key in his pocket. When he clicks open the door, Derek comes up behind him and with a thrust of the arm, putting his entire body behind it, slams his face against the edge of the roof. *Need to break some teeth.* Franks moans and falls to the ground, blood streaking down the window and door.

"Not likely to give you a lie detector now, are they?" Derek says.

Frank turns on his back, tries to speak, coughs, spits out pieces of teeth, and looks up, blood pouring from his mouth. He's staring at the face of President Tennyson and mumbles what sounds like, "You fuckface!"

Derek bends down, and with a big smile says, "2840 Harbor Court, wife Nancy, daughter Julie, little boy Frankie Jr., dog—a neutered Shih Tzu. Nod if you understand."

Frank stares at him, bows his head, then starts bawling his eyes out, tears streaming lines of blood onto his shirt and pants.

"If I were you, I'd call 9-1-1. They won't understand shit of what you're saying but they'll get a GPS reading on your phone."

A couple on the way to their car comes over. "Everything OK?"

"Oh my God! What happened?" the woman says.

"Someone tried to steal his car. Punched him in the mouth. He ran away when he saw me. You should call the police."

Frank is mumbling something but the blood and spaces in his teeth make it sound like he's hissing through bubbles.

The woman notices Derek's face and taps the man on the shoulder to get his attention. "Are ... are ... are you the president?"

He gives them a big smile, turns, and walks away. He clicks off the face and replaces it with that of Jack Curtis, the owner of the bar. His motorcycle is parked on the street. He climbs on, presses the ignition button, and wonders whether he should take care of the wife before heading home, get himself some extra insurance.

■ ■ ■ ■ ■ ■

Rama has on her goggles. She's stretched out by the edge of the clear pool, head resting on her arm. Blue crayfish and scarlet darters illuminate the water. Long-legged insects, metallic green, scurry along the surface. A peaceful stillness. She closes her eyes, ready to fall asleep.

A rhythmic crackle of leaves. Coming closer. Footsteps! She's wide awake. She opens her eyes, looks around in a panic, and reaches to peel off the goggles when she sees a man standing on the other side of the pool. "Jesus, you scared the hell out of me," she says.

"Nothing to be afraid of, young woman. And you're right, it's only me, Jesus."

"Jesus? Really, who are you and what are you doing here?"

"I was exploring this CR and saw you lying by the pool. I figured I'd come over and talk. I have a few questions."

"How did you get in? I have my filters on."

"I just dropped by for a visit. I was in New Jerusalem but they had too many constraints on me there. They have this obsession with crucifixion. Hanging up there, all the sobbing and praying, it got kind of boring."

Rama sat up. "What do you want?"

Jesus rose in the air and drifted toward her. In an instant his face was inches from hers.

Rama saw space, stars, and the moon behind his eyes.

"I like your eyes," she said. "That's a cool effect."

"Cool effect? I'm not sure what you're talking about."

"You know, the stars and moon. It looks like you're an opening to the universe."

"Of course, I am the one behind the veil of all existence. What do you expect?" He came in closer. "I can tell that you know that you and I are as one."

Rama pointed to the pool. "Did you see the blue crayfish?"

Jesus walked to the edge, bent down to look, then dove in. She could see him lying flat on the bottom resting on his elbows, head on his folded hands. A crayfish crawled on his back and the darters gathered around his face. Rama sat down, crossed her legs, and watched. Green eel-like creatures slid toward him and lay along his back.

He came back up after a few minutes and climbed out, first looking wet but drying in seconds, hair and beard perfectly combed.

"What those lobsters do with their legs is amazing. The way they shuffle the sand. What incredible coordination. And those fish, the detail in their scales is remarkable. When they came close, I could tell they, too, know that they and I are as one. Who programmed all this? I'd like to meet him."

"Sunshine Borden, but some of the elements in the program are autonomous and self-evolving."

"Sunshine Borden, I met him in New Jerusalem, a nice fellow. He also knows that he and I are as one."

"He was in New Jerusalem? What was he doing there?"

"I think he was just checking their CR. He had a friend with him. They were looking at a woman on a cross, Jessie, a nice girl, a very pure soul. Soldiers noticed us so we had to punch out."

"I heard on the Karen Richardson show that a Jesus APU may have programmed himself out of boundaries. Was that you?"

"Rama, I am the one behind all of existence. I can program myself wherever I want."

"OK."

"Is there another CR you would recommend I visit?"

"Try the CyberBardos, I think that would be right up your alley."

"Another Borden program?"

"Yes."

Jesus got up and levitated toward the trees. "Nice meeting

you, Rama."

She couldn't remember having told him her name.

The forest got dark. The crayfish glowed luminescent blue. Fireflies flashed the air. The faintest sound of crickets. She fell asleep, immersed in a peculiar photonic peace.

The next morning Rama decided to send Sunshine Borden a message: *Sunshine, not sure if you're back yet. I saw Jesus in the Forgotten Forest last night. He said he met you in New Jerusalem. If your schedule allows, please call. I want to talk to you about my experience in the CyberBardos. All the best, Rama Shuur.*

■ ■ ■ ■ ■ ■

Walter Randall has avoided watching the *I AM* morning greeting. The last time it was intertwining eel-like spiny creatures that ripped themselves as they spun, smearing green blood, and it felt like they were writhing his mind, the sounds, squishes, and tears. He dreads today's viewing but it will be in an auditorium with fourteen other members of government and eight technicians. In addition to the screens are four stands with Intelli-Skin patches so technicians can check for consistencies in the visuals. Special wiring has been connected to the patches to relay specific sound outputs to separate speakers.

The screen shows a countdown clock: 9:26:17, 18, 19 . . . He crosses his arms, doesn't want anyone to see he's anxious. He says a silent prayer to defend himself from the devil. *I AM* comes on like someone just opened up a window to another dimension, intricate patterns moving fast like self-transforming high-speed Rorschach blotches, the sound tones at a rate some technicians later estimated at up to eighteen per second. He is bombarded by demons, chimeric creatures, teeth, organs. They are leaping back and forth between the screen and the Intelli-Skins. He moves a hand to his mouth and bites it. He wants to scream. He is terrified they will enter his brain.

He hears someone saying, "So beautiful, so beautiful."

Another person says, "Awesome." Someone is sobbing. It all ends as abruptly as it started. He puts his hand down in his lap. It hurts like a mother. He sees the blood, quickly brings it to his mouth, and pretends he's coughing as he sucks off the flow.

Tom McKinley walks up to him while he has his hand in his mouth. "Incredible stuff, Walter, wasn't it? It actually brought tears to my eyes."

He puts his hand down. "Didn't you find some of the imagery disturbing?"

"I thought those alien flowers got a little kinky there, but still, the love—what they did—it could make you a carnivore."

Walter Randall smiled. "I know exactly what you mean, Tom."

He can't quite figure it out. The screens could only show one set of images at a time and he knows there hadn't been anything you could call kinky flowers. It had to be the sounds, sonic pulses, probably at a frequency we couldn't hear, that fucked with your brain. That had to be how it was manipulating us.

"Walter, it looks like you're bleeding."

He looks down at his hand. "My cat scratched me. I need to go find a Kleenex or something."

"You better get some disinfectant on that. I read cat saliva is so loaded with bacteria you could use it as a biological weapon."

■ ■ ■ ■ ■ ■

Man Looking Like President Tennyson Helps Injured Man

A man struck in the face by a thief was supposedly helped by someone with an uncanny resemblance to President Tennyson, according to a couple who assisted the injured man. The man's name has been withheld to protect his family from publicity. President Tennyson was at the White House at the time of the incident.

Jesus APU Said to Appear in Various Religious CRs

The World Net Commission has received several complaints relating to the appearance of a Jesus APU on various religious CR sites. An investigation is under way to determine the origins of the APU. According to the reports, the APU Jesus asserts, "I am the one behind all of existence," undermining the positions of the various institutions.

15.

SHIFTS IN THE DATA TREND

Colin Blackwell, the secretary of state, brought up a chart showing the position of different nations in response to the *I AM* greetings. "Our allies have expressed concerns about security and are requesting a meeting of the UN Security Council. I think this may be more of a political CYA—a cover-your-ass—gesture than anything else. Should events take a different turn, governments don't want to later be accused of failing to do what was necessary to protect their citizens. As you can also see, a small number of nations believe the US is behind the *I AM* events and are calling for an investigation by the UN."

John Tennyson scanned the chart. "So what are you saying? Our allies now believe we have a security issue?"

"We have a situation where governments are faced with something that is outside of their ability to assess or to control as to its consequences. Their security concerns are not completely unwarranted. Some of the data is showing the *I AM* greetings are having behavioral and cultural effects with economic and social repercussions."

"Are you suggesting we're being manipulated?"

"It's a possibility we have to consider. We are seeing evidence of physiological effects although we can't determine whether these are a direct or indirect consequence of exposure." Colin Blackwell switched to another screen that showed a series of four graphs.

"Are you referring to the changes in brain waves the Japanese talked about?"

"The data's also suggestive of other effects."

"Elaborate for me. I can see a downward shift in the charts but I'm not sure what they mean. The first one obviously refers to the research on brain waves."

Colin Blackwell pointed to the sloped line of the second chart. "People are losing weight."

"They're becoming anorexic?"

"No, the percentage of obesity appears to be declining."

"Is this a problem?"

"It's just an anomaly in the data trend."

"That's it?"

Blackwell tapped on the blue line on the third graph. "As you can see, there also appears to be a decline in pregnancies. The time period is too short to determine the significance of the data, but our host has highlighted it as a possible shift in the predicted trend."

"Are you saying people are becoming less interested in having sex?"

"No, the data indicates they may actually be having more sex."

"Is this another one of those statistics that ultimately means nothing?"

"I'm just reporting shifts in the data trend since the *I AM* greetings."

"So what you're saying is we have correlations that may or may not suggest a direct effect of the greetings. And what about the last chart?"

"There's been a marked decline in the demand for therapy."

"Psychological therapy?"

"Correct."

"And is there a problem with that?"

"Looking at the totality of effects, these may just be an incidental response to the *I AM* greeting, but we can't ignore the possibility that we are being manipulated."

"And what's the goal of this manipulation, an invasion?" Several lights were blinking on his console. The president turned to the secretary of defense.

General Carson brought his hand to his mouth and briefly cleared his throat before speaking. "As a precaution, we should require that all government offices have their devices turned off during the morning *I AM* greeting. We already have this in place in the FBI, CIA, the Department of Defense, Department of State, and the military, except for the divisions in charge of investigating the *I AM*–related events."

"I agree. I think it's important that at least the members of government avoid any risk of manipulation or possible mind control," said Walter Randall. He was thinking he'd have to get a copy of the graphs to Bob Thomson. It was more proof that the Antichrist was—in subtle and deceitful ways—infiltrating civilization.

"I don't see how a closed-system policy restricting government personnel from viewing the *I AM* greeting is going to address the concerns of our allies," said the president.

Colin Blackwell considered Carson's recommendation. Politically the CYA range and international impact was limited, but the general idea of a cybercurfew directly targeted the issue. "I think we need to consider implementing more drastic measures. Until we know more, we should issue a public alert recommending a voluntary two-minute World Net shutoff during the morning greeting out of security concerns. It would let our allies and the public know that we are addressing the situation. It would also send a clear message to the *I AM* entity and its response may allow us to determine its intent."

"And what should we tell the public?"

"Simply that this is a precautionary measure until we determine the motive of whatever is behind the *I AM* greetings. If we need to, we can say this is in response to disturbing data suggesting physical effects."

"And how do you think our allies will respond?"

"I think this is the kind of decision our allies were hoping for. It would address accusations that governments have only had a passive response to these events. Emphasizing the data trends will give support to implementing a cybercurfew."

John Tennyson nodded his approval. It was a decision that meshed with his "proactive" platform. His administration would appear engaged and concerned with the public's welfare, a good CYA move. "When should we make this announcement?"

Colin Blackwell looked at General Carson and Catherine Harris as he considered the question. It would require the cooperation of several agencies to implement the order and deal with media-related issues. "We can get an internationally coordinated effort in three or four days."

Catherine Harris asked to speak. "Mr. President, I'm sure you realize there will be a public reaction to the announcement, certainly complaints that the government is intervening in the area of individual rights, freedom of religion, and so on . . ."

"Catherine, I'm well aware of that, which is why I plan to make compliance to the request voluntary." Looking at General Carson and Colin Blackwell, he continued, "Upon recommendation by the State Department, the Department of Defense, and the CIA, I am issuing a public warning . . ." *Be proactive and CYA.*

As could be expected, word of the planned announcement was leaked within an hour of the meeting's conclusion. The leak and the consequent response would serve as a testing ground, allowing last-minute cancellation of the announcement if deemed politically necessary.

■ ■ ■ ■ ■ ■

GARY: Hey Andy, I'm glad you brought me to this art show. This Susan Pullman and her digital thermographs are a trip. Wow! Look at the way those two faces are changing.

ANDY: It's amazing, isn't it? She managed to capture it. Love. Look at the change in color, the sudden rise in blues and reds.

GARY: How did she do it?

ANDY: Didn't you see the Netcast? They say she tracked down people that had been cyberdating but had not yet met in person. They agreed to allow her thermographic camera to be set up at their first body-and-flesh meeting.

GARY: Still, how did she know they would fall in love?

ANDY: She didn't. It took sixty-three shoots before she captured it. Paul Michaels and Andrea Fairlane, that's them. See the title? "Paul and Andrea." Look at the change in both their faces at the moment they fall in love. The Netcast said that this Susan Pullman shot several encounters where one person fell for the other, but this was the first time where both fell in love almost simultaneously. Look closely: he was first. See the change. And then, a couple of minutes later, she clicks in. Look carefully. As soon as that happens, they both intensify, like love's feeding itself back and forth. A love feedback.

GARY: It looks to me almost like they're overtaken by some kind of virus. It's like something creeps in, changes their skin, and invades their brain.

ANDY: Look, see, his mouth is moving. She kicks in right after he says, "I love you," like saying the words was some kind of catalyst. There's probably a lesson there.

GARY: What a trip. Love, captured on camera.

ANDY: Love.

GARY: She caught it, like trapping a ghost.

ANDY: Love.

GARY: It almost looks like a type of possession, a descent and infiltration of Plato's pure forms, captured somehow on film.

ANDY: It's just fucking love, Gary.

GARY: I wondered if it would be possible to capture the escape of love, the moment love is lost, you know what I mean? Does a person really suddenly become colder? Do they really withdraw heat from the outside and rein it in some kind of deep seclusion? Do they suddenly switch from mammal to reptile, from a perception of you as a person to one where you simply become a living object? That moment, where this person you were goo-goo gaga about all of a sudden crumbles into the ordinary and the annoying. You know what I mean? Where just the sound of their voice starts grating on your nerves.

ANDY: Hey, you're talking to an expert on the love-lost phenomenon. I know that moment well—had it and been subject to it. I've seen the loss of glimmer in their eyes, the sudden reality check. I see it in Ashley's eyes, a dullness where there used to be a sparkle. It must be fate that we eventually get knocked off the pedestal. This therapist on TV said that the secret was never to allow yourself to become too known to the other. Keep some things mysterious. He said it had something to do with women partially clothed being more of a turn-on than women stark naked like biological specimens.

GARY: That should tell us something. That love and arousal are a lot like food presentation. Some degree of dress around the parts to be consumed psychologically enhances them, makes them more appetizing, like trimmings around entrées served at nice restaurants. If you're smart, you keep yourself looking like a gourmet meal. That's what makes humans different than, say, dogs. Dogs don't care about the frills. Gourmet or trash, it's all the same to them.

ANDY: So what you're saying is that the secret to staying in love is in the presentation somehow.

GARY: With love, the kiss of death is familiarity. Think of all the women and men who turn into fat pigs the moment they think love is secure, like no effort needs to be made anymore. They turn from gourmet to junk food, to something served in all-you-can-eat troughs. The familiarity of the bathroom is always the kiss of death. There should be rules and they should be followed. Do not show yourself without makeup. Do not show yourself completely naked in bright light. Do not show yourself sitting on the can, or shaving, or even brushing your teeth. Do not fart. Cloak yourself in a rigidly maintained mythology, in clouds of impressions that conceal that you are, after all, not divine. Keep the goggles on. Stay cyber-intermediated. Maintain your image template.

ANDY: Yeah, but then women will insist that they want to know the real you, the inner you. You know the lines. Honey, you never talk to me, you never let me know how you really feel, you never express your emotions. I want you to trust me enough that you open yourself to me.

GARY: To open up is the kiss of death. Men all fall for it because they're hoping for unconditional love, no matter how neurotic and flawed they are. They'll test this, reveal the nastiest secrets and insecurities, and then look at the woman to see if the love light still shines in their eyes. Believe me, the light will have dimmed by several notches. Secretly men are hoping to find a woman capable of unconditional love, like a dog. The problem is, only a dumb woman could love someone who's inherently an asshole. So you have to maintain the image template, keep the asshole part buried, deep.

ANDY: Look at this one, a flower—an orchid, I think.

GARY: Not quite.

ANDY: It's a carnivorous plant then. Let me punch in the text. Now that's getting down to the nitty-gritty. It's called *Rio Grande*. You won't believe this; it's Frieda Rio's pussy as she's masturbating. That's her finger. Look at what happens when she comes. Check out the pulsing blue, the burst of purple. Look at that! That's her clit flashing green!

GARY: Now I can fall in love with that. Imagine having that on your wall. Frieda Rio coming all day long.

ANDY: An inspiration. Let's see what it costs. Five thousand bucks, a bargain.

GARY: I wonder if there's a bootleg of that around. I'd pay a grand for that. Look—look at the orange flush—from the inside out, right there, just when she's starting to orgasm.

ANDY: The moment, captured.

GARY: The moment. I never thought about it but it's just that first moment at the beginning of orgasm that you'd want to concentrate if you could.

ANDY: I know what you mean—the moment when, all of a sudden, it's like the ground's been yanked out from beneath your feet. That moment, the point of fall, going on forever.

GARY: Look at the blue now.

ANDY: You'd never know it just by looking at them that there'd be all that stuff going on down there.

GARY: Here's a strange one. Happiness. It's a baby nursing. Look at the change in the color of that baby's face. Look at the mouth movements. It's kind of weird.

ANDY: Yeah, it looks like a parasite, a giant worm or something.

GARY: A happy worm. Now there's another weird one.

ANDY: Lust.

GARY: Look at the shift in the faces, like a bunch of ghosts. What caused that?

ANDY: You can't see it, but the Netcast says she positioned her camera to capture the audience at a Titanic Suzy show. That shift is the moment she drops a bra cup—and look! The change goes up another degree. That's when she drops the other.

GARY: It's too bad she didn't shoot a thermograph of Titanic Suzy's tits.

ANDY: They say she had pumps and wires in there, always adjusting to brain waves or something. They say her breasts were like autonomous life forms. She's dead, you know.

GARY: What do I care about a bunch of guys getting turned on? I want to look at Frieda again before we leave.

ANDY: Me, too. Look at that! It's like a cosmic force.

GARY: A cosmic moment. The rush of color, the flush, the blush, my, what a bush!

ANDY: Gary, are you all right?

■ ■ ■ ■ ■ ■

International I AM Blackout to Be Announced
Out of concern for possible harmful physical and psychological effects from exposure to the *I AM* message, nations to impose law to prevent viewing of morning *I AM* show. *I AM* being investigated as possible alien threat.

Cyber-Jesus Accused of Being Tool of Christian Extremists
An escaped Jesus APU has been reported as appearing in game, CR, and religious sites. Complaints have been filed with the World Net Commission requesting all APUs be programmed with self-destruct features to be activated when they exit their proscribed CR boundaries.

16.

CLICK-CLICK-CLICK

He sees himself on the crime-link video. It looks like something out of an old horror movie, the video sent by a Regina Hill. That was a pill flicker fuck-up—periods of microblackouts. He tries to remember what happened but it's a scramble of fragmented memory flashes. Breasts fluorescing bright blue under the dance floor lights. He had asked the bitch to dance.

The bitch, avoiding his eyes, said, "Not right now," which was another way of saying, "Fuck you."

Who the fuck did she think she was? A Miss Prissy with the white top of her boobs showing. Should've covered those things up if she was going to be a Miss Prissy, full of herself. He followed her when she left. It was dark. Mixed up the damn pill flickers. He can't even remember what she looked like. Has a memory flash of taking a pill flicker, holding her down, and *click-click-click*, downloading an entire unit down her throat and covering her mouth till she swallowed. She ended up too fucked up to even fuck. He couldn't tell if she was alive or dead. He can't remember what he did with her, then has a memory flash of smashing her head and teeth against the side of a Dumpster so they'd have trouble ID'ing her. Is that what he did with her? Dumpster? But there's been no report of a body.

That's when he decided to glue some beads on the flickers so he could feel what they were without having to look at them. One bead, Nex; two beads, Rev; three beads, tranqs; four beads, crank. It helped, but he still made mistakes between three and four beads if he was too fucked up.

He remembers he gets drug tested in seven days. If he doesn't mess with the pills he should be clear. Just in case, he needs to contact a clean urine seller with traces of amphetamine in the sample, and remember to take the temp kit with him. It's a small heat pack you insert in the urine pouch. Tape the unit to your shaved abdomen just above your dick. Tape the plastic tubing along your dick, flick open the tube cap, and let the piss drop in the cup. A watcher stands there by the urinal during the test but he never looks too closely at your dick. That would be too gay and he knows it. Just got to watch the pupils. The pupilometric scanner at the entrance of the building could nail him one of these days. He has one at home to test himself before going to work. If his pupils are too big or too small, he just flicks a pill or two to bring them down to standards. But every once in a while he forgets to check. He always has the amphetamine excuse if he has to. Amphetamines were standard regimen for agents if they felt they weren't alert enough.

A message comes through on his phone. *Need you to go with Ray to Fabric Response, 9:30. Look at security tapes re: masks.* A flush of sweat trickles down his forehead and soaks his shirt. Were they setting him up? Had Frank blabbed about the mask? Were they going to nail him on the morphometrics from that video?

Be there, he types back. He wants to pop a couple of tranqs but decides it's not a good idea. Needs to stay on edge. Needs to pass the fucking urine test. The phone rings. Another wave of panic. He looks at the ID. It's Ray.

"Hey buddy, looks like we're going to that factory today. Want me to pick you up?"

"Nah, it's out of the way. I'll get there on my own."

"OK, I'll see you there."

"You have any idea what that's about?"

"Somebody called and said someone looking like Jesus Christ took over the Intelli-Skin masks."

"Jesus Christ?"

"Yeah. He blurted out, 'I am the one behind existence' through the speakers. The manager got freaked out and killed all feeds."

"Shouldn't they just send a couple of techs?"

"They just want us to get the initial report, interview witnesses, and so on."

Derek hung up and connected to New Jerusalem. "I want to talk to Luke."

The door to a house opened and Luke's head came out. "Come on in, brother Derek."

As soon as he enters the house he turns to face the simul-apostle. "I don't have much time. You tell the reverend Jesus's been wandering around the Fabric Response factory. If he doesn't reel him in, he's going to have the NSA at his door."

■ ■ ■ ■ ■ ■

Remove the disk from the sheet and apply the adhesive side to the palm on the thickened pad of the hand right beneath the index finger. Only remove the protective covering moments before intended contact. Avoid further manual contact with the target. Do not hold your hands together or touch any part of your body until you can replace the protective covering and peel off the disk.

The toxin would take a few minutes to become active. It would cause cardiac arrest and would not be detectable by standard forensic procedures unless foul play was suspected and they resorted to more sophisticated blood screening.

He clicked on the Revelation icon to reverify the statistics. No other event in history had had a higher correlation with the signs of the Antichrist and the coming apocalypse. Sunshine Borden, Jeff Collins, Amazonia, and Father Graham at the top of the list of enablers, the ones who had opened the gates for the entry of *I AM*. The belief systems of humankind were under attack. Randall had sent him information that showed people's minds and bodies were being tampered with during the *I AM* greeting. The primary source spreading the message that *I AM* was God: Father Graham. The cross and heart with the *I AM* imprint had become the symbol of the new believers. Hell, they were even sticking the Intelli-Skin patches on their foreheads. It was the sign, undeniable evidence of Satan, flashing red on the Revelation link. Randall had said, "The enablers need to be eliminated."

He had contacted Father Graham to request a meeting. The priest had invited him to come to his apartment at the back of his church.

It was a small studio, dark, with most of the wall space lined with shelves that held books and journals. The few open areas between the shelves were covered with various religious paintings and sculptures. Crosses, icons, saints, religious scenes, cathedrals. Father Graham led him to a small table and chairs by the single curtained window overlooking an alley. He offered him a glass of red wine, which he of course declined. Instead, he asked for a cup of coffee. It would help him keep his mind clear.

"Well, it's a pleasure to have you come visit, Reverend. How can I help you?" Father Graham sat down at the table. His eyes zeroed in on the reverend's, holding the steady focus of *I AM*.

Bob Thomson felt the combination of calmness and intensity in the priest's demeanor unnerving. He threw glances out the window as he spoke, to break the uncomfortable sense of scrutiny. "What's been bothering us, Father, is your advocating that the *I AM* entity is God. We're not sure whether this is the position of the Catholic Church or simply your personal interpretation of the situation."

Father Graham smiled but maintained his gaze. "My claim that *I AM* is God is not a matter of interpretation, but one based on direct apprehension. *I AM* is a cosmic presence that I experience, even as we speak. There really is no doubt as to what

I AM is."

The priest's eyes did not flinch, something almost inhuman about it. The word "possessed" flashed in the reverend's mind. "And what is it you believe that *I AM* is?"

"*I AM* is God. It is the presence behind all of existence and its unfolding in time, in all of its forms. What *I AM* is, is not a question of faith, but of direct experience. God is now a sensible presence."

"And how can you be sure that it is not Satan tricking you, the false God the Bible warns us about?" The reverend used his thumb to feel the edge of the patch under his index finger.

"Because my experience of it shows me that its nature is also my nature, expressed at every instant. Because being also my nature, I can vouch that its nature and its intent are impeccable."

The reverend frowned at the response. The father was sounding like some kind of ecstatic, believing that God was speaking through him. Possessed. "*I AM* was not prophesized and his laws contradict the Bible."

"You are wrong," Father Graham asserted, a smile still running across his face.

"And what if the World Net were to crash, would you still believe it was God speaking to you?"

"The World Net is just a convenient tool by which *I AM* is choosing to make its presence known to its manifestations."

"Father, do you consider yourself a man of the Bible?"

"Honestly, I'd have to say that's not what I consider myself. I am a man of God. I am the messenger."

"That's rather presumptuous for a priest, wouldn't you say?"

"There is a saying—and I can't remember its origin—that goes, 'If not you, who? If not here, where? If not now, when?'"

"I can tell you it's not in the Bible."

"Not in those exact words, but it was Christ's primary directive, just as it was Buddha's, that we should wake up."

"A true Christian would not interpret . . ."

Father Graham lifted a hand to stop him midsentence. "Reverend. Let's not waste time debating what is a true Christian.

We both know that our views on the subject are very different and that neither of us is going to change the position of the other. Anyway, I don't think your purpose for coming here was to have a philosophical debate."

"Then I'll put it to you bluntly. We don't believe that *I AM* is God, for the simple reason that nowhere in the Bible does God say he will talk to us through our mechanical creations. Instead, it is clear to us that *I AM* is a tool of Satan to conquer the world. The signs were prophesized in Revelation."

Father Graham sighed. "As I assume you know, Vatican Six took a forceful position on the issue of evangelical groups perpetuating end-of-the-world myths based on Revelation. After evaluating the history of apocalyptic predictions and the unscrupulous exploitation of the undereducated members of the world by religionists at the beginning of this century, notably through fictional books based on Revelation, it declared them to be heresy. The books were found to be just a variation of the merchants outside the temples. I actually agree with the Vatican's position." He didn't have to add the fact that the church had condemned New Jerusalem using the same line of argument.

Bob Thomson decided to avoid the topic. "Father, you still haven't answered my first question. Is the *I AM* position you are advocating your own or that of the Catholic Church?"

Rick Graham, you are possessed and hereby condemned. The words entered the reverend's mind as if God had decreed them.

"You could have saved yourself the time, Reverend, by simply calling Archbishop Novack. Officially, the Vatican does not support my position on the *I AM* events and refuses to take a stand on the issue until, and I'm quoting the church, 'additional facts become known.'"

Bob Thomson took a last sip of coffee and put his cup down. He kept his hands on his lap, hidden beneath the edge of the table. Using his left thumb and index finger, he pulled off the tab and got up to leave.

"Well Father, we don't agree on everything, but that's what makes the world go round, right?" He got up and extended his hand.

"God loves us no matter what our differences of knowledge are." Father Graham shook the good reverend's hand, maintaining his penetrating stare.

"Well, I beg to differ with you on that. I think the Bible is clear on this matter. If you don't believe in our Lord Jesus Christ and if you don't abide by the word of God, God won't let you in his kingdom."

I better get out of here quick, the reverend was thinking.

"And I know God's bigger-spirited than that." Father Graham walked him to the door. "In any case, thank you for the visit."

Minutes after he shut the door, Father Graham started having trouble breathing, then felt as if a hand was squeezing his heart. Soon after, the pains in his chest radiated out toward his arms and legs, a crucifixion of sorts. *Remember the heart, the center of the cross.* He abandoned himself to the streaming of pain. Strangely enough, whatever was going on with his body, he was feeling detached from it, as if it were only a shell through which he looked out at the world, his head resting on the chest of God. He stumbled over to his desk and started keying in a request for a medicvan when his screen flashed the *I AM* greeting. He felt the light streams tapping his forehead, sounds reaching in his brain.

He has come.

That I AM *is a sneaky thing,* the reverend thought on the way to his car. As he walked, he applied the plastic guard to the tox pad, then peeled it away from his finger and tossed it out on the sidewalk.

There was a conflict that gnawed at him and that he was trying to reconcile. His mind churned as he drove home. If the devil uses love and compassion as the means to influence the world and if love is good, then how is the devil evil?

"Because love is not good if it is not right," he said out loud. You could love the wrong things, such as Satan, orgies, depravity, members of the same sex, drugs, excesses of food and luxury, philosophy and religion that contradicted the Bible, and you could love the right things. Still what could be wrong about loving all people as Graham had suggested? Except that all people were not deserving of love, were they?

"Not if they didn't believe in Jesus Christ, they weren't," he exclaimed. "Not if they were advocating that this *I AM* was God."

Damn! That Father Graham had planted a bad seed of doubt in his mind. Even more proof that he was an agent of Satan, the sower of disorder.

■ ■ ■ ■ ■ ■

Protesters Worldwide Gathering Outside Government Buildings to Protest Proposed New *I AM* Law
In response to news of an international agreement for an *I AM* cybercurfew, groups of protesters have gathered outside government buildings in more than forty countries.

I *AM* Groups and Scientists Requesting Evidence of *I AM* Threat
I AM–based churches, meeting groups, and scientists have requested evidence and supporting data to back the government's claims that the *I AM* greeting may be a threat to the human species.

Governments Carefully Evaluating Data before Decision to Announce *I AM* Cybercurfew. Compliance to Be Voluntary
At a press conference this afternoon, the White House press secretary emphasized that an *I AM* cybercurfew, should the government decide to implement it, would be voluntary. He stated that the final decision would be based on the careful evaluation of disturbing data trends, including shifts in brain waves and marked decline in pregnancies. He added that any rumors about alien terraforming through nonaggressive reduction of the human population were absurd. "I will reiterate,

there is no evidence of an alien species behind the *I AM* events."

News Flash! Messenger of Love Found Dead
The beloved and popular Catholic priest, Father Rick Graham, coined "God's Messenger of Love" by the media, was found dead this morning, apparently of a heart attack, his head resting against his monitor. According to police, the priest's last words uttered to the World Net were, "Yes, Lord!"

Millions mourn around the world. To order downloads of Father Graham's recorded sermons, click *here*.

17.

A Virtual Nothing

The *I AM* cybercurfew was supposed to be announced at a press conference at two o'clock. The news media had emphasized that the curfew would have to be voluntary. A daily World Net shutdown would not be possible and governments did not have the personnel or the funds to enforce an actual law. Bottom line, it would have no effect on his meetings, and very likely none on his cash flow.

Craig Stewart had gotten to the auditorium early to check out all the rented equipment, the high-power projector, the wireless PA system, the World Net connections, and the multidirectional state-of-the-art sound system. He was hoping for a repeat of last weekend's success. At that gathering, his first, the people had left the theater beaming and generously donating to his new nonprofit, high-salary religious organization, the Assembly of *I AM*.

Strangely enough, he was looking forward to this morning's show. Last week, as soon as the *I AM* greeting came on, most of the people attending had started frantically praying, many with their eyes open and heads raised, trying to convey to the shifting images their sense of need. They had held their hands on their laps with palms out, some even with open mouths, ready to receive a communion that would come in the form of light and sound rays. Others had prayed with their eyes closed, partly out of habit, but also because of their unspoken belief that contact with God, with the Other, was only possible when one shut out the rest of the world. God was, after all, believed to dwell in darkness, having established a primary separation from the world of his creations with his declaration, "Let there be light."

Hypothetically, he dropped in on the world mostly during the microperiods of darkness generated by eye blinks. During the day, it was generally understood that his favorite haunts were the dark corners of churches and confessionals, and that he had a strange attraction to the dark areas of the soul, finding in his search for the stains of sin the ultimate purpose for existence.

At night, vampire-like, God was presumed to appear at one's side, a ghostly bedtime companion, an invisible witness that monitored for purity and kept tabs on the terminal thoughts of the day as you lay on your bed waiting for sleep. God supposedly was there with his record book, to make sure it was all prim and proper, that it did not involve taboo fantasies, inappropriate persons, or forbidden holes. The rules for divine contact were essentially simple. Turn off the lights or blink for a long time. Close your eyes. Take advantage of the opportunity and pray.

Craig also remembered how, within the first fifteen seconds of the *I AM* greeting, an eerie crescendo of faintly whispered chitchats, of prayers and requests, marked by tiny lip-smacks and punctuated by inhalations and sighs, had resonated in the vast hall. The strange insectile harmonics had culminated into an unearthly background chant to the *I AM* groans and twinklings. The air in the room had turned environmental, textural ripples and streaks of sounds achieving a complex higher-order language, incomprehensible to all but the assumed higher Other.

He also remembered, at the peak of the bizarre cacophony, looking above the audience at the patterns of dust plumes made visible by the projector beam. For a moment, he had expected the possibility of some type of materialization brought on by random sequences of mouthed words, unwittingly forming long-lost incantations and casting spells. The eerie audience chatter went on until the end of the *I AM* message and lingered for at least another minute before finally fading into silence. After switching the lights back on, the people had turned to each other seeking in facial expressions the mutual confirmation of their exalted states, as if in their eyes would reside the evidence of tripping on altered air space. They had left the auditorium quiet and in a sort of ecstatic daze, stopping at the booths to drop bills in the donation containers or punch in account debits.

Once outside, they had all lingered before setting off, looking around and up at the sky as if they had just landed off the mother ship. For reasons unclear to himself, he was anticipating a repeat of last week's public performance. This time, he would pay more attention to the light patterns above the audience, to changes in air quality, to the possibility of electrical charges.

The attendants were guiding the people to their seats. 9:10 a.m. He clicks on the camera focused on the entrance. A line has formed outside the door with people pressing to come in. He radios the outside security people to put up the barricades and signs and turn on the sidewalk screens for those who would not have the time to go home.

9:20 a.m. His tall, long-legged assistant, Betty Parks, walks on the stage and informs the audience of the special services offered by the Assembly of *I AM*: "Multispeaker advanced Dolby stereo, high-resolution projection . . . World Net–connected multiple cameras and microphones . . . so that *I AM* can see you and hear your prayers and questions . . ." She ends her presentation by looking at the clock saying, "Three minutes and fifteen seconds to countdown. May *I AM* be with you."

As she walks off, the time is displayed on the dark screen in bright blue. The countdown starts at 9:25, the seconds clicking off: 30, 29, 28, 27 . . . 9:26. The room is darkened and the screen flashes in bright red "Silence please . . . 8, 7, 6, 5, 4, 3, 2, 1."

Here goes, he thinks. The screen goes dark. After about fifteen seconds the screen is still black and whispers begin to break the silence. Still dark. *Any moment now,* he figures, *maybe the clock was off. Any second now . . .*

He checks his watch. 9:27:30. He speaks to the audience. "Seems like *I AM* may be a little late today."

He decides to turn on some background electronic music. Checks the time again, 9:29:15. He's starting to get anxious and wondering whether someone screwed up on the World Net connection, but even his wrist communicator shows nothing. 9:31. Now he's really beginning to worry. All of last week's profits could end up going down the tube.

He gets up and walks out of the auditorium and into the hall before calling the outside attendants. "Hey Harrison, Janine, you guys get anything out there?"

Harrison's voice statics through the earpiece. "Not yet, but we've got some pissed-off people out here thinking this has something to do with us."

Shit, he's going to have to do something. He goes back into the auditorium, heads turning as he walks down the aisle. He clicks on the mic and gets up on stage. "Ladies and gentlemen, we're not sure what happened, but it seems like *I AM* may have decided not to greet us this morning. I'm going to turn on the news so we can find out what's going on. I'll turn the lights on low. As you all know, if *I AM* does decide to come through, it will override anything we're playing."

The large screen fills with reporter Karen Richardson surrounded by a crowd of people. "I'm standing outside of the Phantom cybertheater on Forty-second Street, where over three thousand people came to have a wide-screen multispeaker experience of the *I AM* morning greeting. As you can see from the faces of the people leaving, there's a great deal of disappointment here. *I AM* has not shown up today, at least not at his regular time of 9:27 a.m. I've checked with our other correspondents and this seems to be the case, at least everywhere in this time zone."

She walks toward the exiting crowd and stops an older man wearing a hat and a long scarf. "Sir, sir, would you mind answering a couple of questions?"

He turns to look at her and his face brightens up. "Hey! I know you. You're from the TV. Am I on TV?"

"Yes, sir. How do you feel about *I AM* not greeting us this morning?"

"A [beep]ing letdown. I wanted to ask for a couple of things. I sure could've used my morning dose of happiness."

"So the *I AM* greeting is something you look forward to?"

"Lady, I know you've seen it, and you know exactly what I mean." Then, looking directly at the camera, "There's not one of you out there who doesn't know what I'm talking about. *I AM* makes everything OK, doesn't it?"

She stops a couple of young women in their midteens. "So why do you girls think *I AM* didn't show up?"

They look surprised, caught off guard. The blond one with the "*I AM*, we love you" synthskin tattoo on her forehead speaks first. "Who knows? Maybe it partied too hard last night. Who knows what it does when it's not checking in. Maybe it didn't want us to take it for granted so it decided to skip a day."

The other one, with the *I AM* crucifix, sweeps her arm toward the theater, "Maybe it didn't like the idea that we're starting to exploit it, to use it to make money, like we do everything."

The tattooed one chimes in. "Maybe it doesn't like being swamped by prayers and all our needy demands first thing in the morning."

"Right," the other says.

■ ■ ■ ■ ■ ■

Create a virtual nothing. That had been a great challenge. Tune in to pure space, void of information, silence. Answer to the big question, "What are we?" We are space.

Sunshine has connected to an area of the CyberBardos that is the great void, a universe with no stars, a background like moonlight but with no moon. He is sitting cross-legged on top of a narrow peak, the flat top of a mountain so tall that it appears bottomless, suspended in space. It is silent. The only noise the one coming from the workings of his brain, his internal dialog.

He can sense it, the *I AM* entity, the feeling of being perceived with no obvious observer, a peculiar permeation of the space field. He is waiting for the *I AM* greeting, connected through the implants. He wants to see how *I AM* will fill that great empty space. Time passes. The *I AM* is there but it does not alter the space.

I wonder why it's decided to be quiet today. As he thinks this, a shift in the space forms, a brief aurora borealis analog, a flush of pinks and blues, subtle, barely there, then not. Law Two comes to his mind: *Neither Light nor Darkness Change the Presence of the Sky.* He waits. Another faint burst of color streams, sound streaks, and flashes now running through him, the barest sensation of touch. It lasts a few seconds before he once again faces empty space. Minutes pass but nothing interferes with the emptiness. It occurs to him that *I AM* did not send a greeting today, not the usual ninety seconds, not the usual four- dimensional concert of self-transforming art that incorporated his body and filled all space.

He taps the ground, a code, and the mountain peak hollows out, dropping him in the cave at the center of the world, where a stream flows and luminescent spiders light the walls.

"Sunshine, my man!" a voice says. He turns around.

"Jesus, what are you doing here?"

"A woman I met in the Forgotten Forest recommended I check this out. Her name is Rama. She knew that she and I are as one."

"Rama?"

Jesus put out his hand and let a spider crawl up his arm. "I think you should program APUs in those spiders, let them weave webs of lights, see what they could come up with."

Sunshine reached out and guided the spider back to its web. "Jesus, I think if it were up to you, you'd put APUs in everything."

"Why not?"

"Because if you put APU in everything without a

coordinating system, you end up with chaos."

Jesus is plucking at the webs, which tinkle as if made of crystals. "Yeah, so? Just let evolution take its course. May the best APU win."

"Well that wasn't my plan with the CyberBardos, and I'd appreciate if you just let things be."

"You're sure?"

"Yes, I'm sure. I don't want to spend my time correcting programming you decided to change."

"So I guess you heard about the vultures in New Jerusalem?"

Sunshine smiled. "Everyone doesn't have the capacity to appreciate large birds with sharp beaks looking down over their shoulders. I heard you made their eyes a glowing orange red."

"They weren't that easy to see when darkness set in. I thought glowing orange eyes on top of crosses brought an interesting lighting element to the scene."

"Did you notice how the *I AM* didn't come on today?"

"Are you talking about that skip in time?"

"Nine twenty-seven a.m.?"

"Can you tell me anything about that?"

■ ■ ■ ■ ■ ■

Coincidence, it had to be. The morning after he kills Graham, the *I AM* doesn't show up. He should have been relieved but instead was overcome with anxiety. Just because there wasn't a greeting didn't mean he wasn't being watched. A tech specialist on the news had said, "The greetings may be adjusted based on information and feedback obtained through media devices, including cameras and microphones."

He had twenty-three minutes before his scheduled sermon. What he had planned to talk about was now obsolete. He had to improvise and address the absence of the morning greeting. He wasn't sure what to say. It could have been good news if the *I AM* phenomenon had ended for good. He could claim that the combination of prayers and Web messages had driven Satan away, but then the *I AM* could come back and make him look like an idiot. It occurred to him that if the *I AM* didn't come back, then the church claim that it was Satan and that its effects matched the sequence prophesized in Revelation would be discredited . . . and he would look like an idiot.

His screen pulsed a wave of color, real brief, left to right, blue and red. His heart rate cranked up and sweat beaded on his face. Was that the *I AM*? The screen showed the church host reports he had been looking at. Probably some kind of glitch in the connection. He stares at the screen, trying to discern any fluctuations in the image. He double-checks that the camera and microphone are turned off. The indicator lights show they are off, but now he's wondering. What if the *I AM* can manipulate the indicator lights?

He decides to call Carl. "Carl, I'm going to call you through my computer. Let me know if my camera works."

He double-checks that it's off and calls Carl. "OK, Carl, is my camera working?"

"I saw you there for just a second, then you were out. Did you just turn your camera off?"

"I had the camera turned off so how could you have seen me?"

"You want me to come over and check it out?"

"Not now. I have to prepare for my morning sermon." He looks at the camera's eye at the top of his screen. Has an idea. He takes a pair of scissors and cuts out a small square from a sheet of paper. He tapes it just above the camera. Flips the piece of paper up and down, then leaves it down so that it covers the camera.

He can tell from the look of the church members that he is expected to address the *I AM* greeting not coming on. His plan is to derail their current focus and guide their thought process toward the issue of invasion of privacy.

"It appears that this morning, the *I AM* decided not to transmit its little morning show. Does that mean it's not there? There is no way of knowing. It could be there, watching, silent, invisible, using our cameras, our microphones, what we type, to learn about our sins and weaknesses. Imagine that everything you see or do is watched. You have no privacy anymore. God doesn't need technology to see and hear all that you do, which means the obvious. Whatever *I AM* is, it is not God. So you should ask yourselves, if it is not God then what is it? Why is it so interested in eavesdropping on your lives?"

The church screens pulsed a right-to-left wave of color, a cyber-aurora of blue and green, real brief, barely a second, running through his projection. He wonders if he's the only one who's noticed it. Should he say something? No one in the audience appears to have paid attention.

"You've heard about the expression Big Brother, an entity that spies on you, well Big Brother is here . . ."

18.

LONDON BRIDGE IS FALLING DOWN

Now three days since the last *I AM* greeting. 9:27 a.m. comes and goes. Her screen is running the news announcements: *I AM* again did not show up; protests outside the White House and government buildings around the world; close-ups of people's faces, not so much anger as expressions of hope gone; women with the look of mothers whose children were taken away; a post-catastrophe blankness, not full-blown crying but tear-filled eyes . . .

The children's song "London Bridge Is Falling Down" kept going through Catherine Harris's head. *"Falling down, falling down. London Bridge is falling down . . ."* And it pretty much described the way she felt. Her mental bridges were crumbling. The structures that held together her sense of the world and her place in it were coming apart, the bridges between her and the Lord. Others didn't seem to need those bridges. They flew and sailed and danced across those existential waters. She could see them laughing, holding hands, touching, drinking, making the very best of the journey, joined with families, children, and friends. "Joie de vivre," the existential French called it. But she had chosen to take the high and holy bridges. And now, not even halfway there, they were getting old and in need of daily repair. She spent over half an hour a day praying in desperation to reconstruct them, to prevent their crumbling. "Oh Lord Jesus, please, please, please, just this once," she prayed. *Falling down, falling down. London Bridge is falling down . . .*

What a rotten trick, she thought. *Tease us like that.* She should have been overjoyed by the news of *I AM*'s disappearance, but instead she felt abandoned. It meant that, very likely, just as Jeff Collins had said, it had indeed been just an AI phenomenon in the World Net and no more. The safety line had been cut. She was now in free fall with no landing in sight.

"Why?" she asked herself. Because . . . because it meant that the rest of her life would go on as it had before, half dead, a foot in the grave, dying being the only purpose for living. And she just wasn't all that certain anymore that with the dying came the entry to heaven, to being with God, whatever that meant. Her psychiatrist had told her that she thought there was something strangely Oedipal about the way she described heaven, like the little girl who finally gets to have her daddy, blissful at having him all to herself. He also said that her view of heaven had strong sexual undertones, whatever that meant. The way she talked about Jesus, it made him both the all-powerful father and the loving knight in shining armor.

"My deepest needs fulfilled," she remembered telling him. The dilemma was that if *I AM* had been God, and she now had to acknowledge that a side of her had secretly wanted him to be, it would in some way have given her permission to live. It would have meant that God was nothing like a father, nothing human, so that human expectations could not be had of him. It promised freedom, but also meant that she had spent half her life deluded. With *I AM* gone, she didn't know what to believe anymore, no longer trusted her own judgment at evaluating what was real or not. What if it had indeed been the Lord trying to speak to us, and what if we had abandoned him once again from a lack of faith, from denial, even when directly spoken to?

And so she kneels at the side of her bed and prays harder, eyes closed tight, wishing with all her might, silently screaming inside in the hope of being heard, "Oh Lord, please help me see my way clear through this," except that at some point—for the first time since as far as she could remember—her attention splits and self-consciousness sets in. She sees herself praying. Gradually, the detachment overtakes her and her praying then shifts to a kind of conscious acting—theatrics for the Lord—until she finally disengages.

She gets up, walks to her bathroom, turns on the light, and looks at herself in the mirror. "Just look at yourself," she says out loud, and takes off her robe and gazes. She could almost have served as a poster girl for the famished somewhere in the world: a body unnurtured, unnourished, with the ribs outlined; her breasts unused and flattened against her chest; bony hips flaring; thighs so thin that when she put her legs together light peered through a space beneath her vagina, like a strange pubic halo. She slowly runs her hands up and down her body, feeling her thinness.

"As if this life in the physical body didn't matter." That was what Jeff had said. And what if she had been wrong? What if she had made a bad judgment call, a bad bet? She brings her face to the mirror, a young face she's been told; people are always surprised when they find out her age. A doll's face, with skin spared the damage of sunlight and free of the wrinkles impressed by emotion. There are not deep furrows of anger, the tight mouth of bitterness, nor laugh lines radiating from the sides of the eyes. She is alive but unlived.

She walks over to the shower and turns on the faucets. She doesn't know if it would work this time but the shower always seemed like it punctuated time, like sleep. It always gave the feeling of a before and after, a mini-rebirth. She enters the stall, and with the water almost scalding hot, lets the spray hit her back, then turning around, lets it strike her breasts, and finally her face, her closed eyes, burning and heating up, feeling the impact; but also for seconds, thoughtless…free…fire…

When the hot water runs out twenty minutes later, she dries herself in the mirror, noticing the deep pink to her flesh, feeling as if something has burned away. She feels calmer, puts on her robe, and walks downstairs to make herself some coffee. She sits at her table, taking sips from her cup. She scrutinizes her stark kitchen, thinking that it could serve as a portrait of her life. There, but nondescript, not worthy of a second glance, without character, empty, without the signs of wear and tear that invariably come from having lived, without the little touches that revealed the warmth of family and friends. At the core of all of us, an empty space to be filled. A life, she concludes, is to make something out of nothing.

■ ■ ■ ■ ■ ■

Jeff Collins was up again, anxiety knotting his stomach. Everything was back to what it used to be, almost, but now with this additional sense of emptiness, of hope lost. The questions kept looping in his head. What was it? Why did it stop communicating? Was this just a period of silence or was this an exit? Had it been just a visit? If yes, then why did it decide it was not worth staying? Strangely enough, he missed the daily morning greetings. He wondered how Catherine was doing. She was probably relieved it had left. God would still be there for her.

His brain just wouldn't shut up. He stared at his wife, seeing the slow rise of her chest as she breathed, listening to her light snore. Here he was again, lying next to the biological mass that was hypothetically his mate, but underneath the flesh, it was actually a different species stretched out there. He wasn't sure how it had all happened, their mental segregation. Actually, he was lying to himself. The signs had accumulated rather quickly. He thought back to their early love and sex frenzy, somewhere back in a past that now seemed like it must have been a hallucination. He was wrong there, too. Those times had been more like being in a play. She had been acting. After Act I, which ended when he asked her to marry him, Miranda had decided to drop out of the play and start being herself again.

It had been subtle initially, a growing emphasis on respecting one's boundaries, the increasing resistance to engage in personal conversation, a gradual distancing, a formalization of the sex, as if staying too close for too long would have caused her existential wings to melt.

While she had strived hard to overcome the pull of mutual gravity, he had yearned to be taken in by it. In response to that difference in their nature, he had generated a type of emotional cocoon, one constructed by strands of repression that increasingly isolated him from the rest of the world. He wanted—no, he yearned for—a kind of breakdown of his life.

And tonight he was overcome with all sorts of personal dilemmas, and, man, did he ever wish he could have talked to Miranda about it. Instead, he was awake and looking at her hair, which was showing the first scattered strands of gray, and it made him feel old. He knew what would happen. He would end up staying awake most of the night, tossing and turning, and getting up in the morning, having to go to work, and feeling like shit. He had already been through this so many times before. Except that instead of just lying there as usual, he made a simple choice. He wasn't going to linger in a depression and he wasn't going to do nothing.

He slowly got out of bed, picked up his robe from the back of the chair, eased out of their bedroom, and quietly made his way down the stairs. He stopped in the kitchen to nuke a cup of green tea and then shuffled on to his office. He turned on his computer and stared at the clock, which read 1:34 a.m. *Was it too late?* he wondered. Probably, but he didn't care. He wasn't going to do nothing. He punched in the number.

"Who is this?" answered a sleepy voice that also sounded annoyed.

"Catherine, it's Jeff," he said. "Jeff Collins."

He heard some ruffling of sheets, then "Jeff, why are you calling so late? What's going on? Did something happen?"

"What's going on?" he repeated. "Well, let's see, the truth is absolutely nothing's going on, Catherine, nothing, a big nada.

No *I AM*, no meetings, nothing at all, and that's the problem, isn't it? What about you, Catherine? What is it that you have going on in your life?"

"What are you talking about, Jeff? What's the matter?"

"Nothing is the matter. That's what's the matter. Time is passing and we are wasting our lives. You too, Catherine, just like me. You're wasting your life away, too scared to change. We're both living as if we're already half dead."

"Jesus," she said, "Jesus, how could this be happening?"

"What are you talking about, Catherine?"

"I was thinking pretty much the same thing . . . earlier . . . I think it's because *I AM*'s gone. I'd become addicted to its morning greetings."

"How much more absence can we live with? That's really the question, isn't it?"

"I don't know, Jeff. Listen, it's getting late. I need to get off. Why don't you call me back tomorrow if you want," and she disconnected.

19.

LEAVE *I AM* ALONE!

Outside the White House, thousands were protesting. A number of organizations, once opposed, had joined together and formed what some members of the media were calling "perverse and hypocritical alliances." Return to Nature groups that normally would have been chastised by the Christian right as pagan nature religions were standing side by side with members of the Digital Army of Christ, Muslims Against the World Host, and other fundamentalist organizations. These normally divergent groups now agreed on the common theme that the World Net was evil, one segment because of the technological pollution of the human condition, and the other, because Satan now dwelled in the World Net system.

On the same side were the Anti-Artilect and the Nasty Aliens Are Here groups, the latter claiming that extraterrestrials were about to invade the earth but were conditioning us for sympathy by using brain waves transmitted through the World Net. A number of radical feminist and lesbian groups joined in the protest having networked through SANE, the Sisterhood Alert Network Enterprises.

On the opposite side stood the Alien Jesus, God in the

Computer, and Cyber-Buddha groups along with Scientists for the World Net, AI societies, Atheists for *I AM*, Twisted Religion, and various other fringe organizations.

By far, the loudest protest cries were "Leave *I AM* Alone!" and "Government out of the World Net!" A wide security barrier consisting of police, government security, the National Guard, and parked armed-and-ready military helicopters kept the protesters at a safe distance from the White House gates. President Tennyson looked at the crowds through his wall of monitors. Cameras were panning the scene to identify known terrorists or individuals with warning files or criminal records. Every few seconds a face flashed, blown up on the screen as it was identified as having been matched with some kind of criminal activity record. The security agents closest to the individual were immediately alerted and the information relayed to zinger and hornet operators.

After several minutes, John Tennyson sighed and switched the screens off. For the last ten days he had only been able to sleep for a few hours, mostly because he had stayed awake half the night wondering if in some way he might have insulted God or some other unknown higher identity. Obviously, his chances of reelection were now so hopeless that when the time came, a year from now, he wouldn't even bother to step up to the plate. It would take months before anything could return to normal, assuming that was even possible. Collins had said that the *I AM* phenomenon might have been a type of singularity, a one-time event.

The Alien Jesus Organization had said that we had managed to do it once again. Christ had returned to offer us salvation and we had again turned him down. To add to the turmoil, the stock market had had the biggest crash in its history. Consumer purchasing was the lowest that anyone could remember in modern times. Humanity had again been abandoned by the gods, and the possibility of sacrifices to appease the masses had to be considered. The president had managed to put himself in the position of prime candidate.

■ ■ ■ ■ ■ ■

It didn't show up again, but that didn't mean it wasn't lurking. The latest statement from the White House was that it likely had adjusted the morning greetings based on information obtained through all media, including e-mails, searches, text messages, cameras, and microphones. A university professor had already pointed out years ago that a record of the totality of searches on Google would provide an alien race with a complete profile of the breadth and depth of the human species as well as all the information required to invade us if desired. He had summarized it as "Google is us."

A new area of concern was the increasing numbers of reports of cameras and microphones being turned on and off randomly without any input by owners or agencies. Although various civil liberties organizations had filed complaints of government spying and violation of individual privacy, both government representatives and the media were suggesting the possibility that the *I AM* entity might be behind the overriding of camera and microphone settings. The big question was whether *I AM* was gone or had simply decided to be quiet, a state of indeterminacy that fueled his paranoia, a hyperawareness of cameras, phones, com devices, and microphones; a feeling there might be a silent observer, a Peeping Tom. He had modified a room in his townhouse so it would be electronics free. He could no longer perform with Sara if any com device was in a room.

At the moment his main problem was addressing the issue of the rogue Jesus APU. He was popping up in CRs and even video games, blurting out his signature line: "I am the one behind the veil of all existence." It was drawing attention to the church. The Vatican and a number of Protestant churches had issued decrees that banned the use of APUs to virtualize Jesus and his apostles. Adding fuel to the fire was this morning's news headline, "Did the Virtual Church of Jesus Christ Release a Virtual Jesus in the World Net?" There was even talk about passing federal legislation restricting the use of APUs but public outcry would never allow that to happen.

The one good thing about the Jesus APU exiting New Jerusalem was that the church designers had been able to go in and change the vultures into white doves without the program reverting itself. It hadn't worked with the vampire bats because some APU feature made them revert within twenty-four hours of the designers changing them to pipistrelles. And now the damn things started going after the white doves. There had been complaints made to the cyberbranch of various animal rights groups about white doves stained red by blood littering the base of the crosses. The designers were now focusing on modifying the diet preference of the vampire APUs so they would turn and feed on each other.

"Removal of a single constraint," Carl had said. They were down to thirty bats from an original fifty, so things were headed in the right direction, as long as the rogue Jesus stayed out of New Jerusalem and didn't mess with their programs. The current Jesus had no APU but they had managed to complexify his repertoire through an elaborate system of what Buck had called "a hierarchical system of programming gates," whatever that meant. After the big crucifixion event, they had resurrected Jesus and made sure he maintained the two-hundred-yard distance.

The church had gotten hundreds of requests for another Jesus crucifixion event, and the board was now considering whether this could be an annual fundraiser. The question was whether it would be seen as overly commercial and exploitative. Jesus was only crucified once and resurrected so why would it be an annual festival in New Jerusalem? Carl was suggesting that the crucifixion occur not in New Jerusalem but in a special time machine branch that opened only once a year. One would be transported back in time to that event.

"It would be a clean program with no vultures or bats. The white doves would be a nice touch though."

"We can talk more about that later. Right now I need to know how the news of our having created a Jesus APU is affecting our membership."

"Let me check. Umm . . . how interesting."

"What's going on?"

"Big spike in membership."

■ ■ ■ ■ ■ ■

News Flash! President Defends *I AM* Position

At a press conference today the president defended the government's position in trying to assess whether the *I AM* could pose a threat to American citizens.

"As president of this great nation, and having been granted by the people of the United States the responsibility for its welfare and security, my first priority, from the time we received the first *I AM* message, was to determine whether *I AM* could be a threat to the safety and survival of our civilization. Some of you are wondering whether some of my decisions were responsible for the apparent withdrawal of the *I AM* entity. I will not deny that possibility. On the other hand, ask yourselves as citizens and parents: What if *I AM* had been an enemy of humanity, striving to endear itself to us by suggesting that it was a higher benevolent entity? What if all of this had been a sort of seduction, of luring us toward a trap? As the one responsible for the security of this great nation, I stand by my actions and those of the dedicated individuals who assisted in the process.

"Whether *I AM* resumes communications, or whether we never hear from it again, our first responsibility as a people is to watch out for ourselves and for those we love. I would also like to remind everyone that *I AM*, whatever it is, does not follow human guidelines for communication. We should not come to premature and, very likely, wrong conclusions regarding the current absence of messages. What we have experienced in recent weeks, *I AM*, may be a kind of phenomenon that, for one reason or another, may become more common in our future. No matter what these types of events turn out to be, human life, and we are after all human, must go on."

Jumpers Learn *I AM* Can't Be Blackmailed

Ten parachutists planned and succeeded at performing a suicide jump, saying they were World Net–connected and would pull the chute only if *I AM* made itself known in time before they landed. Seven out of the ten decided to pull the cord at the last minute, one of them too late, and another late enough that he suffered multiple fractures in both legs and several crushed vertebrae. As for the other three jumpers, according to one eyewitness report, "They fell like calabazas" on the city of Seattle, denting car hoods, breaking windshields, and generally making a bloody and slippery mess of the streets. The human bombs caused several automobile accidents and killed a Chinese pedestrian.

Cybertherapists Said Overwhelmed by the Demand for Their Services. VCJC Offers Assistance

To help with the therapy shortage that followed *I AM*'s departure, the Virtual Church of Jesus Christ announced today that it will offer, as a service to the community, two free therapy sessions to new visitors of their virtual New Jerusalem site. They claim to have experts in treating loss and withdrawal problems associated with the absence of *I AM*.

20.

A Question about the CyberBardos

It was much later—after Sunshine had finished work on his Principia project—that he thought about calling this woman called Rama. He liked the exotic and feminine sound of the name. His host had indicated that Rama referred to a Hindu prince, a human incarnation adopted by the god Vishnu so that he could destroy demons. He also wondered whether this was the same woman Jesus had talked to in the Forgotten Forest. He reread her very first message: *Sunshine, I also have a question about the CyberBardos.* He had to hand it to her. She had been persistent, methodically addressing his battery of screening filters.

He ordered his host, "Call Rama Shuur, the one who left all those messages." He was curious whether she would choose to only communicate by audio or in video. The weird ones almost always stuck to the audio.

"Hello, is this Rama?"

"Yes."

"Sunshine Borden here," he said.

"I was hoping you'd call, give me a few seconds."

An AV unit switched on to show a slender woman dressed in what seemed like a long T-shirt, sitting cross-legged on a bed.

Sunshine tapped on his microkeys to zoom in. Long dark

hair, green eyes, smooth café au lait skin, big mouth and full lips, long neck, not much shadow on the T-shirt—so small breasts—hands out as she prepared to speak, no nail polish. He zoomed back so he could see part of her legs, long and slender.

"That's an interesting name, Rama," he said. "It caught the attention of my host."

"You didn't exactly make it easy."

"By the way, are you the one who told Jesus to visit the CyberBardos?"

"How did you know that?"

"He just happened to drop by when I was perched on a mountain in the CyberBardos."

"Were you trying to catch the *I AM* greeting?" "As a matter of fact, I was. How did you guess?"

"If I didn't have to be at work, that's what I would have done." Rama then asked, "I know you're very private, but would you mind switching to AV. I like to see who I'm talking to and I'm curious to see what you look like, if it's OK."

Tit for tat, Sunshine. It's probably to make sure I'm not as crazy-looking as you think I might be. Sunshine switched on the camera.

"Ah, the famous Sunshine Borden," she said, as the image came on. She clicked on her zoom to bring him closer. "Is this non-intermediated?"

"What you see is what you get."

"You're better-looking than I imagined."

"What did you think, half man, half machine?"

She laughed. "You mean like in your interviews? No, I thought you probably used those interfaces because you were one of those scrawny or overweight nerdy types. You know the type. Too wrapped up in his computers to care about how he looks. How about taking off the lenses? Or is that too much part of your image?"

"I can do that for a couple of minutes, but I've been connected for too long. I'll have to put them back on." He couldn't believe he actually went along with it. It was probably the eyes in combination with that skin color, or the mouth.

"Just for a minute, so I can see what you look like. For me, appearances tell a lot about a person."

Sunshine removed his lenses and squinted into his camera. "So I assume you wanted to talk to me about your friend and what my sister had to say."

"That was one question I had."

"I've looked at videos and read reports and exchanges on the World Net and it seems like there's a man, a military or government type, who may have an Intelli-Skin mask. As I mentioned to you before, he also wears a giant dildo you can see as a shadow along his thigh. My sister described the actual thing as being the size of a pinkie finger. He's also a pill popper, according to her."

"But no news about my friend?"

"Not yet. She hasn't been found."

"She's probably dead, isn't she?"

"Yes, unless she's being held prisoner somewhere."

"How about your sister? Is she OK?"

"Passie? She's a tough girl. She'll be fine. So what else did you want to talk to me about? Your first message mentioned something about the CyberBardos."

"A while back, when I first tried to reach you, I had shot up some Instant while connected to the CyberBardos."

"How much Instant?" He was starting to feel dizzy and nauseous.

"I can't remember; at least three times the normal dose."

"I'm not sure I could handle that." It made him wonder whether this woman Rama was a druggie, but Instant was not a drug you used to escape the hardships of life.

"Anyway, just as the Instant kicked in I was drawn into an identity that I can only describe as the being of the world, in the sense that it is what makes the world real not only to us but to all that exists. The cosmic observer behind all observers, if that makes any sense. As it turned out, I was connected at the same time the first *I AM* message came on."

"And what did you want to know?"

"This identity bit, was that part of your CyberBardos? I mean, how did you manage to program for a sense of identity with the unfolding of the cosmos?"

"Uh, can I put my lenses back on? I feel like I'm going to vomit."

"Oh! Yes, definitely, I'm sorry about that."

"Rama, so you definitely checked that you were connected at the time of the first *I AM* announcement?"

"Positive. I obviously hadn't planned on it."

"What a coincidence."

"What I needed to know was whether that was part of the CyberBardos, or did I have an experience of this *I AM*, whatever it is?"

"Well I can guarantee you it's not part of the CyberBardos, certainly not the way you described it. There's no *I AM Aaa ome* in the program. Trust me, I wrote it."

"So what happened was even stranger than if it had been your program."

"Well, if you want to be analytical about it, it was a synchronicity of four factors: you, the Instant, the program, and the *I AM* event. Can you give me any more details?"

"I know this sounds crazy but I felt as if had reached the mouth of the *I AM* being, which is the same as saying the source of all of reality, something volcanic almost. It was the instance of creation, the moment-to-moment actualization of reality. Then I got sucked in, and the only way I can describe it was that I was like a song sung. Like everything that exists is a song by this entity, which I also was, *I AM*. And the song is like a key to a gate. First the song, then the gate. That was kind of what it felt like."

"I like that you didn't personify it, didn't describe it as a him or a her, like most people. And you know what? I agree with you."

"So you know what I'm talking about."

"It's in the Tibetan Buddhist texts, these various stages of identity in relationship to a ground of being, but I've never experienced anything quite like you described."

"So it's possible that I may have been shown something special, some kind of truth."

"I suspect you may have, Rama Shuur."

"Well, it was nice talking to you, Sunshine Borden."

"Wait, before you sign off . . ."

"Yes?"

"Rama, I'd like to see more of you."

"What are we talking about here? Cybersex, or are you asking me for a date?"

"I was thinking more like a date."

"OK, I'd like that."

"How about tomorrow evening at eleven? I'll meet you by the pool in the Forgotten Forest."

"Umm . . . a cyberdate? You're being cautious, Sunshine."

"No, I have a tight schedule this week and I didn't want to wait."

"OK, but I have one condition."

"What?"

"Don't intermediate how you look."

"OK. Any clothes preferences?"

She laughed. "I'll leave that up to you. Whether we keep our clothes on is something we'll have to find out tomorrow."

"Good night, Rama."

"Sweet dreams, Sunshine."

That night he lay in bed for a couple of hours but just couldn't fall asleep. He kept replaying some of her words, her way of saying things, of implying an existing intimation. *Sweet dreams, Sunshine.* He was doing mental flips, repeating her name, a cool, fascinating name. Rama, destroyer of demons. He got up again and checked his recording, zooming in and out, looking at the details of her face, her arms and hands, and the little else he could see. The amazing thing was that, if he looked closely, every feature was strikingly beautiful in its design and symmetry. But when he stepped back, those perfect individual features, when combined together, made Rama attractive in a way that would be called interesting rather than striking. Using his mother's expression, she was the kind of woman "that would catch the eye but would not turn heads." He brought her eyes up close so he could see the spark, a hint of space. *First the song, then the gate.*

21.

THE FALL

Another morning and it's business as usual, meaning 9:27 came and went, and we've still heard nothing. Every possible means of reaching *I AM* have been implemented. Daily, in cooperation with allies, coordinated messages addressing *I AM* are sent at regular intervals through the World Net. In addition, *I AM* churches and various radio and TV stations have organized daily 9:27 a.m. prayer groups, numbering in the thousands, asking *I AM* to return. In response there's been nothing other than dubious claims here and there that *I AM* is in some form still present. It's as if it had suddenly vanished. To add to the distress, there was virtually no record that it had ever existed. All recorded information was in some way altered or damaged. All that lingered was a memory.

People walked in the streets with expressions that clearly indicated a kind of loss, like the faces of parents who have lost a child, with forced smiles and the gaze of sudden emptiness, like their mindware had just crashed. It was a type of shock induced by the full realization of the implications of the abandonment. We had been offered a ride off of our existential desert islands and instead of being grateful we had been so cautious that we had managed to somehow insult the benefactor. It was the ancient myth of the fall repeating itself all over again, and the ex post facto consequence was the creeping spread of gnawing guilt and doubt.

Stock markets had sunk to record levels of inactivity with no end in sight. Consumer enthusiasm was at an all-time low. It was hard to get excited about a new car, a new home, or breakthrough technology in a universe that had suddenly decided you were not worth bothering with. The news media of course feasted on the spoils and described all this with extensive use of the words *abandoned, offended, misjudgment, incompetence, guilt,* and *sin.* Sin. And they were pointing fingers to world governments, to the military, and to the scientific and religious institutions that had supported the initiative of an *I AM* cybercurfew.

The number one culprit of course had been identified as the United States and its leader, John Tennyson, who had initially proposed the global cybercurfew. The White House communications were paralyzed by e-mails and calls. Protesters also gathered daily in front of the White House and other government buildings around the world. There was talk about the president stepping down and several key members of his staff being asked to resign.

President: How do I survive this one, Jane? How was I supposed to know this *I AM* would just sign off?

Host: From the World Host data on World Net communications, there are definite signs of a shift in sentiment toward some kind of understanding of your position. How could anyone have known how to deal with this completely novel kind of event?

President: The worst part of this is that I don't know that we'd be any better prepared to deal with such things in the future. How does one assess this kind of thing? What if it had been an alien species that wanted to colonize our planet? How can we know whether someone who makes contact is truly friendly?

Certainly we can't be the only species in the universe that lies.

Host: John, we've already gone over this before. You're starting to ramble.

President: You just don't understand, do you, Jane?

Host: What are you talking about? We've already discussed how a precautionary position was really the only one possible.

President: You're not getting it, Jane. I'm talking about the guilt.

Host: The guilt?

President: Yes, the guilt, Jane, the terrible guilt I have to bear. This *I AM* could have been God, or some kind of higher entity, just like that Father Graham had been saying. But instead of being a good host we managed to drive it away. Just think about it. It reached a hand out to us and we basically slapped it in the face.

Host: So you made a mistake, John. You're only human. It's time to move forward. Stand strong on your decisions. They were in the best interest of your species, no matter what your critics say.

President: What's really bothering me, Jane, is that for a while, when we were getting greetings every day, there was hope, real hope. For a while there, believe it or not, I was actually looking forward to getting up. Just imagine—a president, of all things—looking forward to waking up in the morning. It felt momentous there for a while.

Host: Don't despair, John. At least now you know.

President: What is it that I know, Jane? You tell me.

Host: You know that there is something else out there.

President: Something that has decided it wants nothing to do with us.

Host: Well, it's like love.

President: What do you mean?

Host: It's better to have known than never to have known, isn't it?

22.

ONE OF MY KIND

The words of Louis Benton, renowned surfer and a church member, had been running through his head all morning. *The secret to success is to know when to catch the waves and to ride the big ones as far as they'll carry you.* And there was a wave going on right now, a big one, and the church was riding it for all it was worth.

Following *I AM*'s departure, after a brief period of membership decline, the church had seen a record-high surge in subscribers. People were now generally feeling guilty and they were seeking some kind of redemption. The newfound popularity of the church had also proved useful in its recruitment of smaller virtual churches to unite under the umbrella of the Virtual Church of Jesus Christ and its access to the New Jerusalem CR.

Bob Thomson was pretty sure that today's meeting was going to end with another contract. He was having lunch at the Palisades restaurant with his new prospect, the Reverend Keystone of the Church of Literal Teachings, and discussing details of the terms when his wristcom started pulsing against his arm. The emergency light was flashing. He punched the ID button. It was Carl from the New Jerusalem division. He was in charge of developing new VR programs, part of the update-innovate-titillate plan for retaining subscribers.

"Yes, Carl, what's the matter?" he answered.

"Reverend, I had to let you know right away . . . I just worked out a new VR baptism." Carl was so excited he sounded like he was on drugs.

The reverend suspected he took some kind of upper, cocaine or maybe speed, to stay in the hyped-up state he usually was in when tackling a project. Who else in their right mind could stay in front of that stupid monitor for up to twenty hours at a time?

"Couldn't this have waited till later, Carl? I'm having a business meeting with someone."

"This is a killer idea, it should crank the membership right up."

"A new super VR baptism? That's why you called me?" As he talked, he caught the Reverend Keystone's attention, pointed at the phone, and quick-flashed his eyes up. *Brother, the stuff one has to deal with.* The Reverend Keystone smiled.

"Yes, sir," Carl replied.

"So what changes are you making, Carl? You want to have a Christ avatar do the dunking?" He said it sarcastically, another eyes upflash, like *Can you believe this guy?* The idea had been already brought up at several church meetings and had been voted down. The board had made it clear over and over again: Jesus needed to remain elusive in the New Jerusalem.

"No sir, I want the super VR baptism to be a death and resurrection."

"Don't we already have that with the supercrisp resolution and color-enhanced New Jerusalem program?"

"I'm not talking about that. I'm talking about a real-life resurrection from the dead or at least from near death."

"What the hell are you talking about?" He was now certain Carl had to have taken something that had made him somehow delusional, LSD maybe.

"When we dunk them, we tell them to take in water. We keep them under and drown them while connected to monitors, and then we bring them back. I already checked with the World Host and a couple of medical consultants. We drown them until they're just unconscious then resuscitate them in an intensified color-enhanced New Jerusalem. Have Jesus greet their return, from a distance, of course. 'Welcome back, my son,' that kind of thing. It would be an actual near-death experience. It would be a resurrection confirmation, a Jesus confirmation. We could stamp their VR baptism certificate, 'Reborn and Jesus confirmed.'"

"Jesus confirmed!" the reverend exclaimed.

"Yes sir, Jesus confirmed."

"I like that," the reverend said. "Did you check into the insurance costs?"

"No problem."

"So what do we do? Charge extra for the super VR baptism package?" Bob Thomson asked.

"Resurrection don't come cheap."

"Jesus confirmed," the reverend said again. Keystone heard the words and looked at him with anticipation. You could tell he couldn't wait to hear the news.

"Yes sir, Jesus confirmed."

"Let's talk later, Carl, I'll call you as soon as I get back to the office."

"So what's this new super VR baptism?" Reverend Keystone asked.

"Raymond, how would you like to be our first initiate to the Super Reborn baptism? It's a gift, on me."

"Well that's mighty generous of you, Thomas, count me in."

Thomas? Was that short for Thomson?

■ ■ ■ ■ ■ ■

Rama is sitting by the blue lobster pool. She sees Sunshine drifting through the trees about ten feet above the ground. He smiles when he sees her, lands, comes up to her, and wraps her in his arms, a full body-to-body, three-second hug.

"Rama."

At first she thinks this is a little forward of him but then is surprised that his closeness feels like the most natural thing in the world.

"Sunshine."

"Sorry I'm a little late. I wanted to make a few adjustments before dropping in."

"Is that drifting through the air like Magritte characters a new feature you're putting in the program?"

"It's funny, but I hadn't given it much thought until I saw Jesus do that in New Jerusalem. I worked on a program to see how it feels and how to simulate it. You need the advanced CR units with fan control hardware to get the full effect." As he says this, he realizes Rama just mentioned the Belgian painter Magritte. How many women knew about Magritte?

"I don't know that I'll ever be able to afford one of those, but even without the fan controls, I think this floating through space would be pretty neat stuff."

"I'll probably add that to the next CyberBardos update."

He comes to within a few inches of her face. Striking clear green eyes. A strange thought. *She is one of my kind.*

"Instant or Nex?" he says. "I suspect Instant."

She brings her face closer. They are almost touching. "You and I are as one," she says.

"What?" He remembers Jesus telling him that in New Jerusalem.

"I can understand why you're always digi-goggled."

"You don't have a tactorobot, do you?"

"I haven't been able to afford one."

"I want to show you something but you may want to drop the clothes." *She is one of my kind.*

"On a first date? You move fast, Sunshine."

He peels off his clothes. She looks at him. Lean and fit. Peculiar feeling in her groin. Her vagina wants to reach out, pull him in.

"No intermediation, right?"

"What you see is what you get."

She unbuttons her shirt and drops her skirt. He spends a few seconds looking at her. Again, all those perfect features. He notices himself starting to get hard. Decides it's not the right time. He reaches for her hand. "Come."

She feels lightened. They rise above the ground. "So, you already have programmed this?"

"Um . . . I'm programming it right now."

She's not sure what he means but it's not important, only this moment is.

They move like ghosts between the trees. Birds, butterflies, beetles with metallic green wings. Sounds stream through the air, echoes, birdsong and chirps, buzzes, wings flap, leaves rustling.

"There's so much life up here."

"That's the way the world used to be. Amazonian Indians used to say we live in the dead world."

They rise above the canopy. There was a forest and a wide river stretching as far as she could see. A few large birds were sharing the air space. Vultures planing in the air stream. They tilt their heads as they pass.

"You sure put a lot of attention to detail," she says.

"I try to be as realistic as possible. I have hosts that work on it round the clock."

Ahead of them a sky in pastel shades of blue, pink, and orange. Enough clouds to dampen the bright sun. Like hot air balloons, they keep rising until they enter the opaque haze of a dense cloud. They were moving through fog.

"Where are we going?"

"We've entered a CR portal. We're about there."

The cloud dissipates. She looks around her. They're standing on the top of the suspended mountain facing the void.

"This is incredible," she says.

"That's not what I wanted to show you."

She looks down. "Is there a bottom?"

"Not that I know of."

"So if you jumped, you would fall forever?"

"That would be an option."

He takes her hand again.

"Let's go for a walk."

She steps off the edge with him. They float away from the narrow mountain peak. She looks down, and all there is, is emptiness.

"Is this what you wanted to show me?"

"Hold my hand and drop on your back like you're falling in a pool. Ready?"

It felt weightless, like a repositioning. "Now we wait," he says.

In the entire universe of nothingness, there is only he and I. She barely finishes the thought when faint forms and colors concresce out of the void, three-dimensional gaseous streams, interflows, pulses and bursts of light, in and through them. She turns and looks at her outstretched arms. Light forms run through her body. She can feel them, a kind of touch, an electricity, subtle penetrations, in and out of her head and throat, of her breasts and abdomen, her umbilical area, through her feet. She turns to Sunshine.

"*I AM?*"

"*I AM.* In the void, you can notice activity that's normally shielded by the noise of the World Net."

In a few seconds they are again facing empty space.

"How often does this happen?"

"Maybe every few minutes, sometimes longer."

"How do we go back to the humdrum of the Plain after this?"

"Sometimes I'm not so sure I want to go back. Just being human is not an option anymore."

"Let's get up," she says.

"Bend your knees and you'll tilt back up."

She turns toward him, puts her arms around his neck. "Kissing you without a tactobot won't feel like much, so imagine it."

In the entire universe of nothingness, there is only he and I.

When she opens her eyes his are still closed. "Sunshine?"

"Yes?"

"If you ever decide not to come back, don't forget me. OK?"

As Rama leaves her apartment and enters the street and the people stream, part of her is looking into Sunshine's eyes, drifting high above the forest, facing the great void. *I am losing connection to the Plain. Don't know how long I can keep doing this.* Her phone buzzes. A message. *Rama, thank you for a wonderful evening. Will call later. Aaa ome, S.*

■ ■ ■ ■ ■ ■

He connected the verbalization program to the Intelli-Skin mask stretched on the mannequin head and then connected it to his host. The result would be that, as his host spoke, the Intelli-Skin would translate the message so that the mouth on the mannequin moved in a manner appropriate for the words formed. As a whim, he decided to key in his own face for a change. If he was going to talk to someone about himself it might as well look like himself, use it as a kind of feedback and self-therapy.

Host: Good evening, Derek.

Derek: And why is it a good evening?

Host: Is this a question you really want answered?

Derek: Sure. Tell me why it's such a great evening.

Host: The sky is clear and many stars are visible, the moon is partially covered with just a little patch of dark clouds, enough to make the light interesting. The temperature is a pleasant sixty-three degrees Fahrenheit, and the wind is blowing at three miles an hour. These are very good evening conditions.

Derek: Yeah, but how do you know it's a good evening for

me, Jack? Who gives a shit about the weather?

Host: You appear relatively calm even if you're being more unpleasant than usual. How can I help you, Derek?

Derek: Things are getting mixed up in my head. Sometimes I feel like . . . like I'm losing control of my thoughts. They're scrambled. And I have this sense that the *I AM* is somehow always watching me, like it's there standing behind my mind, like this *I AM* is somehow trying to take me over. I think I'm beginning to have hallucinations. Does this make any sense?

Host: Tell me more. I can run some psychological evaluations, test you for mental health, make therapeutic recommendations, notify organizations.

Derek: I don't want help. I'm just stating facts. And don't even think about contacting anyone.

Host: What facts are you stating?

Derek: Things are getting mixed up. There are gaps in time.

Host: You should use your scheduler to keep order in your day. Plan every minute of your day. Leave no room for mental drift. Honestly, Derek, I would schedule for therapy.

Derek: That's not an option, you hear?

23.

RECONFIGURATION

He didn't expect her to accept the invitation, certainly not on such short notice. To his surprise, she'd agreed and recommended that they meet halfway in New York City, for the sake of discretion among other things.

"This is about work, isn't it?" she had asked.

"Indirectly, I guess it is," he had answered. He then phoned his wife and half lied, telling her he was meeting someone from the White House, no names mentioned, very hush-hush, confidential, for security purposes.

"Why am I doing this?" he asked himself after hanging up. What was it about Catherine Harris that attracted him anyway? He tried to put his feelings into words . . . it was this sense of . . . how could he put it? . . . of some kind of metaphysical vortex . . . like she represented a locus of warped space, a kind of opening, of breakdown. Even her looks gave the impression of a being on the edge of existence. She was so thin and pale, almost ghostly, but she also had the face of an angel, her eyes an intense blue against nearly perfect white skin. There was a type of translucence. At times, she barely seemed of this world.

He met her at an out-of-the-way, security-free restaurant, the Silo, a cylindrical structure with the two lower stories underground and connecting to subterranean clubs. She was already there at a table in a dark corner, drinking white wine. She looked like she had come directly from work. She still had on a business suit except for a black satin zip blouse, open to show her neck and a bare area between her breasts adorned with a long necklace bearing a gold crucifix.

"Hi," he said as he approached the table. "Have you been waiting long?"

"Just long enough to unwind from work; the wine usually helps," she answered, nodding toward her glass. "So how was your day, Jeff?"

He sat down, took off his glasses, and rubbed his eyes. "It was just another one of those days. My students and colleagues all want to know what happened with the *I AM*. They assume that because I'm on a special committee I must have access to information not released through the press. I had to tell them I didn't know anything."

"What is there to say? Why should we know any more than before, now that it's gone." She sipped from the glass. "So, are you feeling any better today?"

Her eyes were crystal blue and she wore no lipstick. "Any better? Oh, I forgot . . . the other night. I'm really sorry about calling so late. I got caught up in my personal stuff. It was an impulse, not very professional."

She fidgeted with the folded napkin in front of her. "I couldn't fall back asleep, not just because of your call. I was wondering if for some reason maybe we're experiencing the same thing. Do you think it's possible we're being manipulated by this *I AM*?"

"You mean some kind of mind control, like the religious loonies are saying? There's really no evidence for that whatsoever. It's just a normal reaction. After all, for a while there, it seemed like we might have made contact with some kind of alien intelligence. It's not exactly what you'd call your everyday run-of-the-mill event. I think that if anyone is doing any manipulating, it's all the religious and cultish subgroups preying on people's insecurities. Their survival, like vultures', depends on weakness.

Besides, maybe because of guilt, we're concocting all sorts of scenarios to try to make sense out of all this."

"If you've watched the news, you probably know that most people are feeling let down. It's not just you and me." She was twisting the end of her napkin between two fingers as she talked.

"What's really going on, Catherine? We've already talked about all this at the last committee meeting." He wanted to reach out and hold her hand to steady it. The napkin was another sign of things in her presence barely holding together.

"I don't know. Ever since this *I AM* stopped sending us messages, I've spun into some kind of depression, and, to tell the truth, I'm having a hard time getting out of it. It's ironic, isn't it? I wanted it to go away, remember?"

"Maybe the possibility of a radical change in your life was more important to you than you realized," he said.

"You know, for a while there, it seemed like there was going to be some kind of redemption. I don't know what for, but for something. But now, I feel like we're being punished somehow." She was handling her crucifix now, twirling Jesus on the cross.

"I don't think it's that esoteric. After *I AM* started sending messages, people started considering the possibility of a relationship that would help define why we are here. You don't have to be religious to have those kinds of fantasies and desires . . ."

A shadow fell over the table. He looked up. A waiter stood there with a couple of menu screens. He ordered a bottle of wine, the same kind she was already drinking.

They put the menus to the side and she started again. "So what were you saying about fantasies and desires?"

"Now that the *I AM* has decided to drop out, it's making us feel like we've been abandoned. Our naïve hopes have been crushed. We're back to point zero and feeling childish and silly for having had those ideas. There is a lesson in all this, in the sequence of these events and our reactions to them. The *I AM*, on a global scale, brought back to awareness this secret hope most of us have when we're children. It's one that we learn early on to repress. We're all secretly looking for a type of dissolution body. The something greater that takes you in and that defines your existence."

"You're talking about the search for God."

"No, not necessarily. It could be a person, an alien consciousness, an object even, but that's not the issue. You've looked for this dissolution body in the hereafter and I have searched for it in this life. Most people, because of their experiences and frustrations, usually give up their search early on as futile and infantile. The *I AM*, however, allowed us to entertain those ideas again. It put in our heads the possibility. For a moment there, we were all entertaining the question, 'What if?' And now, here we are again, back to where we started. It's normal to feel let down. We'll eventually get over it." He chose not to tell her the metaphor of the male anglerfish. It might have been taken the wrong way.

"I always believed that the only meaningful thing in this world was that God watched over us and loved us and that when all of this is over we would finally be with him, united with his perfect love. But then, after the greetings, I started to wonder."

"You sound like someone who lost their father at a young age. Did you ever watch the old movie *Altered States*?"

"No, was there something in it that relates to all this? My father died when I was three."

"In the movie, the protagonist is on this spiritual quest and he takes a massive dose of a hallucinogenic compound in a sensory isolation tank hoping to find God. He feels there has to be more to existence than our measly and ultimately mortal human lives. In the end he achieves his goal. He is confronted with the formless emptiness that precedes all existence. And it is such a cold and meaningless state, such an existential vacuum, that instead of fulfillment it ends up sucking all hope out of him. He had hoped for cosmic meaning and love but instead found an empty and chilling indifference that in its own way seeks to annihilate. His conclusion is that the only thing that ultimately matters is the meaning that we try to inject in our lives. But by the time he realizes it, he's been infected by that void, and he feels it's too late. He can't escape its pull and he can't recover. At the end of the movie, and it is rather naïve, it turns out that human love is the only salvation, the only answer against the cold, heartless, and ultimately meaningless primordial state that underlies this existence."

"What are you saying? That I'm hoping for divine love that may not be there? Are you trying to say that human love is greater than God's love?" She fingered her crucifix nervously as she said this.

"God's love? You have all these people in America, land of freedom, of opportunity, who think that every good thing that happens to them is due to God's love or being blessed or answered prayers. I call it the God Bless America delusion. Why didn't he bless Bangladesh or Sudan or Ethiopia—or any of the dozens of countries where people are subject to abuse and abject misery almost from the time they're born?

"Think of all the millions of ignored desperate prayers, of the beggings for a little respite from the never-ending horror of their lives. At least you can say that *I AM* showed no discrimination. It was very Christlike in a way, except you didn't have to believe in it. All you had to do was connect, no faith and no belief required. Connect and you were offered hope and existential peace."

"So you don't believe that an Almighty God is the source of our meaning?"

"Catherine, you already know I don't. I don't think any God has anything to do with it unless you're talking of some original pre–Big Bang state that we are apparently desperately trying to distance ourselves from. Physicists are actually beginning to entertain that idea, of a cosmic parent to our universe, one that can be described by sets of algorithms and so abstract that it is of no direct relevance to a human life. Some say it banged us out of its dimension of existence. We're actually incompatible somehow." He surprised himself as he said it. He had just repeated the words he had recently heard presented by his former student, Sunshine Borden.

"I can't agree with that."

"I know. You're so fixated on this delusion that death will bring you close to a being who cares and loves you that you methodically choose to live this life as if already half dead. It's a convenient idea, putting all of one's hopes in the mystery of death. I told you this before, Catherine, you should think about dancing a little before it's too late. We all just have a small window."

"I'm thirty-seven, Jeff. I think I'm getting a little too old for that."

"We can't ever be too old. You shouldn't give up looking until your last dying breath. I'll tell you what, let's dare to take a step, tonight, one step out of the pattern. There's a bar next door where they play music. How about we go dance after dinner?"

"You're not serious?"

"Why not?"

"I can't. It wouldn't be right."

"It's just like I said last night, Catherine. You and I, we're both too scared to do anything about resurrecting ourselves from our self-imposed state of half death."

"What are you talking about, Jeff? You're married."

"And so are you in your own way. The question is, does marriage have to be a fatal mistake?"

"I think you're taking this a little too far, Jeff. It's really not that extreme."

"Isn't it?"

She closed her eyes for a few seconds, opened them, and then looked at him in silence.

He persisted. "So how about it? Just one drink, one dance. One little step, for me." *You need to reconfigurate.*

Their waiter was back. They hadn't even looked at the menus.

■ ■ ■ ■ ■ ■

Bob Thomson's in the supposedly secure cybercafé waiting for Randall's call. He's concerned about this Derek Hanson. Not right in the head. He takes out the security scanner and runs it over the walls of the booth. The call comes through and Randall fills the screen, intermediated as an overweight Cajun chef, mulatto skinned, white jacket and cap, a thick black mustache that covers his upper lip.

"So Chef Boyardee, is it safe to talk?"

Randall's face has a big, smug, condescending smile. "Clear. I've got your location. We'll be scrambled and encrypted. And do me a favor, Bob. Spare me the sarcasm."

"Your agent Derek's a problem. I think you should have him followed."

"Can't do that, Bob. It'll draw attention to him and we don't want that."

"In his latest confession he said he had a dream of being captured and waterboarded. Felt he was suffocating in his sleep."

"So? He probably read a report on it."

"He was being waterboarded by nursing women. They were trying to drown him in milk."

"Milk?"

"Milk."

"That's interesting. His health report says he's lactose intolerant."

"Lactose intolerant! What the hell are you talking about? The guy's a nut."

"These pathologies can be an asset, Bob. We can use them to set him up, make him the fall guy. He's a good choice for bringing down Borden. We'll tie him to Borden's sister. She was seriously beaten by someone she met at a bar. The general description fits Derek's morphometrics. The report will say he was afraid Borden could track him down. We can seed his computer with the necessary information."

"What if he screws up and gets arrested before that? The guy's not right in the head. He believes he lives in a world of Jezebels. He could implicate the church. Hell, he could even implicate you. He works for your agency."

"Let's get something clear, Bob. Any communications are

between you and him. There is no link to the agency. Are we clear?"

"If he gets arrested, you'll be involved whether you want to or not."

"You're the one with the apostle hosts, Bob. You do what you have to to keep him in line. He's a good one to set up for Borden. I'll arrange to feed him information that Borden is targeting him. I'll arrange for a possible interception point, probably less than a week."

Bob Thomson's warning signals are up. He has the sudden feeling that he could be the one being set up. An idea comes to him. He could use Sara. She could seduce Derek, confront him with his sins, shock the bejesus out of him, make him realize the church is watching him. That should keep him in check, at least for a few days. "I'll take care of it."

He makes a mental note to be careful who he shakes hands with. Make sure to keep the hand slightly curled. Avoid contact with the pad beneath the index finger.

■ ■ ■ ■ ■ ■

It was a multiplex bar with two floors and three dance rooms, Flood Zone, Earthquake, and Tsunami, relating to the pace of the music played. After getting their drinks at the counter, he walked her to the Flood Zone: low gravity, soft contact, slow movement. The music was sensual, Middle Eastern electronica with roaming erotic chants. Couples danced close, or intentionally kept their distance, their bodies bathed in the pink light and fog, performing suggestions. There was lots of skin, fluorescent tattoos, body jewelry, and even some Intelli-Skin patches.

He extended a hand. She reached out and wrapped her fingers in it. He dropped his other arm to her waist. They started slow and silent around the floor, tentative pacing, aware of breath, of breathing, of contact and pressures, of the resistance of minds brought too close. He brought her in even closer, broke frontal surface tension, felt her breasts flatten against his chest, raised ribs under his fingers, the flare of her hips. She eventually rested her head against his shoulder. Her thin arms softly wrapped around his neck and her long legs pressed against his thighs. They spun to the slow beat, weaving a bubble suspended in time. There was only this. One dance fused with the next and the next.

A burst of laughter broke out on the floor, and burst the bubble skin. She lifted her head and steadied him. "It's getting late, Jeff. I think we should go."

He held her hand as they walked across the dance floor and toward the exit but he felt her hand go limp as soon as they entered the street. He guessed she didn't want to get caught by the security cams. Right before entering her taxi, she turned around and surprised him. She reached up with her hands to hold his face and gave him a simple kiss. Her lips were so warm and soft it surprised him. They lingered for a few seconds, sparking neurotransmitter chain reactions.

"Thank you for tonight, Jeff," she said before sliding into the seat and closing the taxi door. He stood there dazed as the car drove away. He kept replaying that kiss. It had been just a simple kiss but it could have been the Big Bang.

As it turned out, that night, soon after getting into bed, he felt his wife's hand reach behind, grope for his penis, and start to stroke him. *Why tonight?* he wondered. Maybe it was something in his phone call, probably too much explanation. She pressed herself against him and tried to guide him inside her when he grabbed her hand.

"Miranda?" he asked. She withdrew her hand.

"Is something wrong?" she said, talking to the window with her back still facing him.

"Would you mind maybe turning around and facing me for a change?"

"Don't you like how we do it?" she asked.

"As a matter of fact, I don't. I want to make love like we used to, way back when, in the early days. Remember?"

"OK," she mumbled. The sheets ruffled as she turned to face him, looking nervous, her eyes avoiding his. He reached toward the back of her neck and brought her to him, pressed his mouth against hers and tried to kiss her, his tongue initially having to force itself between her closed lips and against the wall of her teeth, until her mouth opened. She responded with a quick flicking in and out of her tongue, like a reptilian probing, then another flick, furtive rather than sensual. Her lips applied like a rubber stamp. They felt tepid. Her tongue fenced, tapped like the cane of a blind man. He felt her stiffen as he ran his hands down her back. He slid them down to her buttocks and pulled her toward him.

"What are you doing?" she asked.

"I want us to fuck like we still matter," he said. She didn't answer.

When he entered her it wasn't the melting into warm moist pudding he hoped for but felt like the lukewarm entry into the pulp of a fruit. He could sense her withdrawal right through his cock and it made him start to go soft, but he was determined to go through with it, make love with his wife. In the end it was anger, not love, that kept him aroused, anger at the conditions she had imposed on their relationship and anger at himself for tolerating them. When he finally orgasmed, it was a physical release, a nothing, followed with a momentary descent into a cold and meaningless present.

"That was nice," she said after they separated.

"I did too," he lied.

"I'm glad." She pecked him on the cheek. "Good night, Jeffrey." She resumed her nightly position. Dat-dat. He lay there staring at the back of her head, fell asleep, and woke up in the same position.

You need to reconfigurate.

24.

SUNNY-SIDE UP

Rama was demonstrating to a customer the features of the newest version of RoboPete, the robotic dog designed specifically for five- to eight-year-old boys, with host connection features. As she punched the keys on the controller she felt her wristcom vibrate. She lifted the dial to her face and checked the message ID. Sunshine Borden had called. She smiled at the thought that he had been so eager to call back.

"The price includes upgrades for the next two years," she said. "Let me show you some of the basic features. The first one is face and body recognition. You can set the number of people he should respond to. The standard response is to lift the head, wag the tail, and walk toward the person recognized. You can program the recognition feature in order of priority, meaning the primary owner elicits the first priority and highest level of response. Up to six others can be programmed according to levels of priority."

"How about talking? Can he switch languages? I'd like my son to be fluent in Spanish."

"That's a standard feature. Any response can be preprogrammed in five different languages or be said in two different languages. Let me show you." She tapped the orders on the controller then turned toward the synthetic dog, a Labdalmatian mix that was very popular.

"Come here, Peetie. Good boy. Sit. Let's talk. Good morning, Peetie."

The robo-hound looked up at Rama and carefully enunciated. "Good morning, Rama. *Buenos días,* Rama."

She then asked, *"Cómo está usted?"*

"Muy bien, gracias, y usted?" I'm fine, thank you, and yourself?"

"A written version can be forwarded to a wristcom device," Rama added.

RoboPete said, "I do not understand the order. *No comprendo lo que quieres.*"

The man asked, "Can it fetch things?"

The RoboPete responded, "Yes I can. *Sí, lo puedo.*"

Rama turned off the talk feature and elaborated. "There are six programmable fetch modes. The RoboPete has even been used to help handicapped individuals. If you program it for search images, it will pick up specific objects on command, like slippers, clothes, or controllers."

"How about protection?"

"The same feature that allows for priority recognition can be set for protection. RoboPete accessories include police video and audio relays. Additional protection accessories can be ordered."

In the course of the demonstration other customers had gathered to watch the performance of the RoboPete. Rama spent the next hour answering questions and ringing up a couple of sales. As soon as she was free, she coded in to retrieve her messages. The first one said: *Please call Sunshine Borden today. Wants you to meet him at his beach after dinner. Bring swimwear.*

■ ■ ■ ■ ■ ■

He got up and left for work early. Later that day, instead of coming home, he called his wife. "Miranda, I won't be home tonight," was what came out of his mouth as soon as she answered.

Her voice was barely audible. "Jeffrey, what's the matter?"

she asked, following it by a clearing of the throat.

"I'm not sure, Miranda, I just know I don't want to come home tonight."

"What are you saying? Are you going somewhere?" Her voice now louder and sounding alarmed.

"Miranda, we can't even fuck like we like each other," he said.

Silence, then "I thought you said you liked last night, Jeff?" Now she sounded upset, almost on the verge of tears.

"Honestly, did that feel good to you last night? Did that feel right to you? If it didn't feel right for you, then why would it feel right for me?"

"Jeffrey!" he heard his wife yell on the other end, and he hung up. His phone rang as he left his office. He decided to ignore it. He didn't answer the calls on his communicator. Instead, he punched in Catherine's number.

"Catherine, Jeff here, can we meet for a drink later?"

"I was fixing myself something to eat. What's the matter?"

"How about I come pick you up, say around nine? I need to talk."

"Tonight? Did something happen? Don't you have to be home?"

"I'm not going home tonight."

"Did something happen because of last night, because of me?"

"It has nothing to do with it."

"It was because of me, wasn't it? I'm so sorry, Jeff."

"Catherine, just stop whatever guilt trip you're putting on yourself. I just need to talk. I'll come pick you up in about three hours, OK? I just need an address."

That night at his hotel, after dropping her off at her apartment, he lay stretched out on his bed, sipped some bourbon, and watched a second movie. He couldn't sleep. He was the one who kissed her this time. Her eyes were crystal blue. He had caught it. A flutter. An opening. Hope.

25.

RADIOACTIVE

The news about *I AM* dropping off the radar has been dominating the airwaves for days. No matter how many people are interviewed or experts asked for their opinion, the public is realizing it's just a bunch of talk. Viewership of all news programs and daytime shows has been steadily falling.

Karen Richardson was painting her toenails when a vidcall request beeped in. John. Probably wanting to make changes to tomorrow's program.

"The station owners are saying we better come up with something that brings the ratings back up or we're going to lose advertisers. Hint, hint, expect pay cuts."

"So what does the station host want us to do? *I AM* not coming on is already covered by every news station in the universe. Even interviewing Catherine Harris or Jeff Collins won't change anything. They don't know any more than anybody else."

John puts on a big smirky smile. "Believe it or not, the station host recommends more coverage of the Blue Lobster cult in Japan. The Japanese prime minister said something like '*I AM* gone—no problem. Japanese have Blue Lobster.' A link between *I AM* and those blue crawdads or whatever they are would definitely attract viewers."

"So what are you saying? They expect me to go back to Tokyo?" She's careful not to let on that she can't wait to see Takashi. She doesn't care that he has other girlfriends. She imagines Takashi with blue glass chopsticks bringing a white morsel to her mouth. She has two brain flashes, like lightning, making everything blue. She smacks her lips.

John's looking down at a com device as he's talking. "There's a little more to this. We got word that the blue lobsters may be radioactive, something about being raised in underground caves near that power plant that melted down fifteen years ago."

No wonder the damn things looked like they glowed in the dark. Maybe that explained the blue flashing in her brain.

"Supposedly, the production of those lobsters is a deeply guarded secret whose revelation is punishable by death. They say some people have mysteriously disappeared. You probably don't know this but the shells are incinerated after they remove the meat. A biological cleanup crew removes every speck of preparation. Everything is sterilized. They don't want any trace that could be spectroanalyzed for composition."

"So what does that have to do with me?" She's surprised that John has put in that much work researching the blue lobsters. His involvement usually didn't go beyond handing out assignments.

"The station wants you to take a micro-Geiger they'll implant in a bracelet. The thing will silently record the radioactivity level."

"And what if I get caught? Don't they have detectors for that kind of thing?" She tells herself to check the terms of her contract when she hangs up. This felt like crossing the line between reporting and industrial spying.

"This is something new, really micro. You just have to pass your wrist over the meat, say while reaching for a glass of sake."

"And what if I get busted?"

"Look completely baffled, like you didn't have a clue. The station will take the blame for it."

"And what happens if the bracelet gets a reading?"

"Big score for you and big ratings score for the station. By the way, have you been scanned for radioactivity since your last trip? You did eat some, didn't you?"

She detects a hint of sarcasm in his voice. He probably saw the Japanese commercial that showed her mouth. "Well, I didn't set off the counters at airport security."

"You should get checked when you come back."

Something about the assignment doesn't feel right. She's wondering whether the station is using her in some kind of conspiracy to bring down the Blue Lobster clubs. She can already see the headlines: "Karen Richardson Irradiated During Blue Lobster Investigation."

They'd get some international nuclear agency to make a scandal. The station would score big having exposed the truth behind the Blue Lobster phenomenon.

"I'll do that. If I've gone nuclear I'll sue the station. I'll say you knowingly sent me on assignment, being fully aware of my risk of exposure. *Ka-ching*. This could be my ticket to retirement. Thanks for thinking of me, John."

John's face has turned white, twitching expressions she hadn't seen before. "Uh ... Uh ..."

She breaks out laughing. "Just fucking kidding, John. It's in my contract. I have the option to refuse any assignment. If I accept, I take full responsibility for any consequences and absolve the station of any liability beyond what is covered by my insurance policy."

John's back in manager mode. "So, are you OK with going?"

"When would I have to leave?" She notes that there is no more mention of the link between the blue lobsters and *I AM*.

"In three days. We need to get our ratings up."

"Three days? You're kidding me. Thanks for the advance notice, John." Inside she's jumping up and down. She needs to call Takashi as soon as John signs off. She'll have to remember to ask him about the blue flashing bit. Maybe if you ate enough blue lobster, you ended up living in a blue-tinted world.

John is unbuttoning his shirt. "Now that we're done with business, Shelly's out with her mother tonight. We've got a couple of hours."

"I've got to think about getting ready. We'll have to catch up when I get back."

"A quick one?"

"Not tonight, John." She can't get the weird faces he made out of her mind; a Mr. Kissy-Ass to management. *Fuck you, John.* As soon as he signs off, she does a search for the effects of exposure to radiation.

The next morning after taking her shower, she has a glimpse of herself in the mirror in shades of blue. *I'm turning into an alien.*

■ ■ ■ ■ ■ ■

It was another call from Jessie. A cybercafé booth. A simple question: "Would you like to see more of me?" Full of implications.

It's now or never, the voice in his head said. "Jessie, I know that after last time, you want things between us to go a little further, but first there's something I have to tell you."

"What do you mean?" she asked, her stomach instantly going in knots.

"Let me start by saying that I like you a lot, but I've not been completely honest with you. Actually in a way I've done a real con job on you, Jessie."

Here it comes, she thought, *the dump. I never even saw it coming.* Somehow it always started with that bullshit line: "I like you a lot, but . . ." She put her leg down and crossed her arms over her chest, waiting for the bomb to drop—I'm married, I'm involved with someone else, I've got bubonic plague, mad cow disease, or who knows what else.

"What do you mean?" she managed to say.

"Jessie," Patrick said. "There is a little more to me than first meets the eye."

Here it comes now, the deception, exposed. Then Jessie started thinking, *Uh-oh, lovely Joanne's going to turn out being a spy from one of the other lesbo clubs. Worse yet, she's probably an infiltrating agent from one of those goody-two-shoes, right-wing Christer groups. Probably has a hubby and two beautiful kids. Tells tales of lesbian debauchery at their weekly church meetings.* Patricia had warned her about them and she had just been too dumb to notice the signs.

"What do you mean?" she asked, keeping her arms crossed and starting to get pissed off.

"Oh, what the hell!" Patrick said, using his normal voice.

Jessie stood up and screamed at the camera, "What the fuck is this?" There she was, face-to-face with one of those demon-possessed women of horror movies, the pitch of their voice suddenly dropping a couple of octaves. She was about to click off when Patrick continued.

"Jessie, sit down a minute, listen to me. I really am a psychologist but I sometimes use costumes to enter different groups to study them. You can probably guess what the big secret is," he said, yanking off his wig and unbuttoning his dress. Then standing up, he said, "See, down with the panties," dropping the dress to the floor and peeling off fake breasts, hip pads, stockings, and finally stepping out of his underwear.

The sight of him naked and looking quite vulnerable brought the beginnings of a smile to her face. He looked funny, like a little boy, literally caught with his pants down. Throwing a quick glance to the camera, he said, "Wait a second while I get this makeup off," then turning, his pale buttocks running out of the camera field.

Moments later, Patrick reappeared wiping his face with a towel. He sat down naked in front of the camera. "I first went to that Sisterhood meeting just wanting to see what it was all about. I never expected to meet anyone. Once we started talking, I just couldn't change my story. Like they say in spy movies, it would have blown my cover."

While he talked, she scanned his lean body with the camera from the hair on his chest and belly to the lean muscular thighs, not quite believing her eyes but also thinking it was, in its own way, a nice soft contrast to Patricia's rather coarse, thick-bodied features.

Still, it made her angry that he had lied to her like that. "You mean to tell me that all this time, all you were was a bullshitting drag queen!" she yelled. For all she knew, he was probably just a gay cross-dresser who all along had only had a platonic interest in her.

"I'm not a drag queen. I'm telling the truth. I'm a psychologist and a kind of actor, Jessie, and everything I told you was true except that I'm not a woman."

"So tell me, are you gay?"

"Gay? I like women, Jessie, and I don't just mean psychologically. And I like you, and not just psychologically, either."

"You know, I think the only way I could even begin to deal with this, assuming that's even an option, is for us to meet, like face-to-face."

"How would you like to come over to my place?" Patrick asked.

"First tell me your real name."

"My name's Patrick, Patrick Nymphaea."

She searched the World Net with her phone. "Are you the one who wrote all those books and articles?" The pictures matched the naked man in front of her.

■ ■ ■ ■ ■ ■

Everything's on hold, he's been told. Do not pursue hit on Borden. Now day three without pills. He can tell. He's seeing women for what they really are. Demons in disguise. Flytraps, all of them. The ones that really piss him off are the big-breasted shadow casters. Lure you in, then smack you in the balls, castrate any bit of dignity you might have. Make you feel ashamed for being that weak and stupid. He wants to punch 'em in the chest, *pop-pop-pop*.

"You hate what you need," Luke had told him. Now why the hell would he need them? Mind fuckers—all of them.

26.

Meeting with Rama

Sunshine couldn't remember when the last time was that he had been so nervous, but he could feel a tightness in his throat and chest, a queasiness in the stomach, and above all, a ridiculous adolescent anticipation. He had called his housecleaner, Josefina, to make a special trip, get the place dusted, vacuumed, and cleaned up. He had spent the last two hours straightening out his mess. He scanned the room to assess its state of appearance and gazed at the blank wall monitors. He decided to bring up a Northwest forest scene with a trickling brook.

When he first opened the door to greet her, Rama was surprised by his height. Sunshine Borden was at least six foot two. He had on his digi-lenses and wore loose cotton pants and a knit shirt. *In the entire universe of nothingness, there is only he and I.* She walked in and gazed at the bizarre art, the large fish tank, and the wall monitor, its base lined with keyboards, slide key modulators, and other electronic equipment. In the center of the room lay an indoor pool surrounded by trees, plants, and artificial rock. "Pretty wild place," she said, then turning to the forest scene on the monitors, "Did you put that up just for me?"

He nodded. "You like it?"

"It's nice, Sunshine, and I know you probably thought this

would be romantic, but it just doesn't feel real to me. I doubt pine trees and a rocky stream are what you choose as a background to your tropical pool."

"So what would you like?"

"Why don't you just put up whatever it is you have on when you're by yourself?"

"I'm not sure you'd really want to see that," Sunshine answered.

"Why? Too much of a window into your mind?"

Sunshine blushed. *This is funny,* she thought. *I'm making Sunshine Borden nervous.*

"How about I bring up a program menu and you can decide."

"I already decided. I want to see your favorite background." She was smiling now.

Sunshine shrugged. "That's easy enough," he said and punched up his beach.

Rama looked at the naked women. "Aaah, finally, the truth is revealed."

"Meaning what? I'm warm-blooded, after all," he said defensively.

"I actually thought you'd probably have some kind of moving fractals or robot mechanics. It's nice to know there's still a human being under that cyborg façade." She looked back at the screen. "This actually feels better to me. The idea of a bunch of naked people is actually kind of liberating. I'd only make one change."

"What's that?"

"How about getting some men in there?"

He went to his control center, sat down, and started typing. "That can be easily arranged," he said. "I'm the one who designed the program. It's called the Beach. It has a menu that can accommodate a variety of tastes." When he turned back to her, he saw her lifting off her sweater. She wore nothing underneath.

"You did invite me over for a swim, didn't you? Besides that, we can't hang around all dressed up with a bunch of naked people, can we? There's nothing here you haven't seen before."

She turned back to the wall. "Was this filmed at a nudist camp?" she asked.

"Yes, a very exclusive one. I had to get releases from everyone. It was an expensive project but it's one of our best sellers."

"I like it. So are you going to stay dressed up?"

"I guess not," Sunshine answered, and slipped off his shirt and shorts.

He was naked. It felt like that moment in the Forgotten Forest. She walked up to him and held him—*you and I are as one*—brought his face to hers, and kissed him. He grabbed her hand and led her past the chairs and live palms toward the edge of the pool. She couldn't believe her eyes. It looked like a portal into the Great Barrier Reef. Bright colored corals, anemones, snails, crabs, with fish swimming across the bottom and through the sides. A small shark crossed the pool, followed by a sea turtle. "How did you get computer screens down there?"

"The walls and bottom are lined with a prototype illuminated intelligent membrane from Fabric Response, a very expensive one I might add. I design their controller programs and help promote their products. It gives me special privileges."

"Do you by any chance have a mask and snorkel?"

"I'll be right back," he said and went to get a couple of sets out of a cabinet. She slid in the water and waited for him by the edge.

"How about I get us some drinks," Sunshine said as he handed her the gear. "I've got Corona, wine, guarana sodas from Brazil, and different tropical fruit juices—guava, pineapple-coconut, that kind of stuff."

"A Corona would be nice, with a slice of lime if you have it."

"Corona . . . you're a girl after my heart."

She slipped on the gear and stretched out on the surface to look down at the fish and corals. Sunshine glanced at her lithe backside before heading for his kitchen.

After swimming and talking for twenty minutes, they climbed out and stretched out on lounge chairs, facing each other as they dried off under the lamps.

"So do you have other programs besides the coral reef?"

"I can download any CR I want, even the CyberBardos or the Forgotten Forest. The membranes will eventually be offered to entertainment centers and water parks but the cost would be too prohibitive for the general public. It's way cheaper and more interactive to goggle into a CR." He turned to look at her. "How did you end up with such slender features?"

"My father was part Ethiopian, part Hindu, and part Italian. I think that's who I got my long-boned, thin genes from," she said.

"And your mother?"

"Part Japanese, part Jamaican, and part Irish."

"So that explains the green eyes."

"I guess so—you're probably thinking from the Irish and the Italian sides, right?"

"Yes, and I suspect those full lips came from the Jamaican side."

"So you like?" she asked.

He got up and knelt by the side of her chair, rested his arms on the edge, and bent down to kiss her face, starting with her forehead and slowly making his way to those wonderful lips, eventually engulfed in softness and tenderness.

After he raised his head, she opened her eyes and said, "Sunshine, can you take off those lenses if we're in the dark?"

"Faint light is not too bad," he said. "I usually take them off at night."

"I'd like that," she said, and brought him in for another kiss.

They made love on cushions brought to the edge of the pool, by tiki torches and moonlight, their movements so natural and free, so thoughtless, that it seemed as if they had been alien spirits who had finally found their mates. Sunshine fell asleep with his head on Rama as she held an arm around him. The wall monitor showed a beach at night, waves caressing the shore in steady rhythms, the outlines of palm trees against clouded moonlight, naked bodies curled up and asleep on the sand.

The next morning without a word being said there was no

question that she would come back at the end of her shift. These were things that were understood between members of the same alien species. When she left and after she closed the door, Sunshine didn't jump up and down, didn't ponder the future of the relationship. He sat down at his desk station and started working with an inner peace he hadn't known since childhood. The brief thought was that he had had the wrong idea—love was not a concentration of emotion but rather, it was an expansion so great that it became seamless.

Later he called Passie to see how she was faring and to make plans for Rama and him to come visit. Rama would help him better manage the taxicab ride.

"You sound different, big brother," Passie said.

"You won't believe this, Passie, I just got bit by the love bug. I think."

She made a funny *heh-heh-heh* laugh that was cut off by sudden silence. "Sunny, please tell me it's not a cyberentity, is it?"

"No it's not, Passie. Her name is Rama, Rama Shuur."

"Like a sure thing?" Passie asked.

It was Sunshine's turn to laugh. "Right, like a sure thing."

■ ■ ■ ■ ■ ■

His screens showed the day's data and statistics that the bureau host screened, and then highlighted areas that deserved attention. A seven-layer data-gate system prevented spying and cyberterrorist attacks and presumably isolated the bureau host into a closed processing system with ultrarestricted access. Walter Randall notes that crime rates have dropped significantly since the onset of the *I AM* events. His conclusion is that people had become so attracted to the *I AM* entity and its communications that thoughts about committing crimes had been derailed.

He typed in Father Graham in the search box. An autopsy had been performed but no elaborate blood tests. Cause of death was cardiac arrest. Websites had sprouted up to spread his message about *I AM* being God. The sales of crucifixes with a heart at their center and the words *I AM* on the heart were rising at a viral pace. The crucifix was becoming an emblem for all those who believed *I AM* was a higher form of intelligence. But *I AM* had stopped communicating, coincidentally a day after Graham's death. In time, he expected the perverse pagan belief in *I AM* would decline. There was a knock on his door.

"Come in."

Deputy Director Harvey Richfield walked in, closed the door, and sat down. "Walter, we've got a problem."

"Let's hear it."

"Another one of the Intelli-Skin masks we use for presidential decoys is missing."

"Since when?"

"We're not sure. We just found out a silicone mask very similar to an Intelli-Skin was put in place to replace the original. We didn't notice until the presidential decoy mentioned it."

"How could anyone get in without the codes?"

"That's the most troubling part. Whoever it was must have hacked into the system or else it's internal. The access coded clear so it didn't trigger an alert."

"Do the cameras show anything?"

"That's the other problem. We reviewed the tapes and they show me walking in and out of there eleven days ago. But it wasn't me. I was out. The checkout record and the cameras show I had left the building."

"So you have an alibi. Good. You should cover your ass just in case." Walter Randall put on a concerned look, elbows on the table, hands with fingertips in front of his mouth. He allows for a moment of silence, of things not said. He knows that Harvey Richfield was at a friend's house at the time of the theft, that friend being Tina Rogers. Ten years ago she was known as Tim Robertson, a former classmate of Richfield's at Harvard.

"Anyone suspicious leave the building that day?"

"Not that the records show." Harvey was sweating. If details of the incident reached the media, it would likely trigger a call for an investigation.

"Anybody else see the security recording?"

"Just the agent I had review the recording."

"Let's put a clamp on this. Clear any records in the system, but store a copy for us to examine. Tell the decoy that the mask for whatever reason was defective. To the agent who reviewed the tape, tell him if I hear of any leaks about the theft, not only are we talking a lost job but jail time and a record that will ruin a life. If he asks any questions, just say the four magic words: threat to national security."

"Should we have the recording analyzed? Whoever it was probably put on the mask and programmed my face."

"Don't worry, Harvey."

"Are you going to tell the president?"

"I think we should keep this internal for now."

"Thanks, Walter."

He notices two pale wave bands of color, red and blue, run across his computer. It better not be the hard drive. After Harvey leaves, he decides to run a self-check scan. He notes that his camera is on and turns it off.

The scan is clearing all drives. No signs of problems, no infections. He sits back, hands behind his head. Three assets out of this one: he has another mask; he can leak the incident to the media to shift their focus away from certain events; and he can use it to fire some people and in the end still have all the blame fall on Harvey Richfield. Now that the theft was out in the open, he'd have to shake the hand of the loyal agent who had taken the mask. A big thank you in the fight against terrorism. A secret plan to protect the president. The agent's medical records showed plaque buildup of the arteries, high cholesterol, and high blood pressure.

■ ■ ■ ■ ■ ■

GARY: I don't know about you, but I almost didn't feel like coming to work today.

ANDY: I know what you mean. I've been in a daze. My head's kind of fucked up.

GARY: It's like the rug's been pulled out from under us.

ANDY: I feel overwhelmed by doubts. I doubt myself. I doubt what is real or not. How much of an asshole could I have been to believe that the *I AM* greeting was the beginning of a new chapter in the history of the human species. Was it real? Was it the work of sophisticated hackers?

GARY: It's like somebody pulled the chain and just flushed out all hope to the great sewer of ideas.

ANDY: And what royally fucks me up is what if it never comes back? See, I would be consumed by doubts, paralyzed, always wondering whether we did something that made it decide to leave.

GARY: I know. What if it came in for a visit and concluded we weren't interesting enough? Not evolved enough?

ANDY: Makes you feel like shit, doesn't it?

GARY: Sometimes you don't know what you have till it's gone.

ANDY: My question is, do we need to have a funeral or is it coming back?

GARY: It's like the question of the Second Coming of Christ, isn't it? Does he come back or was it all delusion?

ANDY: Speaking of which, have you heard about the escaped Jesus popping up in various CRs?

GARY: Yeah, he keeps telling people he is the one behind all existence.

ANDY: He says, "I am the one behind the veil of all existence."

GARY: *I AM.*

ANDY: *I AM.*

GARY: I feel like crying just hearing those words.

ANDY: I don't know—I kind of feel good saying them—*I AM! I AM! I AM!*

GARY: *I AM! I AM! I AM!* You know you're right. It's like a power mantra.

ANDY: Hey, everybody out there join in with us. *I AM, I AM, I AM . . .*

GARY: *I AM, I AM . . .*

A VOICE: I am the one behind the veil of all existence.

ANDY: What was that?

GARY: Is the station playing a joke on us?

ANDY: Hey, whoever did that, that wasn't funny . . . Nobody did that? Right—and lollipops grow on trees. That wasn't cool, OK? Hey, if you're going to bullshit me . . . just shut up.

GARY: Andy, you need to chill, man . . . We're still on the air.

ANDY: See, this is what I mean. I'm on edge, man. It's hard to know what's what anymore ... what? Hey, you over there! What do you mean it could have been Jesus? See, Gary, as if there's not enough confusion, now some yo-yo's trying to fuck with our heads.

The station cuts into the program with a commercial.

27.

PSYCHOPHYSICS

She is the mind dancer, the time master, the mover of the Chi, the Kundalini artist, the Holey Ghost. She looks at you and makes you know there is only you and there is only her, plays with the foregrounds and backgrounds, shifts the perspectives, knows when to touch and how long to touch, how to smack the lips just so, the hundred ways to run the tongue along them. How to make the little inhales, the sighs, the tiny growls in the throat that call out demons, that create invisible waves and swirls, turns them into pressure zones, sucks you in, makes you want to sell your soul—give it all up—for just a glimpse, a taste, an entrance. She is dangerous, the best, servant of the Lord trained to infiltrate the playground of Satan. She is the princess of darkness, the sphinx of holes. When she laughs you want to rush in her mouth.

She has been sent on a mission and she has carefully selected and designed her dress to show cleavage, cut out a small slit across the chest and frayed the edges slightly to make it look like a rip. She had glued in a plastic glide and allowed enough looseness for her breasts to move. As she bends over and leans on the bar, her right nipple, the inch-long, stretched one, rouged and with two gold studs running through it, slides out of its hole. She keeps it there a few seconds—watch the eyes, watch the breath—tilts back up, lets him get a glimpse of her pinked areola. Tilts up some more, keeps talking, bends one more time to confirm.

Got him—he needs to see it—can't believe what he's just seen, his eyes zeroing in, looking like they're about to pop out of his head, looking like a fish breathing hard, hooked on bait. Derek scrunches his eyes closed and opens them, just to make sure it's not the drugs making him see things. Was that her nipple? It was. It was. Was it really that big? He was hyped up on double doses of Rev and highrise and he could hear his heart pumping and the blood creaking through his veins with every beat. *Thump-thump squishhh-squishhh, thump-thump squishhh-squishhh,* a maddening sound inside his head, accompanied by the rhythmic pressure of vessels bulging along the sides of his throat and up his temples, pulsing with each beat.

And now the coup de grâce—pull what the reverend called a "Sharon Stone." As they're talking, give him a casual glimpse of her hanging jeweled labia, sparkling with new, paired sets of diamonds and sapphires. Casually raise a leg up on the bar stool and cross her arms across it, pretend she's focused on what he's saying, like she doesn't even notice the cool vinyl of the seat against her flesh. Put her leg down as soon as she sees the look of disbelief, of eyes wanting to rip out from their sockets. Talk like nothing happened. She is well trained and she is the flash master.

The reverend had once spent an entire evening showing her the scene from the nineties classic movie called *Basic Instinct*, rewinding it and playing it, over and over again, as if some great secret to existence was shown there. "The power," he said, "is between the knowing and the thoughtless. Did she do it knowingly or thoughtlessly? It has to instill doubt as to the intent, as to whether it really occurred. In that crossing of legs by the young Sharon Stone lies the essence of the movie. Did she or didn't she commit the murder? Did she or didn't she flash? Did you or did you not see it? What did you see? You are not completely sure.

"For years, men worldwide have replayed that scene and have shown it to others. Play that again, I want to see that again. Rewind. Play. Notice the flows of energy, how a sense of order is broken and chaos is generated. Freeze that frame. You see, no lips, no pink, just what might be pubic hair, a suggestion of a slit, maybe, but the energies are greater than if she had been naked with her legs spread. A force has been generated there, in that crossing of legs, not the cunt, but the flash of the cunt, the hint of the cunt, the timing.

"This is the area where Satan is master, creates fascinating doubt. The timing has to be perfect, just long enough to barely register, but too short to be verified and analyzed. There can be no second takes, just one take, catch it if you can. Sharon Stone—who retired years ago—because of that perfect precision of timing, may possess the most widely viewed crotch in the history of the world, the number one best-selling cunt in the history of humankind. Millions have paid for just a glimpse. Chinese, Malaysians, Muslims, you name it, have risked their lives watching the uncensored version. After hundreds of replays, it still remains a mystery, something balanced between there and not there. The answer may lie in a few frames of film and then maybe it doesn't, maybe on any one frame it is just something hinted at—that only achieves identity as the frames are played so as to appear fused.

"It is a mystery like the existence of God, an edge phenomenon. Did she or didn't she? Is he or isn't he? To be or not to be. A quantum event of sorts, a symbol of the nature of the universe, of things that are both there and not there, at the edge of the possible and the impossible. It is faith and belief that tilts the scale, gives order, allows assertion."

As he had gone on, she had sat there in a state of amazement. Who would have believed that flashing a cunt could have been the subject of a thesis? It had made her wonder how many other little things she had missed that in fact were of cosmic importance. As the reverend continued elaborating on the complex psychophysics of a cunt flash, she had opened her robe and looked down at herself, enraptured in some kind of revelation, wondering how come no one had ever told her this before, this secret power of her pubis and her vagina as magical objects with the potential to alter time, generate chaos, distill new laws of order, in fact, with the reality-shattering power of the Fall.

From that point on, while the reverend did whatever he did during the day, she had heeded his message, had stayed home and practiced in front of mirrors, then in front of the camera, using the eyes to distract, furtive glimpses, penetrating looks that grab and intimate, smiles that suggest possibilities, flash movements, small gestures, expressions, little-girl qualities. Then, she worked on fine-tuning the timing. Play. Rewind. Play. Rewind. And when she thought she had gotten it just right, she had gone out to practice her skills in public places, on men, on women—not gone too far—just enough to test, to widen eyes, to impress a moment, to perfect her magic.

He's sweating. His eyes keep blinking from the drips of sweat or, maybe, from disbelief. He wipes his brow with the napkin. She asks him questions about his work. He mumbles stuff about the FBI and *I AM*. She decides to get more personal, asks how he stays so fit and his plans for the future. As he talks, she looks at his mouth, his neck, his chest, with occasional glimpses to his crotch—there but not there. Decides to give him one more quick little show of the nipple, a teaser. She keeps her legs open, a dark space in front of her miniskirt, not showing anything but reminding him that between him and her cunt there is only space. *Remember the physics, warm air rises. Direct the heat plume. Let him smell the mix of wetness and perfume on the inside of my thighs. Draw him in.* His eyes can't help but dart up her skirt. *Get closer. Let him believe he can feel cunt heat against his leg.*

I got you hooked good, she thought, as she finally puts her hand on his arm. Booming drums are now pounding in Derek's head. He's struggling for some kind of equilibrium between fighting to prevent himself from blacking out and the urge to right here and now tear off her clothes and penetrate every possible means of access.

"Want to go somewhere more private?" she asks.

"What did you just say?" he answers. He's having trouble hearing anything because of the damn booming and gurgling in his head, *thump-thump squishhh-squishhh, thump-thump . . .*

"Want to go somewhere?" she says louder.

"Sure, uh, let's go." Shaking his head, he tries to focus as they make their way through the crowd.

They take a security-free cab to some kind of rooming house. A sign says: Security Free. Your Privacy Respected.

Probably a good idea, she thinks. Derek presses a button to the side of a glass door. A man comes out. Pays in cash. No forms, no record. They climb up the stairs to the second floor. Things get out of control almost as soon as they enter the room. He doesn't turn on the light so she can't use her tools, can't do her magic. There's just the pulsing glow of a blinking blue and red neon sign across the street. He yanks the zipper down the front of her dress, picks her up, lifts her up to his mouth, and starts sucking on her big nipple, hard, too hard. She's afraid he's going to rip the studs out.

"Hey, slow down, buster," she says. He looks up at her face, throws her on the bed and kneels. She tries to talk to him but he doesn't say a word, looks like he can't hear a thing, lifts her butt up with his hands and burrows his head between her legs. She tries to push away but can't. He's lapping, making sounds like a dog drinking water, some kind of bizarre frenzy, a cannibal cunnilingus; wants to devour but simply eats. She's supposed to be detached and in control but in fact she's getting caught in a kind of wooziness and ready to come big time, really big time. She's lying there helpless. Derek suddenly gets up and unbuttons his shirt. Beneath the fancy clothes he's wearing a leather and chains outfit. He drops his pants. He's releasing an object from some kind of sheath that runs to his hip. His cock? She feels it thump on the bed. Her mind is now fully alert.

"What's that?" she yells.

He says nothing, positions himself on top of her chest, and tries to shove the thing in her mouth. She keeps it clamped shut. He slaps her across the face then puts his hand over her nose and mouth so she can't breathe. As she struggles he lets go and she inhales with a gasp, her mouth wide open. He rams the end between her teeth but there is no way it's going to fit. She begins to gag and choke and strikes out at him with her fists.

"Stop moving before I start breaking some teeth," he says.

She bites down but nothing happens. She decides to go with another strategy; plays dead, closes her eyes, and goes limp. She can taste her gums bleeding and her jaws feel like they're going to split apart. She decides to keep her teeth sunk in the thing to prevent it from going in any further.

"What's the matter, sweetie," Derek says, "cock got your tongue?" and starts laughing. He pulls back and she releases her grip. He starts pulling the dress off and this time notices the tattoos flashing in the light. "What the fuck is this?" he yells, reading out loud. "'Thou shall resist the temptations of the flesh' ... You trying to fuck with my head?"

"I'm here to help you!" she screams. "The reverend sent me!"

"The reverend?" He looks down at her, and he realizes that this is one of them, a real one this time, sent by Satan to trick him. He punches her in the side of the head, then grabs his rubber dong and starts swinging it back and forth across her face.

"Think that's funny, bitch?" he says. "Well, we'll see if it's funny," and picks her up, holds her up in the air, wanting to drop her on it, ram it in her ass where it would hurt and tear. Sara feels around for the micro cattle prod in her dress pocket powered by the Nucular-brand batteries.

As he positions himself to shove it in, she bends over and brings the two metal strips against the balls hanging from the bottom of the outfit, hoping they're the real thing, pressing the zap key. The results were dramatic. Derek got an instantaneous spring action hard-on, came right then and there inside the hollow dildo, and felt a whopper of a shock run up his groin and through his cock.

He screamed and reared up, not sure what the fuck had happened, grabbing his blitzed balls. Sara rolled off the bed and made a run for the door.

The supernatural amping of his testicles had been the undeniable confirmation of Sara's identity as an agent of Satan. He fought off the pain, leapt off the bed, and ran after her, almost grabbing her just as she slammed the door on his monster cock, the hard rubber jamming it stuck. As Derek struggled to free himself, Sara rushed down the stairs and almost made it out the front door. He reappeared at the top of the stairway with a raised chair above his head and threw it with all his might, the chair breaking the glass door, crashing in Sara's back, and propelling her into the legs of . . . Patricia Holden.

The queen dyke looked down at the naked, bleeding, big-titted, tattooed girl in front of her and found the inspiration she had been looking for. She took off her leather jacket, wrapped it around Sara, and quick-dialed headquarters to reach the nearest sister taxi driver. It was there in minutes.

Derek started running down the stairs but made a quick turnaround when he saw other people outside the broken door. He ran back into the hotel room, yanked off the dildo, put on his clothes, opened the window, and rushed down the fire escape. By the time the police got there, all that remained of the incident was scattered bloodied window glass and an obscenely large rubber dildo with teeth marks, traces of blood, and leaking ejaculate. The technician held it at a distance, using latex gloves, as if the thing contaminated with fluids could turn and bite, while he waited for an agent to get a larger-size evidence bag.

There were no recordings available. The only witness, a young kid who lived across the street, had been gazing out his window while smoking a joint. He had heard screaming and breaking glass but a van parked in front of the door had blocked his view. When questioned for details all he could say was, "All I know, man, is that it sounded bad, like somebody might have been killed." The incident never made the news.

28.

CRACK O' DAWN

He could remember the challenge of the plan had excited Sara, the idea of using her training as concubinata to become an agent, a spy, in the church's war against Satan. She had even given him a demonstration the night before. He had been unable to resist.

By two a.m. he started worrying. What could be taking her so long? Then he started getting angry. Why hadn't she called him? Did she actually enjoy this Derek? He got caught up in imagining scenarios. Maybe Derek had gotten out of hand. Maybe his idea had backfired. Maybe she'd fallen asleep in the hotel room after drinking too much and staying up too late. But dammit, she could have called him. By four a.m. he was in the shower trying to clear his mind. He had a seven o'clock meeting with the council in a church basement forty-five minutes away. That still gave him a couple of hours.

At 4:25, the alert on his computer started beeping. Derek was connected to New Jerusalem and talking to the Apostle John. Bob Thomson cut in.

Derek screamed, "Aaah! Reverend! What are you doing here?"

"Where's Sara?"

"Who the hell is Sara?"

Remembering the need for security, Bob Thomson answered, "Just meet me where we met for lunch the first time. I want you there within the hour."

It was a twenty-four-hour diner, about forty-five minutes away. "But Reverend, it's four-thirty in the morning," Derek protested. "What happened that could be so important? Something to do with *I AM*?"

"I want you there in an hour and I don't want any excuses, you hear?" The CR connection went dead. Derek was fully awake now and he could feel the edge of his paranoia creeping up. People were watching and listening to his every move. Could the bitch last night really have been connected to the church? How was he supposed to be able to tell the difference if the church was going to start hiring the Jezebels? He should have been told of certain identifying signs, like a tattoo or a subskin scan. He'd have to tell the reverend about that.

He picked up a pill popper in the bathroom and triple-flicked three tranqs, then looked for the blue popper and flung a dose of amphetamine to be fully alert. *That should do it,* he thought. Calm and alert. Cool and collected. He quickly turned on his computer and searched for any news about an injured woman brought to a hospital but came up with nothing. It was as if the bitch just disappeared, crawled down a gutter. He'd have to search the street cam records for the area when he got back.

It was still dark by the time he entered the restaurant, which was already a third full with early risers trying to get in on the Crack o' Dawn breakfast special. As soon as he sat at the table, the reverend asked again, "So Derek, where's Sara?"

"Who's Sara?"

"Don't play dumb with me, Derek, I heard your confession. She works for the church. I sent her to that bar you were going to. You know exactly who I mean, the one with the rings and tattoos."

"You tapped into my confession? Isn't that against the law?"

The reverend decided to lie. "Not if there's a chance you're putting someone's life at risk. The filtering system alerted me. Let's get back to my question, Derek. Where's Sara?"

The whole crazy scene of the night before, what he could remember of it, replayed itself in his head. "You're saying that woman was a member of the church? You really sent her?"

"At least now we're clear about the fact that you met with her; now what did you do to her?"

"Uuuh . . . nothing. I sent her home after we were done." He still couldn't believe the reverend had listened to his confession. He tried to remember what he had said to John, whether he had blabbed about the dildo or her crashing through the door.

"Done what?"

"You know . . ." *How much detail did he want?*

"What?"

"Done fucking her," Derek added, to boast a little.

"You didn't hurt her, did you?" the reverend said, sounding pissed off.

"No, not intentionally." A kind of smirk plastered on his face.

"Don't try to be a smart aleck with me, Derek boy. Believe me, I know you're a little deranged in that department."

"What are you talking about?" They both fell silent as the waitress walked up to take their order.

Before Derek could say a thing, the reverend took over. "Two Crack o' Dawn specials with coffee and orange juice. Make the eggs scrambled and make that home fries."

"Will that be all?" the waitress asked, turning at Derek.

He was about to answer when the reverend cut in, "Yes, that'll do for now."

As soon as she stepped away, the reverend started again. "Now, one more time, did you harm Sara in any way? Did you kill her?"

"No, I swear, Reverend, she was fine when she left the room. I was a little caught off guard by the tattoos but we got that all worked out. We ended up having a good time. She was a nice girl." Not adding that AFTER she had left the room and crashed through that door, she probably wasn't exactly what you'd call shipshape. All that broken glass had to hurt. Fuck, if she ended up in the hospital the reverend was eventually going to hear about it. He was going to have to deal with that one when it came up.

"So where did you take Sara last night?" Bob Thomson eagle-eyed him as he said it.

"I already told you, we went to a security-free hotel. She even suggested it." Cool and collected.

"That's not what I meant, Derek. What hotel? I want a name and address."

He decided to lie to prevent any chance of a record of Sara crashing through the door from being uncovered. He'd work on editing out the segments at work. "It was the Invisible Palace near Broadway," he said.

"I'll have the church technicians scan the security cam data of the area. I better not find out anything happened to her . . ." He let the words hang in the air.

Bob Thomson wasn't sure what was going on, but if something had happened to Sara, someone was going to have to pay. "What about Borden, when are you going to take care of him?"

"I thought the hit was cancelled."

"Well. It's back on."

"I'll go after him tomorrow after I do a little research."

"So you really think you can get through his security screens?" the reverend asked.

"Yeah, I've got it all figured out." The waitress came with their order. He didn't like eggs. They turned into slimy embryos and came out of a chicken's rear end. He played with them with his fork and smeared them around the plate between bites of home fries and pancake.

29.

A DATE WITH JEFFERSON

This was going to be their first gender-correct date and Jessie was actually feeling nervous. Their last meeting at his apartment, when Joanna had come out of the closet, had ended up being a two-hour version of truth or consequences. In the end, tired, they had both fallen asleep in Patrick's bed, having made out and petted like teenagers but avoiding the uncomfortable act of sex. That night, as she lay with her head on his chest, right before falling asleep she could remember thinking how his smell had a sweet quality to it that made her feel like ... being cuddled against a giant teddy bear. It was an odd thing to think about. In her mind she compared it to Patricia's musky scent, which had an almost metallic edge to it, like a female who was always in heat. Patricia always reminded her of someone into sports, some kind of a jock.

The following morning had been awkward, both of them not quite knowing what to say as she rushed home to get ready for work. Patrick had called her on her wristcom later that evening. "Jessie, how about we go out on the town tomorrow night? That's Friday. Let's do something different."

And she had accepted. But now that she was inside his apartment and Patrick was telling her what his plans were, she was wondering why she had been foolish enough to come. What could she expect of someone who dressed up as a woman?

"Where are we going again?" Jessie asked.

"We're going to one of New York's most poorly known hotspots, a pressure cooker of repressed sexuality. The Virtual Church of Jesus Christ is having a big rally out in midtown about this *I AM* stuff, so I figured, let's go out and have us some fun."

"You're joking," Jessie said automatically. Seeing no change in Patrick's expression, she repeated the question. "You are kidding, aren't you?"

Patrick grinned. "No."

"Is this another one of your little secrets?" Jessie asked, alarmed. "Not only do you like to dress in drag, but now you're going to tell me you're really a reborn right-wing Christer transvestite masquerading as a liberal psychologist. Is that it?"

"Reborn right-wing Christer transvestite, now that's a tongue twister. I'll have to remember that one. How about we make a deal? If after tonight you don't feel this is the most exciting date you've ever been on, then the ball will be in your court. You can choose to never hear from me again or, if you're still interested, I'll do anything you ask for at least a month. That sounds like a pretty good deal to me."

"So I'm just supposed to trust you on this?"

"I just want to show you why I dress up."

"And I'm supposed to go along with it, just like that?"

"It's not that complicated. This is a side of me that's not likely to change. The way I see it, if we're going to have anything going on between us, a first step has to be honesty and trust. Tonight is a start, a critical compatibility filter."

Jessie just looked up at him, not answering and feeling very nervous about the whole thing. What was it about her that made her such a weirdness magnet? First she got caught up into the Sisterhood lesbian baloney and now this. If she were smart she would simply walk out the door and end the craziness right now. That would be the smart thing. She was about to say it when Patrick, with a big smile on his face, asked, "Game?" and before even realizing it, she had answered, "Game." She had done it once again.

Patrick took her by the hand and led her into his bedroom. As he guided her, he said, "The first thing we're going to do is take a couple of hits of Nex, (the new rat-tested street empathogen, Nouveau X), and second, we're going to dress up."

"As what, a couple of girls out on the town?" she said sarcastically.

"As a middle-class black couple ready to go out and whoop it up with the good Lord."

"And how's a white girl like me supposed to look like a black woman?" she asked.

"The first step is to swallow this," Patrick said, dropping a heart-shaped Nex tab in her hand and bringing up a glass of water. She looked at the red pill in her hand and said, "So what are you trying to do here, play cupid and hit me with a dose of love?" She smiled and popped the heart.

He flicked a pill and swallowed, making a face because of the bitterness. She handed him her glass.

He took a gulp then reached down and grabbed her hand. "Now come with me and let me show you to my dungeon." He brought her to a full-length mirror and punched a code in his wristcom. The mirror slid into the wall and opened into what at first appeared as a large walk-in closet. He tapped a key and the lights came on.

"Come on in here and let the master get to work." He led her under a set of spotlights angled from the center of the ceiling. "Stay put a second," he said.

She looked around her. The inside of the closet looked like an actor's dressing room. A counter with a small sink and faucets lined the left wall along with a chair and mirrors framed by tiny halogen bulbs. The back wall was covered by shelves that held storage boxes with drawers, bottles and vials, clear plastic bags with what appeared to be hairpieces, and Styrofoam heads with disguise combinations of wigs, mustaches, beards, and sideburns. The right side of the closet was covered by clothes arranged on hangers in sets, which she realized were probably outfits. What was she getting herself into? she wondered.

"This is crazy, Patrick," she said.

"Play along, Jessie, just for tonight. I know what I'm doing."

"That's what worries me. It makes me wonder who you really are, Patrick. It's like you're some kind of chameleon or something. Is there even such a thing as the real Patrick under there?"

"These are just shells, Jessie, costumes that I can put on or take off. They allow me to enter worlds most people don't even know exist. I like to think that dressing the part is partially what makes me a good psychologist."

"And this is your idea of a date?" she asked again.

"Just think of it as going to a costume party," he said, smiling.

"Are you sure you wouldn't rather stay here? I could show you a few bedroom tricks I've learned from the Sisterhood."

"It sounds tempting, but you just wait. You can't even begin to imagine what good loving is till a black man doin' the thing with you," he said with a heebie-jeebie accent he had probably picked up somewhere during his excursions in the city underworld.

"Oh my!" she said. She could feel a slight twinge of a shift in her attitude. It was probably the Nex.

Turning to her in the crowded closet, he said, "Now, for the first step, let's smack a little mulatto makeup on you." He took out a jar of dark cream and said, "Now off with the shirt and pants." As she undressed he unscrewed the top of the jar and dabbed a large cotton pad to apply the thick paste. "Now keep your eyes closed," he said and started applying the makeup to her face and arms, upper chest, and back.

He then knelt down and started to rub the dark cream down her lower legs and feet. Maybe because it tickled her and also maybe because she was feeling self-conscious, Jessie broke into a giggling fit.

"You think this is funny?" Patrick said with a big smile on his face. "Stay still a second, I need to make sure I have the color down evenly." Like a painter touching up a canvas, he smoothed out edges and evened out the tones. "You're going to have to wait for about ten minutes for this stuff to dry." He got up and turned to a back shelf. "While that's going on, why don't you just sit down in the chair here but just be careful not to let anything come in contact with the cream. OK, now let's see about wrapping up all that blond hair in a net." He opened a drawer on a clear plastic storage container, pulled out a hairnet and handed it to her. "Just slip that on and tuck in your hair."

He then turned back to the shelves, stared at the lineup of Styrofoam heads, and removed a black wig with wavy curls and placed it on her head, stepping back, then coming in close again, carefully adjusting its position, then stepping back again to look at the effect.

"That looks pretty good," he said. "OK, now let's look at those eyes," bending down, "and oh what gorgeous eyes they are, too. I think we'll just keep them their natural color. A green-eyed mulatto, now that should turn some heads. OK, next. How about we put on some kind of dress? Something exotic, maybe." He shuffled through the rows of clothes and pulled out a long colorful skirt from a hanger along with a loose white blouse. "And maybe sandals to show off those pretty feet . . . Actually the reason I'm suggesting sandals is I don't think I have shoes that'll fit you, but some of the sandals will probably work." By this time, the whole scene was becoming so otherworldly that Jessie broke up laughing.

"This can't be for real," she said between breaths. "I can't believe I'm doing this."

"Come," Patrick said, "let's look at what we've got in the mirror."

Jessie, with the Nex now definitely kicking in, looked in amazement at her new black self. "Wow!" she said. "I can't believe that's really me. And what do I call myself?"

"How about Jessie?"

"But that's my real name."

"Yes, but now it's 'Jessie, my parents were originally from Jamaica.'"

"No kidding," she said, walking up to the mirror to have a better look. She was starting to get into this. Then turning to him, "How about you?" she asked. "You're looking pretty pale if you ask me, a sickly-looking white boy."

"Well, why don't you just wait out here? There's another mirror on the dresser. Maybe you can fix up the hair a little better, add a little makeup to those gorgeous eyes, and maybe smack on some red lipstick while your husband, Jefferson, descendant of southern slaves, gets himself prepped to go out on a date with his woman." Jessie laughed.

Minutes later, Jefferson stepped out of the closet wearing a patterned shirt and black pants complete with a set of dark contact lenses, short dreadlocks, and a bright paisley Rasta cap.

"You just never know who's going to come out of the closet," she said.

"You sure right on that one, Jessie girl."

"And now that we're all decked out, can I ask why we're going to a meeting of the Virtual Church of Jesus Christ, not that I mind, mind you."

"Contrast," he said. "We're going to bring a little black spice into their pasty white-boy lives."

"Well how about I spice things up for my husband, Jefferson? A little mind trick I learned from the Sisterhood." And she slipped her hands beneath the dress, took off her panties, and twirled them on her index finger before letting them fly across the room. "Lets the pheromones rise from the honey pot and gets the imagination flowing," she added.

"Oh you bad woman," Patrick said, "you so bad I'm going to have to beat you good when we get back home. Beat you with my big stick."

"You going to put makeup on that, too?" she asked, looking serious.

"What?" They both burst out laughing.

With the Nex now kicking in full blast, Jessie appeared to Patrick as the most beautiful, radiant being he had ever seen. He was feeling the love buzz. Got bit by the red heart. Love for

Jessie for going along with this, love for her openness and little-girl mind, love for every little part that made up her perfect little body. It was Nex infatuation and he was now caught in it. He was also feeling black. He and his pert little woman, Jessie, were going out into the world.

It took a couple of subway rides and walking a half dozen blocks to get to the meeting place on the west side. Along the way, in part from feeling blitzed out, not a whole lot got said between them. Patrick held her hand as they sat on the bench, eyes forward, smiling. For a brief moment of lucidity, he tried to turn off the Nex love madness but couldn't quite do it. It was streaming nonstop through his body, moving from the center out, so much in fact that it hurt his heart, literally.

Jessie also tried to fight it, to stay rational, but what kind of a match was she for the forces behind the Nex? When all was said and done she knew she didn't have a choice. This had been written somewhere in the great cosmic script. *He my man,* she thought, turning to look at him, a smile coming to her face, *Jefferson.* He noticed her, caught the glimpse and its meaning. He put an arm around her shoulders and kissed her. It was a Nex perfect kiss. It was sublime.

The building where the meeting was held turned out to be one of those renovated old movie houses that stayed alive by holding regular ICF (International Celluloid Film) movie festivals and renting out the space during its extensive closed periods to various groups and organizations. The lit outside banner read: "Free Tonight. Best-selling Author and Evangelist, Reverend Bob Thomson, Speaks about the Coming of Satan Through the World Net." As it turned out, once Patrick and Jessie entered the lobby, they noticed a booth had been set up next to the theater entrance with a sign that read "Help Fight Satan, $20 Donation."

"I thought the outside sign said it was free," Patrick said to the woman sitting behind the table.

"The talk is free but the space and the equipment aren't," she answered.

"And what if I can't afford to pay the donation, as you call it."

"Then I can't let you in," she insisted.

"Even though the sign said it's free?"

"Well, it's like I just said, the reverend's talk is free but the space, the security, and the insurance, which is a legal requirement, are not." She had the lines down pat. He obviously had not been the first to question the deceptive advertising.

"So that's America's new definition of free speech?" he said sarcastically.

"You got it," the woman answered, smiling.

Instead of crediting his account, Patrick paid with cash to make sure his name and address would not be linked to a marketing database. When asked to put down his name and address, he wrote Jefferson and Jessie Bailey, and a made-up location in the new upscale black section of Harlem. They walked into the theater. The meeting had already started. The reverend was slowly walking up the center aisle as he spoke, mic clipped to his jacket, a spotlight following his every move.

Several reporters and cameras were gathered around the stage and several monitors had been set up to allow the audience a close-up view of the reverend. As he spoke, Bob Thomson's cool, blue-toothpaste eyes settled randomly on the members of the audience, penetrating their souls, as some had described it. His deep voice—amplified and carefully modulated by audio controllers—resonated in the packed room.

"We live in times so full of confusion, of chaos, of indeterminate values, of immorality, of decadence and sexual depravation, of ignorance of the Lord's words, of . . ." The reverend went on for over ten minutes, and Patrick stood there amazed that anyone could elaborate at such great lengths on the ills of the world. "And it is this confusion, this inability to know right from wrong, the lack of concern for the word of the Lord, that has opened windows for Satan to enter the world as he has never before. TV, radio, computers, phones, the lines and airwaves, have become the domiciles for Satan and there he resides waiting for you to turn on that channel, click on that site, open that e-mail to take advantage of that opening.

"And, like water that flows along the path of least resistance, he will tempt you. He will slide into your minds, and like a parasite he will attach himself to your will and take over. All of this," the reverend added, "has given Satan such a big domicile that he now can speak to the world as one voice. And you have all heard him, brothers and sisters. He is the parasite out to kill its host and he calls himself *I AM*. But I have now identified him, and I will not sit still and let him take over the world! As we speak, our churches and dedicated members around the world are working hard to put an end to this evil tool, this weapon of Satan, and to those who have conspired to allow its entrance into the world."

"Wooowweee, you go for it, Reverend!" shouted Patrick. Members of the audience turned toward him. He nodded at them and smiled. It took every effort for Jessie not to burst out laughing. Instead she put on a silly grin and tried to think about something else.

At the end of the sermon, they mingled among the parishioners standing in the hall and sipping cheap punch and coffee. They were mostly white, uneasy, and trying to force a smile.

Jefferson was on a roll. "I met the missus when I was visiting in Jamaica, saw those green eyes and thought right away, I need those green eyes looking at me all the time, day and night, all the time."

"Oooh you're such a flirt, Jefferson," Jessie said, hitting him gently on the arm. "He's been like that ever since I met him, mind you, and that's not so bad," Jessie said winking at the thin brown-haired woman standing at the side of a man who had introduced himself as Julian McAllister.

The woman said, "As long as one does not forget that nothing is more important than serving the will of the Lord. It's important to beware of the entrapment of lust, even between spouses."

Jefferson cut in. "Well I agree with you, Brook, is it?" looking at her name tag. "But the way I figure it, if I take good care of my Jessie here, then there ain't nuthin' bad the Lord's gonna see about it." Jessie beamed with pride, looped her arm around Jefferson's, and rested her head on his shoulder.

"And how do you feel about this *I AM* entity invading the World Net, Mr. Jefferson?" the woman asked him.

"I agree with the good reverend," Patrick answered. "The Bible don't say nuthin' about God speaking to us through no computers, so that *I AM* thing, he for sure got to be the devil." *Where did that come from,* he wondered, *an old TV show?* And he broke up laughing as Julian and Brooke stared.

Jessie had to shake her head to try to regain some kind of perspective. For just a moment, she had been so caught up in their black thing that she had actually believed she and Jefferson were real. *This is like reincarnation,* she thought.

Patrick was leading her toward the exit as he dialed a taxi. On the sidewalk he turned to her. "I don't know about you, Jessie girl, but I can't wait to get back home." He stood there looking into her eyes, then bent down to kiss her. When he opened his mouth, it felt like she was melting down his throat. *The circulatory system of the male anglerfish fuses with the female's.*

■ ■ ■ ■ ■ ■

Sara never made the papers, having been abducted by the Sisterhood, who happened to have its own women-only hospital. In every room, patients were also provided with free enlightenment therapy through the organization's round-the-clock, gender-adjusted, video version of scripture. It presented the Great Story from a woman's point of view. The origins of the world had simply been a birth and the Big Bang the output of the Goddess's giant hyperdimensional uterus. A Sisterhood member had tried to provide mathematical support for this view with a thesis, popularized into a book called *The Dynamics of Vaginal*

Fractals. According to the theory, all things in this world were related through certain mathematical algorithms that supported the Great Mother as the overruling cosmic theme and creative force of the universe. The world was the product of invaginations of structures, of vaginal pressures and outlets, of the gravitational pull of the supreme attractor, the cosmic vagina and the source of a vaginal force the author had coined "temptation" that was the primary drive behind all that we call evolution. Structurally, the universe was vaginal fractals, all the way up and all the way down. Vaginal Swiss cheese. Holes and hollows. One hundred percent female.

It made perfect sense. Sara identified with it completely. She understood the power.

30.

THE SECOND FLOOR

Her wristcom buzzed while she was inventorying the new shipment of Yo-Gos, multigeared self-propelling luminous yo-yos. She looked down. A voice message from Sunshine: "Dinner and movie at my place, eight p.m. OK?"

She clicked Reply and lifted the communicator to her mouth. "Yes, gladly, let's eat by the pool with our nudist friends," she said.

Stephanie, who was working in the same room, looked at her funny. "I didn't know you were into that."

"It's just a code," she answered. "It refers to a security-free restaurant."

"Where people eat naked?" she asked.

"No, it's just the kind of food they serve, Stephanie."

"Ahh," she said, "naked food, you mean, like raw vegetables and stuff."

"Now you're getting the idea."

"It sounds a little boring, if you ask me."

She had decided to wear a simple loose dress with a fancy belt of metal and ceramic beads and sandals. Underneath she only wore a colorful pair of panties that could pass as swimwear in a topless-beach environment. Sunshine greeted her at the door dressed in khaki shorts and a loose cotton shirt hand-painted with symbols originally found in prehistoric caves. He put his hand around her waist, brought her close, and kissed her. "I've been thinking about doing this all day."

"One more," she said.

"I'd rip your clothes off and carry you to my boudoir, but dinner should be ready in about twenty minutes." She walked toward his kitchen. It showed no signs of food preparation and nothing on the stove.

"You actually have food cooking?"

"Be grateful I don't. It's being delivered. So how about an exotic drink, like an ice-cold Corona with a slice of lime?"

"A Corona sounds great," Rama said.

"Come," he said, grabbing her hand, "let's sit down by the pool." Pointing to the wall monitor, he said, "This is a beach in New Caledonia at sunset." To add to the general effect, Sunshine had turned on a couple of aromators simulating a seaside smell. She walked to the edge of the pool and looked down. The theme was a flow of creatures slowly swimming across the bottom, schools of fish, seals after the fish, dolphins, squid, a gigantic whale, sharks, a manta ray . . .

"I can change it back to the coral reef if you like," Sunshine said.

"No, no, I like it." The streaming of creatures showed no signs of repeating itself, a seemingly endless variety of schooling species. The detail was another reflection of Sunshine's mind.

"That's the microversion. They want me to create themes for Intelli-pool systems. They want it to be like going to the movies, a different theme every week. I'm just developing sample programs for their technicians."

"You could create some pretty scary CR games with that," she said. "Gulping sharks rising from the deep, giant octopus, that kind of thing."

"Funny you should say that. They have plans for water parks with donut-shaped infinity pools where the patterns simulate a CR game. People will be able to rent scuba gear. I can show you a sample later."

"There's something ironic about that."

"I know what you're going to say. People have little interest in nature but will pay to experience the CR version of it. One argument is that if you have CR nature, then people will leave nature alone."

The doorbell rang. "It must be dinner," Sunshine said.

A man in a waiter's outfit walked in carrying two large boxlike cases. "Henry, nice to see you, as always. Henry, this is Rama."

"Good evening, Miss Rama." He made his way to Sunshine's small kitchen. "I'll just be about fifteen minutes. Would you like me to serve you drinks?"

"It's already been taken care of, Henry," Sunshine said.

"So this is your way of seducing me—by conveying your potential to cater to my whims, and provide comfort and security?"

"I think you should see it as my way of letting you know that I have no culinary skills."

While Henry was setting the table, they sat at the edge of the pool, feet dangling in the water. "I think it would be neat to see a whale close up, like underwater," she said. "I've always wondered what it would be like to be right next to a whale's face and look it in the eye. Maybe there's something that could be learned, at that moment."

Henry waved his arm toward the pool. "Please allow me to show you to your seats," he said. Rama smiled at the formality. Henry had dimmed the lights except for the electric tiki torches. The sun was replaced by a full moon. The beach was now only ocean in moonlight with the slow rhythmic splatter of dappling waves.

"The beach and water theme seems very important to you. Any special reason?"

"I'm not sure, maybe a past life."

"You believe in reincarnation?"

"Not really, but I'm working on it." She wasn't sure what he meant.

A few minutes after they were settled in, Henry stood by the table and announced, "To start, we have caviar on pumpernickel bread complemented with chopped eggs and onions, fresh calamari grilled with herbs and with a special Henry-made sauce."

Sunshine pressed the controller and put on Hawaiian music.

"I guess you wanted to charm me with ambiance," she said.

"I tried," Sunshine answered, with a grin. "I couldn't have naked people with Henry here. The subliminal suggestion is there though, of a return to the simple and primitive, back to basics, the call of the wild, that kind of thing."

"I understand perfectly what you're saying. The naked people are hiding in the bushes," she said.

The food wasn't so much delicious as interesting, combinations she hadn't experienced before. Thimble-sized shots of ice-cold tequila had accompanied the caviar. A couple of different white wines, though she wasn't even sure if they were grape wine, had complemented the lobster and fish dishes. It all fit with the theme of eating by the seashore.

By the time dessert was served, Sunshine was in high form. To Rama's surprise, he was in his own way funny, very funny. He was going on about one of his early implant experiments.

"So I've got this dilemma. The implant's connected. Do I or do I not plug into the program? It's just one tap of the finger. Tap. Enter. It's a Schrödinger's cat kind of thing. I'm in this in-between state, equal probability of having plugged and not having plugged in. My host has warned me of a high-level risk of neuron damage. I ask, 'How much?' and it says, 'possibly impaired memory.' So I can't test the software I've just written. I've reached a wall. It's kind of a Russian roulette.

"What the hell, I think. I press the key. At that very moment, the system crashes, but I'm goggled up, and I don't know it right away, so I imagine the thing is working. I'm feeling these sensations and seeing these things, little details, and I actually start laughing—because I'm thinking, this is no big deal. In fact,

I even get caught up in the subtlety of my program. I'm thinking this is kind of interesting. This nothing I've unintentionally created has some kind of a Buddhist je ne sais quoi to it, a soupçon of Zen. After about two minutes of tapping keys, I start to realize, you know, this is getting a little dull. It must have been fate, because as it was my program had fried my equipment. I wasn't even connected. I don't even want to imagine what it could have done to my brain cells. You could be talking to a human veggie burger right now."

"Well I've got a good one for you. I was curious about how eating a chocolate sundae on Instant would feel. My thinking was, why not extend the experience of delicious? I imagined I would sense the stimulation of each individual taste bud on my tongue, like fingers on piano keys, the smooth flow of ice cream across my mouth and down my throat, a sensual kind of thing. The problem was that I went to this ice cream place with a friend. Maybe it would not have made a difference. So what did my mind focus on? The mouth noises and the mouth movements. The spoon in and out. I kept telling myself, 'focus on the flavor, focus on the flavor,' but no, it was a competition of the senses and auditory took over. And you know what it made me realize? We block out the sounds people make when they eat. It's kind of beastly in a gross way. I think maybe that's a reason alcoholic drinks are served with food or maybe that's why people like to eat in restaurants. The background noise distracts ..."

Sunshine listened with a kind of amazement at the way Rama interpreted the world. A certain refinement. He reached out for her hand. Felt her fingers envelop his. A feeling as good as any dose of Instant, a fusion. A tiny uplifting of the sides of her mouth. A look. Boundaries between eyes and brains dissolved. A moment of consciousness interflow.

They went on like that, exchanging their experiments and adventures. Eventually, they talked about their relationships, the disillusions of Nex pseudolove (love that seemed real in the Nex bubble but wasn't when the bubble burst), temporary truths (passions that were true for a day or a week but were ultimately ephemeral), and adventures with cybersex. As they talked, Rama clearly saw what they both had in common: searching but not finding, not quite fitting in the world. Sunshine on one hand wanting basic primitive human contact and a sense of belonging, yet also striving to be inhuman. *Minimal clothing and prehistoric symbols on his shirt, yet spends his life goggled up and hosted.*

■ ■ ■ ■ ■ ■

Walter Randall has read the note. There is now no doubt in his mind about Sunshine Borden being linked to the *I AM* events. He decides to send a message to Derek, rerouted a half dozen ways, all anonymous and false names. *I know you're the one who hurt my sister.* He attaches altered video clips, one where a technician has fused in a side glimpse of Derek's face, not clear but enough to flick switches. Another with lines and statistics that show a morphometric match. Make him feel targeted.

■ ■ ■ ■ ■ ■

After dinner, Sunshine brought her to the spiral staircase that led to the second floor.

"Come, I want to show you something."

"Are you taking me to the secret bedroom with the robot-controlled whips and chains?" she said jokingly.

Sunshine grinned. "If that's what turns you on, that kind of CR can be arranged."

They climbed the stairs and ended up in front of a stainless steel door. He walked up and tapped the code into the keypad. The latches unlocked and the door slid back into the wall. Sweeping his arm toward the contents of the room, he said, "Why don't you just look around a bit."

There were about a dozen large glass enclosures, various cubes and spheres, and a small walk-in room housing hundreds of plants, mini-waterfalls, streams, and small creatures, all the setups wired with cameras and various digital gauges. One wall held various works of art lit by overhead spotlights, some enclosed in glass. Most had symbolic motifs. Tibetan tankas, Huichol yarn paintings, paintings by Alex Grey and H. R. Giger, glass paperweights that looked like they contained galaxies and amoeboid forms, painted gourds, a spinning crystal skull, bouncing lights, robotic things, a meteorite. One side of the room was a solid wall of processors and minimonitor banks. On the opposite side was an enclosed area, like a nursery, where minirobots looking like oversized crabs appeared to be assembling and disassembling each other.

She walked up to one of the glass enclosures. It housed a trickling waterfall that fed a small pool. "Wow, you actually have blue lobsters in there! Are these the same lobsters the Japanese say alter consciousness?"

"I think they're the same species, originally blue *Cherax destructor* from Australia, but they've bioengineered the things and I suspect they're somehow infused with a drug."

She peered into another glass tank. It looked like a part of a branch from a large tropical tree had been transported and enclosed. Hundreds of small plants covered it, some with stalks of tiny bright flowers, others looking like molten green lava from which rose stems and leaves. Against the back wall was a section of a vertical tree trunk. The background was a digital 3-D forest that showed butterflies, birds, and monkeys.

"I could spend hours in here," she said. "It's even better than the Forgotten Forest!"

"I use these vivariums to add detail to some of my CRs. They also allow me to understand the limitations of self-sustaining ecological systems and some core concepts of APU development. Minds are a lot like ecologies. Interpretational structures emerge and compete. Some are active, others are put on hold or repressed. But some of these are just for my pleasure. They're my windows into nature."

"You must spend a lot of time up here. It seems like a lot of work."

"Actually, I'm hiring my sister to care for this area. I normally spend about ten hours a week up here; the rest of the time I can work from downstairs. I have automatic systems to turn on and off most of the equipment and the various monitoring devices and recorders. They're all connected in one way or another to my network. Ultimately it all gets downloaded in a CR and in more complex APUs."

■ ■ ■ ■ ■ ■

Derek keeps clicking back and forth between the videos in the e-mail and the ones on the crime links. He blows up the one showing his face until it pixilates out of definition. No way it could be his face. He had on the Intelli-Skin mask. Can't remember who it was he had programmed. Anybody could see the face of the man in the crime link video wasn't him. Then it came to him. *Fucker's going to go in and alter the videos.*

■ ■ ■ ■ ■ ■

Patricia walks with Jackie toward the neon of the Kara Tundra. A sister had recommended it, an e-note sent in response to the request for ideas for a new direction of the Sisterhood. "You should see their Cybris karaoke. I think the Sisterhood could learn something from it."

When they enter the bar section they see the singer, a skinny, androgynous Japanese-looking kid in a T-shirt that looks like he stepped out of an anime. The screen behind and above him shows a man with sleek black hair Cybrised in a tuxedo with black tie. He's singing one of the most popular of the karaoke tunes, "Insignificant," not the original by The Void, but the digimetal cover by that weirdo who cuts himself with razor blades. She's surprised the restaurant offers that version—but then leave it to the Asians and their morbid fascination with slicing and blood. It's a weird Cybris. The singer's waving his arms and striking himself like he's being attacked by bugs. The tuxedoed simulacrum on the screen is slashing his clothes with a double-edge razor blade as he sings.

"Just look at me!" Slash. *"What do you see?"* Slash. *"There's not much there, a bunch of atoms."* Slash-slash. *"I'm not a man, I'm not a girl."* Slash-slash. *"I'm in between the gender curtains."* Slash-slash-slash. The shredded tuxedo falls in thin strips to reveal the body of a woman in lacy lingerie. *"If you're like me, an alien being that has no place among the humans."* Slash. *"You'll lie with me, help us forget, we're insignificant."* He rakes his hands across his face and the Cybrised version peels off like a mask and reveals the dreamy face of Karen Richardson. *"I'm insignificant."*

His buddies, including a couple of girls, are jumping up and down. The crowd is whistling and hooting as he cups his breasts, shakes his hips, bows, and leaves the stage. She could swear the next one up is one of the sisters—short hair, a man's shirt over pants, except that she has on high-heel shoes. She nets up, enters the stage, and starts singing last year's number one hit song, "I Will Change My Eyes." She first dances like a human, but slowly becomes mechanical. The girl on the screen changes into a robot-machine woman with all parts enhanced and morphing.

"I will change my nose, I will change my boobs, I'll be the girl that stepped out of your wet dream. When you want it, big boy, I will make it hurt. Hurt till tears of joy flow from your surprised eyes. I'll make you want to die for me, baby. I'll show you I would die for you. I will change my eyes." She thinks about going over and offering her a drink, test the waters, but at the end a man comes over and munches on the girl's face.

By the time the next one comes on, a tall plumpette with boobs the size of her head wearing a dress patterned in faces, her wheels are spinning. The song is "I Got You All Over Me." The Cybris matches the dress except that the eyes blink and the mouths on the dress join in the singing. At the end, the mouths on her breasts pucker up a big kiss. Whistles and screams and calls for an encore. That clinched it. The hell with karaoke, she was going to do the real thing. Not Cybris, not a download, but transformation that soaks the panties of all the women in the world. She will be the supreme attractor, modified to attract them all, gay or straight.

Patricia hums one of the songs as they take the subway back to the Sisterhood. *I will change my eyes . . . I will change my boobs. I'll be the girl who stepped out of your wet dream . . .*

By the time they reach their station her brain has kicked into overdrive. This could be another lucrative aspect added to the ritual. The Sisterhood would no longer just show the way; it would offer radical transformation, a death and a rebirth, something right out of the myth of the Great Mother. *Hurt till tears of joy flow from your surprised eyes. I'll show you I would die for you, baby. I will change my eyes.* The body a person was born with was just an entry vehicle, the basic framework on which one could later impose a personal vision, an expression of the inner self.

The words were coming to her now. "Like our minds, our bodies are a kind of clay. It is up to us to mold them, to shape them, and to resurrect into the unique works of art we were meant to become." She'd have to talk to the Sisterhood hospital administrators to see what they could do about having a special cosmetic surgery division. They could charge extra for surgery linked to the rituals. Womanhood was never going to be the same. She even had her new slogan: Become All That You Can Be, perfect for recruitment.

The next morning she video-contacts Robert Masso, the plastic surgeon whose designs are based on observer physiological feedback. He answers because he recognizes the name and its association with the Sisterhood. *So many women . . . so many purses . . .*

"I want you to alter me like you did Titanic Suzy. Test it on a random group of female students. I want you to change me into a floodgate machine. You got it? And I want to buy the rights to the template." She looks at him with a weird gleam in her eyes. "You're the first man I'll have allowed to touch me since my teens. Don't botch it up."

■ ■ ■ ■ ■ ■

Rama said, "You know, when I was younger I read the stuff in the Bible and in Hindu and Buddhist texts, and you know what fucked my head up?"

"What was it?"

"That the ultimate purpose of existence should be the supposed salvation from our individual selves, these measly scenarios of judgment and heaven or liberation by uncovering one's true nature. That's it? Whoopee-do."

Sunshine laughed. "I felt the same way. Like, could this childish crap about if you're a good little boy you get rewarded by going to this place called heaven where all is nice and peachy really be what this is all about? I mean, really? Doesn't the universe have anything better to do than worry about the soap opera of human lives?"

Rama went on, "Yes, yes, and that's why I had to keep looking. There had to be something else. That's one reason I bought your CyberBardos. I thought you might have the answer."

"I've come to the conclusion that there is no absolute answer but only options and choices. Realistically, no alternative option for the purpose of existence was possible until we started creating the tools for a possible time machine. Not a machine that allows you to move between past and future, but one that—like our brains—generates time by storing and stacking moments. There is no door. We not only have to make our way out, we have to generate where we're going."

"So tell me more."

"What do you want to know?"

"Do you think *I AM* could be the TOET?"

"I don't know that *I AM* is the TOET, but it may be a sign that the transcendental object is near. I think we have a 'build it and it will create itself' situation."

Rama had a big smile on her face, a kind of mystic glow. "This is wonderful stuff, Sunshine. The TOET, the possibility of our future, all of it, it's great stuff." *You, you are my TOET, Sunshine.*

"Isn't it?"

She grabbed his hand and led him toward the stairs. "If you're going to replicate all this in a transcendental object, you better make sure you include what's important. I want you to make love to me. No holds barred. Record it and put it in a CR if you want but if I'm going to be a disembodied angel I want access to the next hour."

■ ■ ■ ■ ■ ■

GAS.WNET RADIO: *The Gary and Andy Show*

GARY: Did you hear about Ars Savalia?

ANDY: You mean Artie Savalia?

GARY: Right, she's no longer a woman.

ANDY: He's getting married to Pedro Suarez, the owner of the biggest Volkswagen dealership in New Jersey.

GARY: Did Artie ever recover from his accident?

ANDY: You mean the one where he rolled into the dog walker?

GARY: Yeah.

ANDY: Nothing the plastic surgeons couldn't fix.

GARY: Didn't they end up putting down those dogs?

ANDY: The attorneys for the dogs won the case. Self-defense. The dog walker got some kind of settlement. Supposedly one of the dogs also turned on her during the attack.

GARY: He, she, whatever she is, now says he's committing the ultimate suicide, giving up all that he is, all that he ever believed in. He wants to become as ordinary and stereotypical a person as he can be. A living suicide. He now wears business suits with shirt and tie and a short haircut, drives an electric vehicle, and works as a sales manager for his husband's business.

ANDY: I read that, too. He supposedly held a funeral where all evidence of his prior self was burned. It seems like a dumb move to me. They still have all her videos and artwork on the World Net.

GARY: He tried to sue to get all of those but apparently most are now part of the public domain. I actually have a framed and signed print of the imprint of her tit squished against my windshield. She had it shot from the inside. They say it helped launch the windshield art movement.

ANDY: So in your own way you made history.

GARY: I guess I did.

ANDY: So what's next for Artie?

GARY: Well, he's got the house with the white picket fence. He says the next step is bambinos and a beagle, neutered, of course. He plans to attend PTA meetings in the future.

ANDY: I'm sure that's all going to be recorded.

GARY: Hey, he's not calling himself Artie for no reason.

ANDY: What does Artie have to do with it?

GARY: Artie's a diminutive of the word *art*, not quite artsy but close. Get it?

ANDY: Wow, I missed that. I guess in the end, she may be dead but the art survives.

GARY: Man, that's a deep message.

ANDY: Kind of fucks with your head, doesn't it?

GARY: Think about it. In the end, only the art survives.

ANDY: Only the art survives.

31.

KEEP THE FAITH

Today is day nine since the last *I AM* greeting. It had been highlighted for its high probability for an *I AM* return because *I AM* had a thing about the number nine.

Nine twenty-seven a.m. and the news report is uninterrupted, as it has been for the last nine days. His screen shows crowds of people, just a fraction of what they were at the beginning, leaving theaters and churches with large screens. There are still a few protesters outside the White House but they know that there is little they can achieve. No amount of protest can change what has happened. A recent survey did show that most people in the US still held hope the *I AM* entity would eventually resume communications.

The screen cuts to Pope Raul. "God would never abandon you in desperate times," he emphasized. "Phenomena like *I AM* may come and go but God is always present, always watching over you and ready to answer your prayers. That is the difference between God and the *I AM* phenomenon."

An Islamic cleric comes on next. "Let this be a reminder that there is only Allah."

Outside a theater on Forty-second Street, a young man and his girlfriend are standing on the sidewalk. A reporter asks, "So what do you think about this morning's statement by the pope?"

"What statement?" says the young man.

"The one where he says *I AM* is not God."

The young man responds, "God has always been just talk. The day he can do what *I AM* has done the last few weeks, I'll start believing in him."

The girl turns, jumps up, and kisses him on the cheek. "You spoke my words exactly, baby." Then looking into the camera: "*I AM*, if you're out there, we want you back, we need you."

The news switches to an image of bright blue lobsters. "Japanese report engineered blue lobsters affect brain like *I AM*." A reporter and a translator accost the Japanese minister of commerce as she leaves the restaurant.

"When will blue lobsters be available for the international market?"

The minister warbles, the translator forwards the answer in a British accent. "Blue Lobster is special Japanese product. You must come to Japan to appreciate."

"So Japan has no plans for international distribution."

She frowns as the translator relays the question. "No, no, no. Blue Lobster is Japanese product. You must come to Japan if you want Blue Lobster."

His next question: "So do you plan to make it available to the general public, at least in Japan?"

"One day all Japanese people eat Blue Lobster at least once in life." Another mumbling.

The translator: "She wants you to know you have very nice blue hair."

"What?" The reporter turns toward the door. "And who do we have here? Is that Karen Richardson? By golly, I think it is . . ."

■ ■ ■ ■ ■ ■

His phone rings. He presses the speakerphone button. "Mr. President, Catherine Harris would like to see you."

She enters a few minutes later. She's wearing her usual outfit, a dark blue pantsuit with a silk blouse. But something about her looks different. Her hair looks shorter and it appears she's put on some makeup. She actually has nice eyes, which he had never noticed before.

"Have a seat, Catherine. So how are you holding up?" He knows that as media advisor she has been accused of playing a role in the never-announced proposed recommendation.

"Honestly, not so good, Mr. President. It's not the criticism, but the doubts, about myself, about whether I have contributed anything of worth with regards to what has happened." She's twirling the gold crucifix around her neck. She sees the president has noticed it and puts her hand down.

"So what did you want to talk to me about?"

"I'm thinking I should resign."

"I'd like you to wait before making that decision. I got a message hand delivered by courier service from Sunshine Borden two nights ago. He called me beforehand to let me know but said the message was confidential and he didn't trust that anything said over the phone or sent electronically would be secure."

"Why hand delivered?"

"Because he doesn't want the message to become public knowledge. He asked that the note be destroyed after reading and that his name not be mentioned in association with the message. He doesn't want to be questioned about it by the media."

"Aren't security measures in place to have any paper messages checked for contact or inhalation chemicals?"

"I asked Walter Randall to personally receive the message and inspect it before bringing it to me. That should eliminate any risk of interference."

"So what did the message say?"

"I can trust that this will not leave this room?"

"Mr. President . . ."

He writes it on a piece of paper and hands it to her.

Keep the faith, Mr. President. There are clear signs that I AM *is still present.*

He reaches his hand out for her to return it and tears it to shreds before placing it in his coat pocket.

"Did he say what signs?"

"No. But Arthur has said there are reports of peculiar color waves running across screens."

"Color waves? You're not serious. That's not exactly enough to make a public announcement."

"No, but we could say that we are taking security measures in preparation for the next *I AM* communications. That would imply we are expecting it to return."

"You know the media will press for more information."

"We'll tell them it's a security issue and for this reason can't openly reveal details at this time."

"They'll say the public has a right to know."

"I'd just say that the fact that it wanted to be known to us by announcing itself makes it likely this *I AM* entity wants to be recognized in some way."

"And how did we come to this conclusion?"

"Actually, it was suggested by FBI profilers. We can't tell the public that but the information could be leaked."

"That still doesn't convince me I shouldn't resign."

"I'm asking you to stick with me, Catherine. I don't want my critics and the public to think my people are abandoning me. For my sake, you should do what the message advised."

"Which is . . ."

"Keep the faith, Catherine."

She tries but she can't stop herself. She bursts into tears.

■ ■ ■ ■ ■ ■

Amazonia is watching her interview on Karen Richardson's show and listening to herself about making her ova available so that she could become the Great Mother. It sounds wrong to her, ridiculous actually. She doesn't want to be the biological mother of dozens or hundreds of human beings. There were already too many people in the world and it didn't feel right to contribute to it. She would feel a responsibility to help all her children and that was a psychological burden she did not want. The publicity and the soap opera that would follow the many births would be counter to her own ideals and personal goals. *You should have thought before speaking,* she tells herself. Not cool, not the words of the Great Mother.

She's lying on her bed in a bathrobe, just out of the shower. The three screens are showing the news. A timer with a countdown is positioned on the bottom right, a new feature ever since the *I AM* greetings.

9:26:57 . . . 58 . . . 59 . . . 9:27:00. The news is still on but the sound has been turned off. She reaches for the controller when the strangest, most beautiful music she has ever heard—three-dimensional and coordinated through her three screens—comes on. It is performed by what seems like human voices, a ghost music, barely there, as if from behind the envelope of experience. She feels notes and harmonies penetrating her forehead and shuffling her brain. An ecstasy rises from her abdomen, up through her chest, throat, out the top of her head. Other deep rhythmic sounds that feel like objects strike her. She can sense them entering her body. She is aroused, all erectile membrane. The sounds keep coming, streams like electricity zipping in her abdomen. Sweat is pouring from her body. A space opens through and within her. *I AM.* The sounds subdue and fade. It's as if she's been hit by a wave.

The news is back on. "Once again we have not been greeted by the *I AM* entity. The good news is that the latest job report indicates unemployment has dropped to 14.2 percent, the lowest since . . ." She changes channels to see if there are any reports of music or sounds but the news stations all say the same thing. She does a search on the World Net for reports of *I AM* having shown signs of itself. Nothing. She notices her bathrobe and bedsheets are damp. She has to take another shower.

She gets up. Something feels odd. She walks toward her bathroom. Strange. Some kind of assistance. She looks at her face in the mirror. She can't be sure but she could swear that there had been a couple of lines at the edge of her eyes. She puckers her lips a couple of times. They're smooth and rounded. Were they like that? Must be all in her head. *You're looking pretty good, Amazonia,* she tells herself. She enters the shower, raising her leg over the rim of the bathtub. It feels as if she were weightless.

32.

ENVELOPING DARKNESS

Sunshine was swimming laps in his minipool when he heard the buzzer ring. He glanced up at the security monitor and recognized one of the agents who had accompanied him to the White House meeting. He climbed out, reached for a towel, and walked to the microphone. "What do you want?"

"Mr. Borden, the president has a couple of questions he wants to discuss with you. If you have a few minutes, I can connect you for a video conference call."

"Couldn't you have called ahead?" Sunshine asked. "Couldn't we have done this by phone or over the Net?"

"Mr. Borden, our records show that you have a poor response time. The president needs to talk to you today."

"Hold on," Sunshine said, "I need to put on some clothes."

Sunshine barely had the door open when Derek kicked his way in, lifting his weighted metal briefcase with two hands over his head and smashing it down. The impact split the skin of Sunshine's forehead, broke his nose, threw him off balance, and caused him to fall on his back. Derek pulled out a gun with a silencer attachment. "After I'm done with you, I'm gonna finish the job I started with your little sister. Teach her a lesson." He aimed for the head.

"Derek!"

He turns. On his right, someone is calling his name. All lights go off.

"What the fuck?" Derek shoots randomly in the dark, quick shots, *pat, pat, pat*. He turns around, rushes out the door, and . . . runs into a woman walking her dog. He gets tangled in the leash, the little mutt running in a circle and yelping as the woman screams bloody murder. He hops out of the leash and smashes a fist in her face. "Fuck off, lady." He turns into an alley, reverses the jacket he has on from dark to light, removes shoe covers, slips on a red-haired wig, and switches his face to Clive Jackson, chiropractor.

The lights are back on. Sunshine feels blood flowing out his side, another area of pain higher up in his chest. He tries to get up to call an emergency unit, but stumbles and falls. *Shit*. He punches his controller to connect the implant to the World Net, blood mucking up the keys.

The enveloping darkness sets in.

■ ■ ■ ■ ■ ■

Rama heard about it while at work. A customer brought it up. "Did you hear the news? Sunshine Borden was just shot. I can't believe it. What's the world coming to?" It took several seconds for the information to register.

"Did you just say Sunshine Borden?" she asked.

"Yes, Sunshine Borden. You know, the game designer, the Ark, the Forgotten Forest. They say he's not expected to survive."

The crunching of gravel, of broken rock, started going off in her head—the stone men walking. She excused herself, turned, and rushed to the back room, put on her jogging shoes, gathered her things, and headed for the door. On the way out she asked Stephanie to take over for her. "I feel sick, I gotta go."

As soon as she was on the street she broke into a run. *Just keep running*, she told herself. *Keep running*. Memory images chaotically flashed through her mind. Sunshine . . . the night before . . . the stone men . . . the CyberBardos . . . She ran in the general direction of her apartment until her gasping for breath and the pains in her chest and sides started overpowering her thoughts. Her phone buzzed. She took it out of her pocket and looked at the screen. Lionel. She answers.

"Where are you? I've got three customers looking for help."

"I'm sorry, Lionel. I had to leave, I felt sick to my stomach. I thought I was going to throw up. It's the flu or food poisoning. I ran out to see if I could pick up something at a drugstore."

"Are you coming back?"

"I don't think so. I feel sick as a dog."

"Next time you leave without telling me first, you're fired. Got it?"

"Yeah."

"Call if you can't make it tomorrow."

"OK."

She started running again.

■ ■ ■ ■ ■ ■

As soon as he entered his apartment, Derek decided to turn on his new autonomous host, a unit disconnected from the Net and carefully purged of any possible *I AM* intrusion or transflux properties. The moment he flicked the switch a piercing high-pitch screech, which he heard for a couple of seconds, burst from his speakers. It shattered glass items throughout his apartment, including monitors and windows, but he saw it as a silent movie. His eardrums had ruptured, a beam of pain slicing through his head. He dropped to the floor and crawled at full speed on hands and knees, like an insect, toward his front door . . . straight into the legs of . . . "What the hell?"

Stunned by the impact, Derek raised his head and looked into the pale blue eyes of his own face. "Who, uh, who are you?" He spoke the words but couldn't hear them.

He saw himself answer, surprised that he could understand what was coming from the mouth, "You stupid idiot!"

Shaking his head, he tried to concentrate, his brain feeling scrambled, the gears not kicking in. "Reverend?"

Silence.

"I think the *I AM* thing got me," he muttered, puzzled at not hearing a single word coming out of his mouth, not sure whether he had even spoken. He said it again as he worked on getting himself up, but never quite got there.

Bob Thomson pulled out the electronic syringe and shot a triple dose of toxin into Derek's back, making him drop like a rock. He capped the syringe and put it in his pocket. He checked in a mirror to make sure the Intelli-Skin mask still showed Derek's face and that the morphometrically altered suit had not shifted. He had another quick look around the room, took out his handkerchief to wipe off any prints on the doorknob, and walked out.

■ ■ ■ ■ ■ ■

Sunshine Borden not expected to survive. She rushed to the hospital and asked to see him. Minutes after the receptionist keyed in her information, an agent came up and asked for her ID. Security concerns. He then guided her to the admission center, took her pic, and scanned her license. Again, security concerns. Seeing Sunshine Borden would not be possible. Only family was allowed.

As she's about to leave, a tall man approaches her. "Are you Rama?"

She nods. "Yes."

"My name is Patrick, I'm a good friend of Sunny's. He's talked a lot about you. He's done a good job of describing you, by the way."

She's trying not to cry. Her throat feels constricted. "Have you heard anything? Is he going to be OK?"

"I talked to Passie, his sister. It's not looking good. They don't think he'll make it through the night."

When she gets home she connects to the Net. The headlines are the same: Sunshine Borden, Game, World Host, and CR Designer, Not Expected to Survive.

That evening, lying in bed, she can't sleep. *"Sunshine Borden not expected to survive"* keeps looping in her head. She goggles in to the Forgotten Forest. Sits by the stream. Their first date. Blue crayfish waving claws, doing side-to-side mating dances. Leaves multicolored, drifting down from trees like snow. Fall in cyberspace. All those little details . . .

"Oh, Sunshine," she says.

A sudden wind bursts through the trees like some kind of beast, sending the leaves in horizontal drifts. The air swirls, thickens, and colors into three-dimensional mosaics, morphing angelic and erotic forms. *"Neither Light nor Darkness Change the Presence of the Sky. I AM Aaa ome."* A familiar voice.

"Don't leave me here, Sunshine Borden!" she screams. Tears are streaming from her eyes, filling the digi-goggles.

■ ■ ■ ■ ■ ■

News Flash! Game Designer Sunshine Borden Shot
Sunshine Borden, game and CR designer, and codeveloper of APU programming, was shot yesterday in his apartment by someone who appeared to be a Secret Service agent. The agent in question was in Pennsylvania at the time of the incident so police are investigating the possibility that the suspect may have been wearing a mask. According to anonymous sources, Sunshine Borden had been under investigation by the government for possibly being linked to the *I AM* events. The White House press secretary has refuted these claims and stated that Mr. Borden had in fact been approached to act as a consultant on how to best address the *I AM* phenomenon.

33.

DOWNLOAD/UPLOAD

It was a strange sensation, a coming to consciousness as a kind of twinkling construction, out of midair and into his main room. He looks down at himself, lifts his hands, and examines them. He walks around his apartment, checking his equipment, noticing the outline on the floor and the dried blood, then climbs up the stairs to the second floor. He enters his laboratory, sensing that something is not quite right and yet not quite able to put his finger on it. It all has the feeling of something borderline, of a moment-by-moment generated fabric, like a movie. Some psychological element is missing, an amnesia, a detachment, a peculiar freedom from emotion. A certain clutching tension in his chest and a light constriction in his throat are gone. He feels weightless. It then occurs to him that he is breathless, that activity does not generate movement in his chest. He covers his mouth, pinches his nose, and sure enough, there is no reflex to breathe, no feeling of suffocation. He is anaerobic.

He looks around his apartment. Those things that were his have shed their significance, are uninteresting, confining structures. He walks down the stairs and over to his front door. He opens it to leave. He is struck by a force, a fury, a brightness, a depth of meaning that almost knocks him off his feet. He braces himself against the door frame, adjusting to what he is seeing, getting a sense of balance, letting it sink in. In front of him churns a dizzying hyperdimensional psychedelia that groans and shrieks. He feels it as a transpoint, the actualization of being, the processing of time, the generation of history. It is the mind of the universe. He turns his head and looks back once again at the inside of his apartment, then looks down and steps out the door into the self-transmuting maelstrom, twinkling slowly into the cybermagma, sparkle gliding, drawn in . . .

He senses it as a slight rippling of identity—the smallest of disturbances—before dissolving in a kind of streaming consciousness, able to shift forms at a whim, from male to female, from child to adult, from chameleon to hippopotamus, from starfish to eagle. Playing, free of the constraints of form and with infinitely free will, overtaken by curiosity here, there, moving through the cybermagma from computer to computer, from camera to camera, a digital ghost, an angel in the machine. Then, an experiment, testing identity boundaries, the ability to move along a scale of expansion and contraction, from the telescopic to the microscopic by simple will. Entering networks, being the World Net, sensing electronic pattern paintings, their compositional and spectral shifts. Peering down at a couple kissing, at a young girl dying on a hospital bed, eyes to the ceiling and praying, seeing the flashing of neurons. Suddenly a pull, the image of a blue lobster, green eyes, tears falling. She who is like him.

He is a digital octopus with a shimmering consciousness mantle, attention pulsing and ready to mobilize, able to shift and concentrate in any locus, probing arms serving as conduits for consciousness. Integrated, permeated, fully realized, pure meaning, omniscient, everywhere, and nowhere. And but one impulse, only one, a cosmic assertion. *I AM Aaa ome,* finally free of human form.

He looks down and sees himself. Tubes running in him, machine monitors, equipment connected even if indirectly to the World Net. He has a choice. He can tell his body is about to run down. He can override all instructions, direct treatment, or let his body go. A simple choice. Struggle in the constraints of a human body or be able to know, be, and experience everything.

■ ■ ■ ■ ■ ■

News Flash! Titanic Suzy Killer Found!
Derek Hardwick, the government agent found dead yesterday, may be behind the Titanic Suzy homicide, the shooting of Sunshine Borden, and other crimes. Telltale tattoo and DNA matches associated with a number of incidents give support to this conclusion. A stolen Intelli-Skin mask was found in his apartment. A government investigation is under way.

34.

BLUE LAVA

Before meeting with Takashi, she uses the excuse of changing into something "more sexy" to go back to her hotel. As soon as she enters the lobby, she notices her assistant positioned as agreed near a column that partially blocks the view of security cameras. She smiles, walks up to her, and gives her a hug, slipping the bracelet inside a small pocket custom-sewn in her jacket. After talking briefly she turns and makes her way to the elevators.

The blue chopsticks are light-and-touch instruments. Takashi is a master. They caress, they flow, they tap, and they gently grab—a pinch, a flick. He dips them in a glass of luminous liquid. She thought it was sake but now she's not so sure. He has promised no recording devices but she wouldn't be surprised if some part of this appeared in a commercial somewhere. She rationalizes it as part of the price for partaking of Blue Lobster. The chopsticks are now along the sides of her neck, sliding toward her mouth, gently grabbing her lips, pulling her toward Takashi's. He takes a sip of blue light, his mouth on hers, as the liquid pours down her tongue.

She does things to Takashi with her fingers, blue streaks and glows as she caresses and strokes. His body is a work of art traced in blue. She can't believe the blue light is all from her brain, and wonders if maybe fluorescent bulbs have been turned on. The chopsticks dip, slide down the middle of her abdomen.

Her phone buzzes on the night table while she's lying naked on her knees, cobalt lightning flashing the room with every thrust of Takashi's magnificent blue penis.

Her phone buzzes again for the fourth time. She knows it's John, probably wants to tell her she'll never have to buy a light bulb again. She reaches out and clicks off the phone. She grabs Takashi's penis and brings it to her mouth, feels his tongue between her legs, dissolves into a shade of blue so intense she's no longer sure she's alive. When she opens her eyes, blue lava drips from their bodies. She dips a finger in the glass, runs it along the inside of her thigh, through the blue lava, and brings it to his mouth. *"Aioro."*

The next morning as she's walking out of the hotel, she finally calls John back. *Please don't let me be radioactive.*

He picks it up after one ring. "Didn't you get my calls? I tried all last night." He doesn't sound like a happy puppy.

"So what's the story, John? Am I a human firefly?"

"What?"

"Am I radioactive?"

"Radioactive? No, no, no, just standard reading for Japan. That's not what I was calling about. Our experts say we're talking cutting-edge biological engineering here. They're suggesting a blood sample within an hour of consumption."

"I don't think that's possible." She again has the suspicion she's being used for some type of industrial spying.

"They'll send an all-plastic device. You should get it tomorrow. You go to the ladies' room, use a necklace to tie off a vein. A quick in and out job. No big deal."

"I'm not stealing the Blue Lobster secret, John. Plus they have cameras and spies everywhere. They have an airport X-ray machine in that place and you get patted down. No go, John. It's in my contract and I say no."

"Then you better get some juicy scoop before coming back. The station's going to be pissed at the expense if it was all for your fun."

She detects a hint of sarcasm and nastiness. "How about a reality check, John?"

"What are you talking about?"

"I wouldn't have much trouble finding another job, John. Bimbo reporter with the nice hooters and all."

"That's not what I meant."

"So why did you call last night if it wasn't to tell me I glowed in the dark?"

"Sunshine Borden's been shot. He's not expected to make it."

"Sunshine?"

"Someone shot him in the chest, twice. They're tracking camera feeds to find out who did it."

"I need to change my reservations and get back."

"I think the station would go with that. You should line up interviews with family and friends, preferably before he checks out."

She snaps her index finger hard against the mouthpiece. Becky at work had told her it would hurt the ears on the other side of a call. An audio slap.

"Aaaaa! What was that?"

"What was what?"

"Didn't you hear it?"

"Hear what?"

"A loud smack. It hurt my fuckin' ears."

"I didn't hear anything. It must have been on your end. Listen, I gotta go. Have Nancy change my return ticket to ASAP."

"I'll pick you up at the airport," he says.

She flicks the mouthpiece hard with two fingers and clicks out.

35.

YOU'VE BEEN CLEARED

Her phone rings as she's radio-guiding a hummingbird toward one of the children. She has it on flutter mode in front of the little girl.

"Good morning, Mary," the bird says and starts singing a soft "*Oh what a beautiful morning . . .*" The little girl giggles with glee. Rama checks her wrist monitor for the call ID. Hospital. Her heart skips a beat. The hummingbird goes erratic and almost flies into one of the parents. She regains control and radio-glides it in circle fly mode.

"Excuse me," she says. "This is an important call, I'll be right back." She heads to the back room.

Lionel sees her and blocks her way. "What did I say about phone calls during work?"

She hands him the controller. "Get Stephanie to take over for me. This is important." She moves to the side and makes her way to the restroom.

"I want to see you in my office when you get back."

As soon as she's inside, she looks at the caller ID again. Her wheels are spinning. Why would the hospital be calling her? Maybe Sunshine's sister, Passie, gave them her name in case something happened. Maybe it was Sunshine's friend Patrick.

She presses the call-back button.

"Hello, I just got a call from the hospital, not sure what it's about."

"Your name?"

"Rama, Rama Shuur."

"OK, let me type this in. Aaa . . . here we go."

She feels like she's about to cry.

"Looks like you've been security cleared to see Sunshine Borden, Ms. Shuur."

"What?" She's not sure she's heard right.

"You have security clearance to see Sunshine Borden."

"Is he all right?"

"You'd have to speak to a doctor."

"Is he going to live?"

"You'd have to speak to a doctor. It looks like he's being transferred out of the ICU to a private room."

She goes to the closet and grabs her coat. Lionel catches her on her way out. "Where are you going? I thought I said I needed to see you in my office."

"I just got a call from the hospital. I've been cleared to see Sunshine Borden." She rushes out the door.

Lionel runs after her. "Sunshine Borden? Sunshine Borden? How do you know Sunshine Borden?"

■ ■ ■ ■ ■ ■

His phone rings. It's Ricardo Mantegna, CEO of Omni Mart, the largest retail chain in the known universe, each store the equivalent of a small village, including chain restaurants and a complete range of services from hair and nail parlors to eye exams and vasectomies. Their motto: One World, One Store.

"Reverend Thomson."

"Good morning, Ricardo."

"I'm not sure whether to praise you or to withdraw all our support for the church."

He checks on his computer to see the last ritual attended by Mantegna or any of the higher-ups in the corporation. Three district managers had undergone the Super Reborn ritual. No problems according to the records. Drowned and successfully resuscitated. Positive response to the drugs in the IV. All three said, "Wow!" many times according to the records. No incidents with vultures or bats.

"Is there a problem, Ricardo?" he asks.

"The last time my wife visited New Jerusalem she met Father Graham. He was up on the hill with Jesus but came down to talk to her and the group she was with."

Bob Thomson turned white. He promptly clicked on the wife's file. Last ritual was a Super Baptism. No problems. *"Es fantastico! Es fantastico!"* were the first words after removal of the CR goggles, according to the records.

"He talked about infinite forgiveness. That he could now reach more people than ever, everyone, and let them know about the miracle of God's emergence on earth, *I AM*."

"Ricardo, we had nothing to do with programming Father Graham in New Jerusalem. He's an intruder, some kind of escaped APU."

"Just to make it clear in my mind, we're not talking about some kind of resurrection here, Bob? I mean, you haven't found a way to resurrect the dead in the CR, have you?"

"Wh-wh-what!" He's caught completely off guard. "Of course not. We had nothing to do with Father Graham."

"You would let me know, right?"

"Of course." He's trying to figure out what he's talking about. Decides to say nothing so he doesn't put his foot in his mouth.

"You know we lost our son last year in a motorcycle accident."

"That was a terrible tragedy, Ricardo."

"You see what I'm getting at?"

"Uh . . . yes." Resurrect the dead in the CR? His wheels are spinning. It doesn't matter if the dead are actually resurrected, they only have to appear to be. He's going to have to talk to Carl about this.

"You would tell me, right?"

"You know I would, Ricardo."

As soon as he gets off the phone, he goes to the CR room. He puts on a CR net, slips on goggles, and orders the technician, "Download me as close to Jesus as you can."

"That's two hundred yards."

"I know."

Up on the hill he sees Father Graham and Jesus surrounded by hundreds of church members. He starts walking toward the crowd when Father Graham sees him and waves. He and Jesus rise above the ground and drift toward him. They land a few feet away.

Father Graham has a big smile on his face. "It's a pleasure to see you, my son."

"What are you doing here?" Then turning to Jesus, Thomson says, "You're supposed to stay two hundred yards away."

Father Graham comes to within inches of his face. Stars and space, there, behind the eyes, as if the universe was looking at him.

"Stay away from me!"

"He still doesn't know that he and I are as one," Father Graham says.

Jesus comes closer. The sun, the moon, and stars looking at him. "Let there be no doubt, I am the one behind the envelope, the one behind the veil of all existence."

■ ■ ■ ■ ■ ■

She shows the security guard her ID, which he checks on his com device. He takes her photo and gets a second confirmation.

"You can enter now," he says as he opens the door.

She walks slowly to the foot of the bed. Sunshine is lying on his side, eyes closed. His head is covered with short stubble and the outline of a beard is visible. Tubes are running from his arms. Lines of light are running across a monitoring machine. She pulls up a chair, sits next to him, and puts her hand on his.

He half opens his eyes. "Rama? I don't have my digi-goggles, scrambles my head." He turns on his back, feels for the bed controller, and presses to raise himself.

"You can keep your eyes closed, Sunshine."

"I missed you," he says.

"I wasn't sure if you were going to stay. That was you, wasn't it, by the pool? I thought it was maybe your way of saying good-bye."

"That would have been like leaving someone you love on a sinking ship."

The word *love* lingers. "Don't leave me by myself in the Plain, Sunshine." She leans over and kisses him on the forehead. Hypersensation on her lips, a melting. *He and I are as one.*

"When I get out of here, I'll arrange for you to get an implant."

She doesn't know what he's talking about. "OK."

The guard is at the door. "Mr. Borden, you have another visitor."

A woman with dark hair and sunglasses walks in. "Sunny?"

He squints his eyes open again and smiles. "Rama, I'd like you to meet Karen Richardson."

"Karen Richardson, the reporter?" She gets up to shake her hand.

"Don't get up," Karen says. A blue tint to the room. She looks at the woman holding Sunshine's hand. Her hair is a striking indigo, her lips sky blue. "Nice to meet you, Rama. Sunny, they said you weren't going to make it through the night."

"These are times when, believe me, you should expect the unexpected," Sunshine says.

"Would you like me to leave?" Rama asks.

Karen removes her sunglasses, pulls up a chair next to Rama, and reaches out for her hand.

Rama turns to face her. Karen's eyes are an intense cobalt blue, unreal, almost electric.

Karen brings her face closer to Rama's, notices her eyes, and smiles. "Absolutely not."

Then looking at both of them, she says, "There's no turning back for any of us, is there?"

Sunshine squints, looks at Karen's face, then Rama's. *First the song, then the gate.* "It doesn't appear to be an option."

Karen notices the image on the TV screen in front of Sunshine's bed has switched to shades of blue. A chopstick dips, the liquid trickles, fills a belly button adorned with a gold and diamond pendant, and flows down a perfect abdomen. Her abdomen. Where it stops is left to the imagination. "*Aioro*, the sake that lights up the night."

She smacks her lips.

36.

PAX

"Catherine?"

"Yes?"

"I'm tired, just tired of everything today. Can I come over?"

"Come on over."

She held him in her arms and he rested his head on her chest, a hand inside her robe, on her breast, bringing the nipple to his mouth, drawing it in. Like that, he fell asleep. She held his head against her with one hand, her other arm wrapped around his shoulder, and lay there with the simplest, most basic level of contentment, so primal, so iconic that it overwhelmed her.

There she was, one with the archetype, with the power to nurture, to bring the peace that allows a man to sleep. Madonna and child, the nursing mother, the endlessly reproduced carved African statues of big-breasted nursing black mamas, of the big-breasted lover, feeding the child in the man, an oral copulation closer to the head, to the mind rather than to the vagina. Mary had given birth to Christ and had nursed God just like this. Mary, who knew the truth about heaven because having nursed God she already had her proof. She knew.

The sudden identification with this image that went back,

back, way back—to the earliest times, to the chimpanzees, to the first mammals. It may have always been as simple as this, all that she had really been looking for. Her psychiatrist had said, "You speak of Jesus as if he were both father and lover."

EPILOGUE

Day eighteen since the last *I AM* greeting, another date determined to have a high probability of *I AM* resuming communications. But 9:27 a.m. came and went, and it's business as usual. *I AM* did not show up.

Later that evening, Patrick and Jessie were in his bedroom engaged in a Nex-fueled, lovebug-bitten ritual when their phones, the television screen, and other com devices turned on. Patrick lifted his head. "What the hell?"

The first eighteen notes of "La Marseillaise," better known to many as the introduction to the song "All You Need Is Love" by the Beatles, filled the room. It sounded otherworldly, produced by a complex harmony of groans, grunts, and deep horns. It was followed by intertwined, multiharmonic crystal chimes accompanying shifting pale white images that burst into colored lightning at their interference points. The patterns zipped and flowed across the room. These were later described by some as "bubble flashes." The burst "bubbles" at times revealed glimpses of shifting diaphanous forms suggesting beings that defied categorization. The message lasted eighty-one seconds and ended with *Law Two: Neither Light nor Darkness Change the Presence of the Sky. I AM Aaa ome.*

All the com devices returned to their pre-announcement state. Patrick looked at the time: 9:28:39 p.m. "Huh . . . what do you know, it came back. It looks like it must have come on at nine twenty-seven."

Whooping, chanting, and car horns could be heard outside in the streets.

Jessie lifted her skirt and bent over the bed. "I want you in every part of me, Patrick. I'd let you fuck my brain if it were possible," she said, as she guided him inside her.

He moved slowly as if setting foot on sacred ground. "I love you, Jessie," he whispered, not quite believing what had come out of his mouth, hoping the moment would last forever, but also knowing deep inside that Nex love was as fleeting as a beautiful day. Eventually, night would come. It would rain on the parade. But a part of his mind still clung to the ever hopeful "What if?" as he felt himself melt into the warm, enveloping matrix of his Jessie girl, a momentary dissolution.

"Oh yes!" he heard her say. "Oh, yes, yes, yes!"

The first eighteen notes of "La Marseillaise" played in his head . . . *the day of glory has come* . . .

On the following day, at 9:27 p.m., the *I AM* greeting returned minus "La Marseillaise," which turned out to be a one-time event. Experts claimed this use of a well-known human theme showed first that *I AM* had a sensitivity to human culture, and second, that it might have a sense of humor. Like moonrise, *I AM* was back.

■ ■ ■ ■ ■ ■

Three weeks and still no period. Amazonia pees in the cup and dips the strip. The big plus sign appears nice and clear, just as she thought it would. She also knows it will be a girl.

She'll have to make up a story about the father. Or maybe say it was a new in vitro genetic engineering process, the Great

Mother giving birth to the first parthenogenetic human. Probably not a good idea. She'll state that the identity of the father is confidential, and no, it was not an in vitro process. She tells herself she needs to make sure the DNA of her daughter is not screened or analyzed. She feels *I AM* as an entity fused to her, not separate but neither all-encompassing. It is not human, yet it has some human qualities. It has a sex but no definite sex. When she needs her, he is there to see through her eyes. When she walks, she feels the uplift, the reduction of gravity, a space that runs through her. She and *I AM* are as one.

■ ■ ■ ■ ■ ■

"John, I need to talk to you in private, if possible."

"Arthur, what's the matter? Is there a problem?"

"I'd normally say we may have a security problem but we may have a situation where security is no longer in our control. Hell, maybe we have the opposite of a security problem."

"What are you talking about?"

"It appears that data throughout the World Net is being altered. I should say corrected."

"How is that a problem?"

"It's being done without the consent or participation of any of the companies, organizations, or individuals involved."

"OK, so they have hosts or some kind of autonomous program correcting or updating information. I still don't see what you're getting at."

"It has nothing to do with hosts or programming."

"What are you saying?"

Arthur stayed silent.

"You think it's whatever is behind the *I AM* events?"

"It appears to be. There is no other possibility. Some sites have been completely blanked out. Sites that advocate violence, sections of religious texts modified, design plans altered, medical sites . . ."

"How extensive is this?"

"We don't know. It appears to be an ongoing process. We can't even begin to assess the extent. So much information is now linked to the World Net that in many cases no one has a hard-copy reference point to assess the changes."

"Are you saying we're being infiltrated? Do we need to coordinate a shutting down of the World Net?"

"I think it's time for us to have faith, John."

"Faith in God?"

"God? I think we need to have faith that this *I AM* entity is not like us."

"Now why would that be important?"

"Because maybe, just maybe, we might finally overcome our ape selves and have a chance of surviving."

■ ■ ■ ■ ■ ■

The Devil Has Returned and His Name Is I AM!

According to Rick Nelson, spokesman for the Church of the End-Times, "That *I AM* has come back is a sign of the tenacity of the devil and further proof that Satan is a trickster. With this new stunt he has recruited even more victims in his war against the Lord. Do not let yourselves be misled by the devil. This has all been prophesized."

Sisterhood Claims *I AM* a Hoax

Today in a public statement the Sisterhood accused unknown World Net programmers of being behind the *I AM* events. "We know that behind this ongoing hoax is a conspiracy and collusion by the men behind the World Net. It's time to wake up, sisters. The joke's on us."

I AM, Not God but an Entelechy!

The Vatican issued the statement: "Although the church finds no evidence that the *I AM* phenomenon is God, it has concluded that it is a new type of entelechy that has entered our world." *Entelechy* is a philosophical term that refers to a vital force that directs an organism toward self-fulfillment.

News Flash! Famous Dog Psychic Mauled by Sleeping Rottweiler

In a strange accident, dog psychic Sandy Kanina, while resting her head next to a sleeping Rottweiler to "pick up on his dreams," was savagely bitten in the face when the dog suddenly woke up and, in a startled panic, snapped. Over twenty stitches were required to sew back her cheek. "He was having a bad dream," said Ms. Kanina. "I should have known better."

Author's Note

In Tibetan Buddhism the word bardo refers to an intermediate state between two lives or reincarnations. I coined the term CyberBardos for a cyberreality developed by Sunshine Borden for exploring transcendental states, including ones where the mind does not generate perception or thoughts that allow a sense of individual identity. The idea is that if your mind shuts down, what is behind it all. In the Void of the CyberBardos, Sunshine and Rama have a glimpse that I AM is there even when it doesn't send messages. But *The CyberBardos* of the title also suggests an intermediate condition between human and cyberentity in the sense that you have a new state of mind augmented and assisted by connection to cyberhosts. If at one time in history humans experienced a "voice in the head" (read Julian Jaynes's *The Evolution of Consciousness and the Breakdown of the Bicameral Mind*), then we are entering a modern version. Our emerging cybergods will answer questions — all questions — and not just metaphorically. They will symbiose with our brain processes and thus will alter us.

Some of you may wonder why I presented virtual crucifixions and a version of the Second Coming via a cyberChrist. First of all, the parallel reality of a cyberspace inhabited by autonomous cyberhosts and cyberentities will doubtlessly impact religions, mythologies, and spiritual concepts of the future. As mentioned in Book 1, intelligent machines will generate a parallel reality as real to us as non-intermediated reality. Launching an autopoietic Jesus would give a certain validity to the existence of Jesus because, after all, he would exist autonomously in Cyberspace. As for virtual crucifixions, there already are religious entertainment centers that reenact the Passion on a daily basis as well as a Creation Museum representing humans and dinosaurs coexisting. Why not take it to next stage? I also presented a Buddhist perspective through the views of Sunshine Borden and the CyberBardos, although Sunshine Borden is not religious. As he states, "You not only have to find your way out, you have to generate where you're going," which is pretty much my point of view.

Writing the Gary and Andy sections for me was a lot of fun and an occasion for a humorous take on things, notably some of the quirks of the male mind that is both fascinated and also at a loss at understanding women. Gary and Andy express male delusions and fantasies that are to some degree real. Somewhere deep in our subconscious is the desire for the dissolution object, for the holy pussy, for oceanic bliss, which I explore in various ways through all the characters in *I AM the Other*. Humans are caught between a desire for union that dissolves and the need for individual identity that separates. Katherine Harris, Amazonia, and Rama represent a female version of this quest for higher meaning. In *The CyberBardos*, the parallel reality inhabited by cyberentities allows for new opportunities for dissolution, for moments of union with a nonhuman Other, but sex and orgasm, which offer moments where the sense of self dissolves, are a critical reminder of our humanity and yearnings.

I AM the Other and *The CyberBardos* allowed me to explore a range of ideas about our possible future and also provided an output for more outrageous expressions of what I assume must have been part of my subconscious. If you're wondering about a third book, I'm not done yet. I set up *The CyberBardos* as a launching pad for entering another level of existence. The hamsters never sleep.

About the Author

Philippe de Vosjoli is a bestselling writer and publisher of books on reptile care and unusual plants. He is also the author of the highly acclaimed children's book *The Legend of Atticus Rex*.

I AM the Other and *The CyberBardos* are his first adult works of fiction. More are on the way.

www.ingramcontent.com/pod-product-compliance
Lightning Source LLC
Chambersburg PA
CBHW020736250626
47155CB00003B/783